The Mayfair Moon

THE MAYFAIR MOON

The Darkwoods Trilogy - #1

J.A. REDMERSKI

This book is a work of fiction. Any references to real people, historical events, businesses, companies, products, or real locales are used fictitiously. Other names, characters, places and incidents are products of the author's imagination, and any resemblance to actual events, locales, persons living or deceased, is entirely coincidental.

Copyright © 2012 J. A. Redmerski
All rights reserved, including the right of reproduction in whole, or in part, and in any form.

In accordance with the U.S. Copyright Act of 1976, the scanning, uploading, and electronic sharing of any part of this book without prior written permission is unlawful piracy and theft of the author's intellectual property.

Cover Art by Michelle Monique Photography | www.michellemoniquephoto.com
Cover Models | Amber Coney & Yuriy Platoshyn
Background Texture Stock by Sean & Ashlie Nelson

J.A. Redmerski | THE MAYFAIR MOON | 2nd Edition
Fiction – Paranormal – Young Adult

ISBN: 1468185527
ISBN 13: 9781468185522

For my mom, Kitty, for always being there for me even when I was at my worst; and to my kids, Devan, Jerricah, and Jonah, for bringing out my best.

1

NO ONE USED THE F-WORD MORE THAN MY STEP-DAD, JEFF. It pretty much made up his already limited vocabulary.

I stayed in my room around this time every night when he wasn't out at the bar. He was a poor excuse for a man, but my mom, Rhonda, 'loved' him. Despite the drunken tantrum, it was a quiet night in our house. But don't get the wrong idea: no one beat me, and my life wasn't all that bad, really. Jeff rarely bothered me or my sister, Alexandra, anymore. He backed off after Alex blackened his eye last year. I'm not afraid of him. Who could be scared of a weasely-looking man with nine-inch nose hairs and who could barely lift an economy-sized box of cat litter by himself?

I sat in the center of my bed with a book in my lap and music playing low beside me. Alex left earlier in the afternoon; she'd begged me to go with her to play pool, but I wasn't much into pool. Besides, I knew why she *really* wanted me to go. She'd been trying to hook me up with Brent Haver-something. "But he's hot," she mentioned on more than one occasion. "And he's a good guy." He probably was hot, and a good guy—she was rarely wrong about these kinds of things— but worse than usually being right, she was so overprotective of her little sister that she would rather pick out the guys for me to date. Only problem was, I wasn't into dating.

It was as simple as that.

I heard my mom shuffling around in her room across from mine. Hangers clanked violently in the closet. Drawers opened and slammed shut so hard the dresser banged against the wall. Her footsteps were heavy as she stomped back and forth, rattling the windows and the exposed light bulb above me in the ceiling.

"What are you doing?" Jeff yelled.

"Why do you care?" my mom demanded. "Your girlfriend is getting warm in there on the coffee table."

Mom always referred to Jeff's beer as his 'girlfriend'.

The only thing I could give him credit for was that it took more than sarcasm to get him to hit her. Not that that was saying much, but it was a small sense of relief for me. My mom, to be completely honest, couldn't keep her opinions to herself—like right now, as she went on and on about his drunken ways. Sometimes I wondered if she was a masochist. I was used to the argument dragging out for at least an hour before Jeff's inner-loser took over and he got physical. Some might say she deserved it (my stepbrother said that once—Alex blackened his eye too), but no woman deserved to be hit.

"Why don't you back off," Jeff said with a slur in his voice. "Crazy, nagging bi—"

"*Nag?*" My mom sounded shocked. I could picture her mouth open in total disbelief, her hands propped on her bony hips. The more vulgar name he had started to call her she was so used to hearing. But 'nag'…no way she was going to let him get away with *that*.

The rest of what she was saying, I ignored. It was always the same kind of argument with the same kind of outcome: drawn-out fighting, which usually ended in lengthy make-up sex that always forced me out of the house faster than the actual fight did.

I hoisted my favorite canvas backpack on after tucking my book away inside it, then raised my bedroom window and slipped out into the humidity. It felt nicer than inside where the heat of the day grew and lingered. We lived in a tiny white house just outside of Athens, Georgia. From the road, the house looked like a dirty speck in an endless yellowing pasture. Not a single tree hovered nearby to help shade it from the blistering southern summers. I hated that house. It was Jeff's house.

Our neighbors were spaced out here and there. Jack and Janice Bentley lived across the street—Janice had a cat-hoarding problem. Old Man Chester lived just around the curve past the proud and famous, Jacquelyn Morose, who had the pinkest house in Northeast Georgia. Though, the house didn't make her famous; she was in a laundry detergent commercial like two hundred years ago and people still talked about it. Anyway, Old Man Chester was older than dirt too, and always wore the same coveralls. And then there was Mrs. Willis who lived next door. Unfortunately, she lived *directly* next door, as in about fifty-feet away on the same acreage. We also shared the same mailbox post and driveway with her and our business was her business, too. One of *those*. There was one in every neighborhood, wasn't there?

Like a vulture, Mrs. Willis watched me walk down the dirt-covered driveway and away from the rusted wire fence overrun by weeds. As if I couldn't see her troll-like figure hovering at the kitchen window. Sometimes I felt like giving her the finger, but I was capable of restraint. I did however, superglue her mailbox shut when I was eleven. On the day she was supposed to get her Social Security check, at that. I could say that looking back on it now, I wasn't proud of the childish deed. But that would be a lie.

Neither my sister nor I were disrespectful girls. Despite Alex's black eye record, she was the most caring and nonviolent person I knew. I learned a lot from her as we grew up; mom had too many unresolved issues to be much of a model herself. Alex taught me how to do a cartwheel, how to cook and even how to drive a stick shift (the only thing that huge field around the house was good for). Admittedly, I wasn't very good at any of them, but that was beside the point.

An antique Ford drove past me, stirring up dust along the road. A gnarly hand poked out the window, waving at me as he went by. Old Man Chester. He waved at everybody; it was kind of customary in these parts. I waved back and kept on walking, slipping past a dozen eroded mailboxes and eventually over the creek bridge, which led to the park. The sun would be gone soon; the sky laced by thin, dark pink clouds on the horizon. I could count four streaks of perfectly straight contrails left by planes, crisscrossing above me.

I sat in the park for an hour under an enormous tree, the one near the outskirts of the forest away from the playground and close to the public fishing pond. I loved it here. But I think a lot of people did. Hard to resist one of those mammoth trees with giant limbs that dip so low you can sleep on them. It was my thinking spot, and where Alex could always find me.

"Adria," she said, walking toward me alongside the water, "Jeff went out, so we can go home now." She wore her trademark hip-hugger jeans, tank top and worn out black flip-flops.

I closed my copy of *Neverwhere* and left my index finger in-between its crumpled pages. The lamppost wasn't putting off enough light anymore to read, and the erratic cloud of bugs swarming around it was beginning to thicken.

"Is Mom home?" I asked.

"She was when I left to find you," Alex said, sitting down next to me on the rain-deprived grass. "But she was on her way out, too."

"Thought you were playing pool tonight?"

Alex shook her head. "I was, but I thought you could use some company."

My sister always thought of me first, always put me before just about anything. She was no eighteen-year-old saint; left me on my birthday last week to hang out with Zach Anthony, but she was still the best sister anyone could ever have.

"Surprised you didn't bring your *friend* along," I said, smirking.

"What friend?" She paused. "Oh, you mean Brent—come on, Dria, he's perfect for you. His dad owns a Honda dealership, and his mom's a doctor."

I really had been referring to Zach Anthony—I admit, I was still a little bitter.

"I don't care about that stuff."

"I know, I know," she said, "but he's adorable—I swear he looks like Ian Somerhalder."

I looked over at her with a roll of my eyes. "Oh please," I said. "Why are you *really* trying to fix me up with this guy? Be honest."

Alex grew quiet and frustrated all of a sudden. "I just don't want you to make bad decisions," she said simply.

Yeah, Alex always had that motherly way about her, and sometimes she sounded like our actual mother *should* have. We grew up quicker than anyone we hung out with—honestly, sometimes we were more adult than some adults we knew. Mostly Mom's loser friends. No surprise there, really.

"You mean like the bad decisions Mom makes?" I confirmed. I had a feeling it was about something like that. She had always been more negatively affected by mom's screw-ups than I was.

I regarded my sister. "I have to live and make my own choices, my own mistakes. You have to let me be me, even if I suck at it sometimes."

"I know, you're right," she said, gazing out at the park.

"I love you for being you, though." I smiled, and she did too, just before she frogged me on the leg with her knuckle.

"Ouch!" I rubbed the spot hard with my palm.

"No cheesy love talk," she replied, laughing. "You know I hate it!"

She eased into a more serious mood then, impeccably.

"I need to tell you something," she said. "I've been holding it in for weeks."

Immediately, I had a bad feeling. I set the book on the grass next to me and turned to face her. I couldn't actually say, "What is it?" as the words were stuck in my throat.

"I think I'm going to move out soon…"

I felt my heart sink. She just kept talking, but I could barely hear any word she said. Absently, I saw the way her dark hair flowed down around her oval-shaped face, and how she kept the corners of her eyes softened as she tried to explain.

"Liz and Brandon said I could stay with them if I want. I'll have to get a job and help keep the place clean, but I'm all for it…"

I didn't want to hear this.

"…I'll have my own space since they have the extra room above the garage. And you can come visit anytime you want. Once I get settled in you can come live with me too."

"*What?*" I said, staring at her in mute.

Alex breathed deeply and let her head fall sympathetically to one side. "We can't stay with Mom forever—you know that."

"So you're just going to *leave*?" I stopped her before she answered. "Mom needs us here."

"Adria," she said, gazing at me with that just-listen-to-me-for-once look. "I don't know about you, but I'm tired of being our mother's mother. She won't leave him. Isn't that obvious already?"

"It doesn't matter, Alex! That's not the point…"

Silence filled the night air in an instant. Alex leaned against the base of the massive tree next to me. I could feel her hand on my leg, patting it in surrender.

"I'm sorry," she said. "I just don't know how much more of this I can take. And it's not just Jeff—it's everything. There's nothing for me in Athens."

"Well, Lexington really isn't that much different," I said, begrudgingly. "I mean, I doubt you're going to 'find yourself' in a place less than twenty miles away."

I didn't mean for it to sound so sarcastic…but then again, maybe I did.

A bug fluttered down and batted its wings against the side of my face. I slapped furiously at the air until I scared it away.

Alex stared more at the ground than at me. She began twirling blades of grass around her fingers; her chin rested on the knuckles of her other hand. I thought about how much she had done for me and I couldn't bear the thought of being on my own and without her. And I knew it was because of me that she hadn't moved out a month ago, now that she was eighteen. Truthfully, Alex would've moved out a long time ago, long before turning eighteen, but she stayed for me.

Maybe I was being selfish.

I glanced over at her; the darkness shadowed her face.

"Alex," I began, "if you want to move in with Liz, I'm really okay with it. And I'm not trying to guilt-trip you, either."

"No," she said softly, her gaze still lingering. "I won't go anywhere if you won't go with me."

After a moment, I said, "I want out of Jeff's as much as you do, but—" I had no idea where I was going with it.

If what I said was true, about wanting out, then why was I not sharing her ideas? Yes, I did want out, but I wanted our mom with us. Somehow, part of me knew that Alex was right about Mom—she would never leave Jeff. God, how could any woman be so blind and stay with a man like him? I knew I would never be like her in that sense. I guess I did learn something from my mother, after all.

We sat quietly for several moments longer, Alex still twirling the grass and me absently watching her. I loved the summer night air, the sound of summer insects and the smell of summer wind. Nothing could beat it. My most memorable moments were of summertime with my sister and even though this particular moment wasn't exactly a joyful one, somehow I knew just sitting like this with Alex underneath the giant oak, would etch itself deeply into my memory. I would never forget the pond and the trees and the smell of honeysuckle and pine. And I would always remember that stupid left flip-flop that Alex had worn down so much that she often stubbed her big toe when she walked. I tried to get her to toss them, but she refused—they were her favorite.

I glanced over at her, down at her feet and just shook my head, smiling.

"What?" she said, noticing.

"Nothing."

"You better tell me, Dria, I'm not playin'."

I just laughed and she punched me on the shoulder.

"Dammit, Alex!" I laughed harder.

Finally, after the moment faded, I stood and slung my backpack over my shoulder. "Let's go home."

She smiled and draped an arm around the back of my neck and we left my special tree. Alex walked with a slight limp on that left foot, but I didn't say anything.

2

MASSIVE TREES TOWERED OVER US, BLOCKING MOST OF THE moonlight from the clear dark sky. The bicycle path through the park was a shortcut to our house. During the day the park was full of joggers and bicyclists, but at night it was desolate and eerie. Even with the sound of the freeway in the distance, I still felt like I was far away from home, lost in the wilderness somewhere.

Catching her off-guard, I frogged Alex as hard as I could on the arm with the bony knuckle of my middle finger.

"Shit, Dria! That hurt!"

"Paybacks." I grinned.

For a moment, when Alex didn't smile back at me I thought she was mad.

"What *was* that?" she said. "Did you hear that?" She gripped her arm, but it was obvious something else was on her mind other than the inevitable bruise. She stared through the trees behind me, and suddenly the hair stood up on the back of my neck.

"No, I didn't hear—."

Then suddenly I *did* hear something. It sounded like growling... sort of. I couldn't tell. But what scared me was the strangeness of it, the shiver it sent down my spine like a cold, ghostly finger. When you heard a dog growling you usually knew right away that it was a dog—this was no dog.

"Sounded like a bear," I said.

We began walking faster. I could see one lone streetlight glowing far off in the distance.

Alex stopped and grabbed my arm, smiling. "This reminds me of the time we saw *Texas Chainsaw Massacre* over at Liz's, remember?"

I guess her sudden relaxed attitude helped calm my nerves because I wasn't as edgy anymore. "Yeah, I remember."

"Like freaked out little girls," Alex added.

We cupped our hands over our mouths to stifle the laughter. But then the wild flapping of wings sucked the calm right out of us again. Birds, hundreds of them it seemed, burst out of the trees and swirled into the night sky like a swarm of bats.

"Alex," I whispered harshly, "let's go." I took her by the arm.

As we hurried down the path, squirrels bounced from tree to tree, all moving in the same direction; there were so many of them I couldn't help but notice.

"What's going on?" Alex said, with suppressed panic in her voice.

The growl now sounded more like a roar; it filled the space all around us; my breath caught, and my heart stopped beating. Alex and I stood back to back, moving in a circle to keep each other safe, but from what, we couldn't have possibly imagined.

A figure crashed through the bushes. My lungs hardened like cement as a naked man stumbled out and fell onto the path ahead. Alex shrieked and gripped my forearm so tight that it stung. I was too frozen inside myself to scream. I think I forgot how.

The man reached out a hand toward us; I could hear the disturbing sound of his flesh scraping against the asphalt as he dragged his body forward with his arms. Alex and I started backing away, trying to gauge the situation before making any sudden movements. We should have just run for it.

"Omigod," Alex gasped. "Omigod!"

"Please..." the man said in a raspy, growling voice, "...run away from here! Go! *Now!*"

I had to shake my thoughts sensible—literally. The sound of his voice held an echoing, demonic undertone and it stunned me into submission. Demonic? Of all the words I thought to describe it, why did I choose that one?

Alex grabbed my arm tighter and jerked me toward her; her fingernails seared my skin. A force, like hot, foul-smelling wind, blindsided me and I felt my face crush into the side of a tree. Furious white spots dotted my vision, shattering my focus. Blood sprang up in my mouth. I couldn't tell if I was still standing, or if the tree pressed against my face was really the ground.

I heard some kind of struggle, but the demonic undertone stood out over everything.

"Alex! Alex!" I had to know where she was, if she was all right.

I looked up and realized then that I *was* on the ground. My vision was blurred for a moment; a canopy of limbs and leaves and stars spun around in my gaze, making me feel drunk. I wondered if I was losing my mind—I couldn't really be seeing what I thought I was seeing: an enormous beast, bluish-black in the moonlit darkness, stood on two legs several feet away. Its head was like a wolf...no, it wasn't like any wolf I had ever seen. It was a monster. Towering at least seven feet, its almost human-like legs and arms were covered in mangy black fur. Its fingers were long, with thick razor-sharp nails on the ends.

The beast lunged at the naked man, burying its massive teeth into his shoulder. An agonizing scream pierced the air, then slowly became a menacing, guttural growl.

I backed my way to wherever I could, gripping the earth with my hands, feeling grains of rock push beneath the bed of my nails. My body jerked forward and I fell face down on the asphalt. Blood pooled behind my lips, the warm, disgusting thickness coating my teeth and slipping down into the back of my throat. Something was pulling me backward, fingers aggressively digging into my ankle. I struggled to kick my way free, but they dragged me slowly off the pathway and onto the dirt. Tiny pieces of rock and grit stung my elbows and ribs.

"Shhh!" demanded Alex. "It's me!"

Relief washed over me, but it was short-lived. We crawled farther away and crouched behind a tree, paralyzed and out of breath. Blood was smeared along Alex's hairline, I noticed.

I watched wide-eyed, my heart banging violently; my legs quivered uncontrollably—I thought I would faint at any moment.

The naked man stood from the ground, pushing the beast off him and sent it crashing through the forest; tree limbs whipped violently around its body as it soared through the air. And then the naked man began to change. His skin began to ripple grotesquely as though something seethed beneath it. He craned his head and pulled back his arms, his fists balled tightly behind him; his stance battle-ready and chilling. His face began to protrude; a snout with terrifying fangs jutted out; and the cracking and crushing of bone sent what was left of my nerves completely over the edge. His human skin changed color, and long, black hair grew within seconds, covering most of his massive body.

I think I finally fainted at that moment—or my mind was running on autopilot—because I couldn't recall what happened immediately afterward. I couldn't guess how I finally got to my feet and began running through the woods. I couldn't say how Alex and I made it to the freeway, or how the cars swerved to miss us, or even if maybe we *had* been hit because when I did ultimately 'wake up', I was in a litter-filled ditch with Alex on top of me. A crumpled soda can and an empty plastic water bottle jabbed me in the small of my back. Cars buzzed by on the freeway above, the booming echo of wheels going over a nearby exit bridge. *Clu-clump! Clu-clump! Clu-clump!* I welcomed the repetitive nuisance. It was strangely comforting, as if it helped me to believe that the nightmare in which made the frightening sounds before it was somehow not real.

"Alex?" I said, squeezing myself out from underneath her carefully. "Are you all right? Alex!"

She didn't respond and I panicked, putting her bloodied face in my hands, feeling for her pulse and listening for the sound of her breath. More blood. The collar of her shirt had soaked it up like a sponge, the ends of her hair clumped together in a sticky mess. Finally, I saw her breathe as bubbles of red formed in her nostrils—her nose had been busted—and I noticed a gash on the side of her head as she began to stir, groaning.

"Alex!" I hugged her close to me.

She opened her eyes in a jolt. "Where is it?" she screamed. "It's going to kill us!" She had never been so hysterical. The whites of her eyes seemed whiter; the skin stretched over her forehead tight like plastic. She dug her nails deeply into my shoulders and would've broken the skin had they not been protected by the fabric of my shirt.

"No, no, calm down!" I tried to hold her still.

"It's gone, Alex." I hugged her tighter. "It's okay. We're going to be okay."

A part of me felt like I was lying to her.

Getting home that night proved mentally and physically exhausting. Alex and I hardly spoke, too traumatized to talk about what happened. What *did* happen?

I cleaned up, taking the longest shower I'd ever taken in my life, watching fragments of dirt and rock and blood disappear down the drain. Lifting my gaze to the mirror, I was relieved that a thick layer of moisture refused my reflection. Tiny bubbles of liquid gray covered the glass in a sheet of delicate humidity, threatening to evaporate at any moment and reveal the devastating truth. The truth I had already begun trying to twist into something it wasn't.

My hands were propped solidly against the edge of the counter; my whole body throbbed, stung, ached. I had to see. And so I swallowed hard and wiped away the veil with the palm of my hand. A girl with a busted lip and a heavily bruised face stared back at me. I didn't look like I'd been punched in the eye; I looked like…well, like my face had been bashed against a tree.

I was so tired, but too afraid to sleep. I laid in bed for hours, taking greater notice to every little sound around me, every movement. Mrs. Willis' headlights shining directly on the *Supernatural* poster above my desk as she pulled back into the drive; the every-other-night Bentley Family cat fights underneath our house; the summer song of crickets and frogs; the remote control hitting the floor in the living room after Jeff had passed out on the couch.

I knew all of these sights and sounds intimately, yet they still managed to put me on edge as though completely new. But this was nothing like the night we saw the horror movie—this time the horror was real.

I *know* what I saw.

I know what attacked us, but to say it aloud was like verifying it, sealing the deal, confirming that I believed in something certifiably insane. I wasn't ready yet to admit it to myself. There had to be an explanation. There was always an explanation, right? I just didn't know which I wanted more: to find it, or to forget about it completely.

Two days came and went and we didn't go to school. Alex never went farther than the restroom or her bedroom. She still wasn't speaking, at least not about what happened. She hardly said two random sentences to me, like how the heat was too much for her (our air conditioner was broken), and something about a fly in her room that was driving her 'bat shit'. But as far as I knew, she never made any effort to plug the fan back in behind her dresser, or get the fly swatter and smack the insect into oblivion.

On Wednesday, there was an unfamiliar knock at the door, which made me jump to alert. I knew it was someone I'd never met before, someone important, or maybe a delivery driver.

"They're both in their rooms," my mother said. "They haven't been feeling well."

My mom was never the type to invade our privacy, which was why we could get away with playing the sick-card.

I couldn't let her see my face.

"Yes ma'am, I called the school yesterday and told them my daughters were sick." I could easily detect the offense in her voice, the same way she sounded when our neighbor, Mrs. Willis, would show up at our door after a Jeff and Rhonda Bradley fight.

I heard a woman's voice say, "If you don't mind, we'd like to speak with your daughters. It will only take a minute, and if everything is fine, we'll be on our way."

I knew exactly where this was heading.

Child Protective Services took me away that day. I protested futilely. I even made up an elaborate story about how Alex and I were attacked by a group of girls in the park. Useless. They didn't believe that our bruises were not the work of Jeff Bradley.

They didn't believe it because—

"Jeff did it," Alex told them.

I felt the air hit my teeth as my mouth fell open. I couldn't speak for what felt like forever. I just looked at my sister, confused, baffled—*angry*. I began to shake my head slowly in protest, my wide eyes darting between the social worker and my sister.

How could you do this, Alex? I wanted to say.

But then I realized why she'd lied—it was our way out, my way out with her.

"Would you like to file a police report?" the social worker said to Alex as she sat impassively with her back pressed against the wall of the Child Protective Services building.

"Yes," Alex said simply.

I dropped my head and looked down at my hands, my fingers tangled nervously between my legs.

Alex said nothing else to me the rest of the day.

I couldn't put my finger on it, but something in her eyes haunted me, something more than revenge for years of Jeff abusing our mother, something deeper and darker than Jeff could ever be. Her face held no emotion. A single strand of hair lay stretched across her nose. She did nothing. She said nothing. Was she traumatized by what happened to us? It was all I could make of it.

She was eighteen and free to go if she wanted, but not me. I was officially a ward of the State of Georgia.

I overheard them talking in the sterile-white hall of the building, something about a witness and a written statement. I knew then that Mrs. Willis probably had everything to do with it. She was the one who called the police many times before. I was sure she told the police that Jeff beat us. She had seen me once, the day after the incident, when I went out to check the mailbox. I tried to hide my face, but she definitely saw it.

I spent six days in the care of the State, and on the seventh day, I was sent to live with my Uncle Carl and his new wife, Beverlee, in Hallowell, Maine.

Thankfully, Alex went with me. I guess she got her wish, after all.

3

I HATED EVERYTHING ABOUT MOVING A THOUSAND MILES away from home in Georgia, except for the weather. Of course I loved my southern summers, but September in Maine was like heaven. The rest of it, I quietly kept to myself, I wanted no part of. I loved my Uncle Carl, but really, the last time I saw my dad's brother was when I was twelve. It wasn't as if he sent Christmas cards every year.

But I had to admit, Uncle Carl's place was nice. He lived in an isolated two-story colonial-style house mostly surrounded by woods. It wasn't a rich place by any means; the outside could've used a new coat of paint, and by the looks of the yard, Beverlee—Uncle Carl's new wife—wasn't much the gardening type. The plants hanging in pots on the porch were mostly dead, and what might've been a little garden on the east side next to the shed, was nothing more than a square patch of dirt overrun by weeds.

Alex and I both had our own rooms, and just like at home, ever since 'the incident' she said little and did less. In her room, on the other side of the locked door was where she stayed. The one time Aunt Beverlee knocked on Alex's door to offer breakfast, Alex responded: "If I was hungry, I'd go downstairs and *make* something."

I didn't know whether to be mad at her for being so hateful, or to worry about what was happening to my once loveable, charming sister who'd never treated someone the way she was treating Beverlee.

"She needs more time," Beverlee said, sitting in the chair on the porch next to me later that afternoon. "She'll come around. What you two have gone through is a lot to deal with."

That was a serious understatement.

It only took about a week before I began to let the changes in my life just happen. And before I knew it, I was eating dinner downstairs with Carl and Beverlee and watching TV with them in the den every night.

I always thought about my mother though. I worried about her constantly. Apparently, Jeff only spent a few days in jail before they released him. I asked Uncle Carl if my mother was the one who bailed him out (it didn't matter to me that he didn't actually do anything this time).

Uncle Carl didn't answer.

My first day at Hall-Dale High School was just about the way I expected it to be. Uncle Carl dropped me off on his way to work, and the few students hanging around out front stared at me as though they'd never seen a thing like me before. I slipped down one long hallway lined by art-filled walls and made my way to the front office. It smelled of cinnamon candles and hospital soap. A man in a navy work jumpsuit stood high atop a ladder with his hands buried in the flickering fluorescent light fixture above him.

"Good morning," a woman at the front desk greeted. "How can I help you?" She wore tons of gaudy jewelry on her wrists and around her neck.

"I'm new," I said. "Adria Dawson."

"Ah yes, I have your class schedule right here." She pulled a sheet of yellowish paper from somewhere behind the low counter and handed it to me. "Great to have you."

I smiled my thanks.

"If you have any questions," she went on, "or you need help finding your way around, just ask Julia."

I glanced around and behind me. The janitor repairing the light, grumbled a curse under his breath and briefly sucked on the end of his fingertip.

"All right, it's up and running, Mrs. Wiles," a girl said as she came around the corner from an office door. "Just let the upload finish."

"Julia, this is Adria…" Mrs. Wiles paused and glanced at me briefly, looking for confirmation.

"Dawson," I repeated.

"Yes, Adria Dawson is new to the school," she went on. "And if you wouldn't mind showing her around, that'd be wonderful."

The girl tucked a book underneath her arm and smiled over at me, though she seemed faintly irritated. "Julia Morrow—I'm *everybody's* hall-guide." She walked around the counter, positioning her bag strap over her shoulder.

I gave her a questioning look.

"Oh no," she said, realizing, "not that I mind at all really." She went to the office door, and gestured a hand. "This way—let's get started."

I followed.

"Wait." Julia put up her arm in front of me.

I froze at the door half a second before stepping into the hall. A small group of students walked past, gossiping about how some girl really 'screwed up her hair'. Not until they were out of sight did Julia let me pass.

"Drama Club," she said. "As soon as they spot you, they'll either try to recruit you, or you'll be their next target."

She led me out of the office just as the first bell rang. Students shuffled casually down the hall while a few darted past so quickly I felt the wind stir my hair.

"Well, I'm not into Drama," I said, "so they won't be recruiting me."

Julia smiled over at me. "Not like real Drama Club," she said. "They just stir up a lot of stuff around the school."

Oh, that kind of drama, I thought.

"Hey Jewels," a guy said to Julia as he approached with a single book in his hand. He looked at me then, and Julia introduced me.

"Adria—cool name," he said. "I'm Harry." He was tall and lanky with stringy black hair; cute in a strictly brotherly sort of way.

"Who do you have first period?" Julia asked, taking my schedule from me. "Same as you Harry—Mrs. Scott. Good luck with that," she warned. "The woman's Bipolar or something. One day she's disgustingly cheery, the next she's snapping your head off for answering a question wrong." Julia pursed her lips looking down into the paper. "Well, at least you can get the worst out of the way early. Looks like the rest of your teachers are pretty cool."

"Let me see that," Harry said, snatching my schedule from Julia. "No way, Jewels. She's got Coach Green."

"What?" Julia grimaced and snatched my schedule back from him, peering into the text more raptly.

She looked up at me then and shook her head. I thought maybe I'd just been sentenced the Death Penalty.

"Coach Green is a retired Drill Sargent," she said. "Too bad you didn't get Coach Little."

Oh great. A potential failed course. It wasn't that I was incapable of the more physical classes, just that I never do anything well under pressure.

We made our way to an open classroom and stopped outside the door.

"This is us," said Harry. "I wonder what it'll be today: hyped up on Poppins happy pills, or her head spinning three-sixty."

Their mockery of mental illness bugged me a little; my mom had been on medication for depression for three years. But I thought they probably didn't really mean anything by it.

"I guess Harry can take it from here," said Julia. "Catch you again next period."

Julia left quickly and slipped into a class at the far end of the hall.

I spent one class with Harry, then second period Spanish with Julia, and then I was on my own until I met up with Harry again in Geometry.

But school was the furthest thing from my mind, and halfway through the day I realized I barely remembered any of it.

What happened in Georgia, I remembered.

And I knew, that no matter what changed in my life, or how hard I tried to, that I would never forget it.

4

AT LUNCH I HUNG OUT WITH MY NEW FRIENDS, PLUS TWO more, Tori and Sebastian, who were a couple. The five of us sat outside on a stone picnic table underneath a shade tree. I was glad to have found my group of friends so quickly, rather than wandering around the school for days until someone had pity on me and decided to take me in. And I did like them all very much. Harry was naturally likable and probably didn't have an enemy in the entire school. Tori and Sebastian were too into each other, she sitting between his legs with his arms wrapped around her from behind, for me to figure either one of them out so soon, but I liked them, nonetheless. And Julia, she talked a lot, but it didn't bother me.

"So why did you move to Maine, anyway?" Julia said and then put a can of Mountain Dew to her lips, gulping down the last of it.

"My mom sent me to live with my uncle," I lied, "because she took a job traveling." It was all I could come up with on such short notice.

"Hey look," Julia said then, gawking toward the street as a muddy Jeep with big tires pulled onto campus. "I wonder what her excuse is for today."

I was relieved the focus shifted so quickly. Any conversation about why I moved here—or about Alex—made me uncomfortable, and I got the feeling that telling them I had a sister was just a few questions away.

The Jeep pulled up to the front of the school and a girl got out on the passenger's side. The first thing I noticed was her short spiky white-blond hair. She tossed a black bag over her shoulder and carried a stack of books in the fold of her other arm.

There were three guys in the Jeep, too, all looking in our general direction. The girl glanced over at us once before heading inside. I didn't know why, but I thought that was weird.

"She's only been at this school a week longer than you," Julia began, "and she's been late every day so far. I helped her around the first day, too, but I got a really bad vibe from her."

Tori stopped fingering Sebastian's bootlace long enough to say, "I have her in fifth period."

"She looks older than a junior," Julia added.

Tori used Sebastian's hand as a notepad, drawing random curlicues with tiny hearts on the ends. "Well I don't like her," she added, without taking her eyes off her work. "She creeps me out."

I glanced back at the Jeep as it slowly pulled away from campus. I wasn't the only new girl at school. This was a good thing.

"Hey, Adria," said Harry. "Do you skate?"

The question caught me off-guard. "Ummm, what like regular skating, or skateboarding?" I hoped this wasn't some kind of dating inquiry.

"Do I look like someone you'd find at a rink?" He laughed. "There's a skate park not far from here. If you want, you can go with us after school."

I looked first at everyone else, waiting for them to confirm or deny that they were going.

"You don't have to skate," said Julia, jumping in to save me. She likely saw the expression on my face that I didn't realize was so loud. "Harry's the only one that skates; Sebastian doesn't even do it."

"Yeah, he sucks at it," laughed Harry.

Sebastian reached over and playfully punched Harry on the shoulder. Immediately, the act reminded me of Alex the night in the park. Already that memorable night was proving to be just that. Unfortunately, the night air and smell of honeysuckle and pine was eclipsed by the more terrifying event afterwards.

I shook it off quickly and turned my attention back on my friends. But then I started thinking about the girl from the Jeep with white-blond hair. I was intrigued by her and I couldn't figure out why. It was a strange but insignificant curiosity. I let go of it until I met up with her in the hallway after school was over.

Her locker was on the same wall as mine.

She glanced at me once and nodded. Her features struck me instantly: she had an ethereal look about her; the white hair and perfectly applied array of gray eye shadow brought out her rounded angelic face. It was as if a painting had come to life in front of me. I felt so inadequate, so plain.

For a moment, it seemed like she was going to say something, introduce herself, spark up conversation, but instead she closed her locker and walked down the long hallway in the opposite direction. She went toward the bright sunlight shining in through the double glass doors at the exit. I could hear a small fashionable chain hitting softly against the back of her jeans as she walked.

Uncle Carl and Beverlee were both sitting in the den when I got home. The house smelled of pork chops and Macaroni & Cheese.

"So," Uncle Carl began, "do I need to ask?" He was not too great at the parenting thing, but he was trying.

"What he means to say is," Beverlee interrupted, "was your first day a good one?"

"Yeah, it was nice."

"So then you made friends?" Uncle Carl added.

"Uhhh, yeah. I didn't have to eat lunch alone on the first day, so that's good."

He nodded and buried his nose back inside his Scientific American magazine where it felt more comfortable.

"I'm going to…well, I mean if it's all right, I'd like to go to the skate park with them later." I wasn't used to having to ask permission to go anywhere. My mom let Alex and I go wherever we wanted.

"Sure you can go," said Beverlee. Her eyes were bright, probably happy to see that I was fitting in. But then the smile faded and she lowered her voice and said, "Maybe you could see if Alex might want to go, too."

"I'll ask her," I agreed, though somehow I had a feeling it would be a wasted effort.

And it was.

I thought it would be the perfect opportunity to talk some sense into my sister; getting her to come out of her shell and talking to me about what she was feeling, at least. It didn't take a psychiatrist to know that Alex needed professional help—my sister was as different as winter and summer, suffering from PTSD, surely. But I wasn't about to suggest it, professional help. Knowing what I knew about what made her that way…no one would believe her, much less help her—they'd just lock her up.

Alex was sitting on the edge of her bed, staring out the window when I walked in. Her room was a disaster. Suitcases were tossed on the floor where clothes and other various things lay scattered around. A plate stained with remnants of last Tuesday's meatloaf sat atop her chest-of-drawers, the fork stuck to the carpet. Absently, I counted six bright red plastic cups sitting on her nightstand and dresser.

"Wanna get out of the house for a while?" I asked, hopeful. "We could go for a walk, check out the town." I remained standing near the door. It was the first time I'd ever felt unwelcome in my sister's room. Secretly I studied her. She wore the same white scoop-neck tee she had on yesterday; the same jeans; her dark hair was oily and matted.

She had always been more organized than I was; everything she owned always had a place. She was orderly and clean and sometimes overly meticulous. But this, the way her room looked now—the way *she* looked now—was incredibly unlike her.

She never responded to my comment, so I moved farther inside the room, stepping over a box that contained her *Precious Moments* collection, each one wrapped carefully in old newspaper. Our great-grandmother had given them to her, one for each birthday up until she died. Normally, that box would be the first thing Alex put away safely; she would never even take the porcelain bisque figurines out to display in her room, she was so afraid they'd get broken. I was surprised to be stepping over them in the middle of a dirty, cluttered floor.

Alex hardly seemed to move and it scared me a little. I began to doubt that she had even blinked since I walked into the room. Her pale, oval face held no emotion. No anger. No sadness. Absolutely nothing.

"Have you talked to Mom at all?" I asked, leaning against the dresser.

"No," she said, still not looking at me, her voice flat and uninterested.

I hesitated, crossing my arms.

"Well, for what it's worth," I said, "you were right."

Still nothing. I went on.

"I was mad at you at first," I said, "about telling them Jeff did that to us, and for getting us sent here—or *me* sent here; you're free to live wherever you want. But Alex, I know why you did it. And I understand."

Alex brought both hands up and ran them roughly over her face and head, dragging her fingers through her hair. I got the sense that she was getting irritated, that she didn't care about anything I had to say.

Change of topic again. Now *I* was getting irritated.

"You know," I said, trying to keep calm, "you didn't have to come here. You could've just gone ahead with your plans to move in with Liz and Brandon."

Finally, Alex looked at me. Just barely. The natural blue of her eyes seemed much darker. Black circles had set in, and a red tint outlined the skin around her lower lashes like an infection. Her jaw was pulled into a subtle, yet noticeable hard line as if her teeth were pressed together bitterly. I noticed then that the bruises and cuts left on her face and neck from the night in Georgia were gone. Hers had been much worse than mine, yet I still had a few faint bruises, and I thought my mouth would stay sore forever.

"Why did you *come*, Alex?" I finally snapped, my voice laced with frustration, "if you're going to be this way?"

Alex swallowed hard and looked away from me; her dark bangs fell down around her eyes. "Because you're my sister," she said simply, staring toward the window again.

Her answer sparked a tiny bit of hope inside me. It was an opportunity to open her up, though a small one, and I didn't want to lose it. Uncrossing my arms, I bent over and picked the box of *Precious Moments* figurines up from the floor and went toward her closet, trekking through a bit of everything on my way.

"I'll put these up for you," I said, as I shoved a mound of sweaters away from the door with my foot. Finally getting the closet door open, I wasn't surprised to see it completely empty since everything she owned was everywhere else. Pushing up on my toes, I carefully slid the box onto the top shelf. A tiny white rope dangled from the ceiling. I reached up and pulled it, clicking the closet light on. I could see the lines on the carpet where Beverlee must have vacuumed before we came here. I had hardwood floors in my room, I briefly noted.

"I can clean your room for you," I offered, still holding onto that hope. "Help you get set up and organized."

I began with the trash: the plastic cups, various wrappers of snack cakes and plastic grocery store bags; I stacked the dishes into a small pile on the edge of the dresser, not surprised to find more dirty plates underneath her bed. Mold was setting in. Embarrassed to let Beverlee see how disgusting Alex had let her dishes get, I couldn't resist throwing one plate away that a fork had been stuck to, held together by mold that looked more alive than Alex did.

Alex never said a word. She never looked at me, even when I was standing directly in front of her. It still seemed like she hadn't blinked.

In minutes, I had cleared enough off the floor to make a suitable path from the door to the bed. I filled a laundry basket full of clothes, though most of them had never been worn.

Finally, I was getting overwhelmed, but I think it was more due to her silence than the cleaning.

"What's wrong with you?" I walked toward the window and sat on the desk chair that Alex was using as a closet. It was time to confront her. It had been long enough for her to start dealing emotionally with what happened, but instead, she was getting worse. I felt bad for her. How could I not? I was there with her when that…*beast* attacked us and when that man…*changed*. We both went through the same hell, but I was learning to put it behind me. Alex was supposed to be the strong one. She was my big sister, the one who had my back if I ever needed her.

Now she was reduced to someone I didn't know.

"Please, Alex," I said, when still she refused to acknowledge me. "It scared me too. No, it *traumatized* me. But it's over now and we need to put it behind us."

"I don't want to talk about it," she snapped, still not looking at me.

"I think we *should* talk about it, so that we *can* put it behind us. You're not yourself; you're this rude, selfish hermit. You never come out of your room, and you treat Uncle Carl and Beverlee like shit."

She was getting mad, I could tell right away. But I didn't care—she needed to hear this.

"Why can't you snap out of it?"

Her fists clenched against the sides of her legs; handfuls of the plaid white and yellow sheet she sat on, crushed in anger.

"I *said*"—her emphasis on the word struck me numb—"I don't want to *talk* about it, Adria." Lines around her eyes became noticeable, deepening furiously.

"But—"

"No!" she roared, jerking her head fiercely to look at me. "Please, just stop."

I paused, stunned. "Fine."

I closed her bedroom door harder than usual when I left. I was done. I was through. If Alex wanted to talk to me, I would be there to listen, but I wasn't going to try forcing it anymore. So I stayed away from her completely. For the next few days I kept busy by sitting outside on the wraparound porch, alone with my thoughts, until Beverlee would join me and play the fill-in mom. I didn't mind so much; she was kind and concerned and becoming more of a mom to me than my real mom ever had been. And I began to learn some things about myself just talking to her, that I never knew before.

I never really had much time to think about how badly I wanted to get away from home. I was always too worried about my mom, but once I *was* away and could think about myself more, I realized how miserable I truly was in Georgia. At Uncle Carl's, we had spacious bedrooms overlooking an awesome landscape of trees in the back and a field in the front. The air conditioning worked here, but we didn't have to use it because the weather was nearly perfect. Beverlee cooked breakfast and dinner every day. She and Uncle Carl were the type that would do just about anything for us—they even bought me a bike—it was no car, but it was something.

But other than the material things, what was truly important and made me see the misery was that there was no fighting here. There was no Jeff. I didn't have to worry about leaving the house to avoid the belligerent idiocy of a violent, always-drunken man who my mom thought so lowly of herself that he was the best she could do. I didn't have to fall asleep under a tree in a park alone at night because I didn't feel safe in my own room. Or risk catching Jeff peeing off the front porch because he was too drunk to realize he wasn't standing in front of the toilet.

I thought maybe it was for the best that I was forced to leave home. Not only did I have a better home in a better environment, but I hoped that with us gone, our mom would somehow wake up and get away from there, too.

But most of all, this new life in this new place was the only thing I had to help distract me from that night in the forest in Georgia. Because the truth was that in some way like Alex, I was far from being able to put what happened to us behind me. I had a long way to go before I could come to terms with it, or understand it.

Maybe I wasn't so different from Alex, after all. I was just better at hiding trauma than she was.

5

I met up with Harry and the others at the skate park before dark, surprised I found the place as easily as I did. It was a relief when I rode up on the bike Uncle Carl bought for me, to see that I wasn't the only person without a car. But Harry had a car, and music blared from two enormous speakers in the wide-open trunk. Skaters whizzed by on the ramps; the sound of wheels hitting the concrete and metal was somehow louder than the music. There were only a handful of skaters, outnumbered by those like me who came only to watch.

I had to give Harry credit: as much as skateboarding didn't appeal to me, it looked to take a lot of skill.

"Over here!" Harry shouted over the noise.

He jumped down from his board, stepping on the end of it in a fancy, strategic sort of way so it popped up into his waiting hand.

"Glad you came," he said. "Wanna try it out?"

"Uhhh, no that's all right," I declined, though I knew he was mostly joking. "I couldn't even begin to understand how to do any of that stuff."

"Ah, nothing to it," he replied.

"Yeah, right."

"Adria!" Julia came up from behind with Tori and Sebastian following hand-in-hand. "Have trouble finding the place?" she added.

"No, your directions were perfect."

Julia gestured for me to follow. "Let's go sit down over here. It's far enough away from the racket, but not too far away we look like snobs."

I assumed she meant the skateboards when she said 'racket'.

"Unless..." she paused, raising a brow, "you *want* to sit closer to the skaters."

I caught on. "No, no, I think your spot will be great."

"You sure?" she said, pulling me along. "Evan is hot, and so is Layne; he's the tall one over there in the *Fight Club* shirt."

Tori jumped in with, "*Julia*, I thought you hated Layne?"

"I do, but that doesn't mean he's any less hot."

"Why do you hate him?" I asked, only slightly curious.

We came to an area with two stone picnic tables. A park grill stood nearby; remnants of charcoal lay scattered about. A bright red and black sign had been nailed to a tree that read: 'No Camping'.

"Well, I don't *really* hate him," Julia answered.

"No, she used to *date* him," Sebastian said, with a twinge of laughter. It caught me off-guard since he hardly ever spoke.

"We never dated." She flashed Sebastian an infuriated look, and then ignored him, which I thought a little strange. "So anyway, Adria," she finally went on, looking over at me again, "was it just you that moved here?"

Really, the question was just her way to distract everyone from the subject of her and Layne. And it worked. Suddenly, all eyes were on me and I was stuck tiptoeing around the topic of Alex. But how were they supposed to know that the very mention of her made me uneasy and even a little annoyed? Or, that talking about her only made me think about the night she and I were attacked by a wer...well, by *something*, and that they were making it more difficult to put it behind me? Making it more difficult for me to convince myself I was a stable member of society.

"No," I reluctantly answered, "my older sister, Alexandra, came too."

I was glad they didn't probe further; just asked the basic stuff—How much older was she? Where is she now?—and then they were onto the next topic.

Suddenly our circle got quiet and everyone looked up and toward the street.

"You've *got* to be kidding me," growled Tori.

The muddy Jeep with big tires drove slowly into the skate park. The same three guys were with the spiky-haired blond girl from school. Once again, they were looking in our direction and this time it made me uneasy. I glanced at Julia and then Harry, lastly at Tori and Sebastian, but saw that everyone seemed as perplexed as I was. I had hoped that *someone* might know what attracted their obvious stares.

"Thank God," said Tori, as the Jeep pulled away from us and went toward a nearby parking lot instead.

I watched across the long stretch of grass and trees that separated us from them. Pulling into a space, the driver killed the engine and only he and the spiky-haired blond girl got out. Bracing her palms against the hood, the girl hopped up and sat atop it, letting her legs hang just over the tire. The driver walked around to the passenger's side and leaned against the back door, crossing his arms over his chest and his legs at the ankles. Vaguely I could see his lips moving as he spoke, apparently to the guys that still sat in the backseat. I got the strangest feeling. I knew they were watching us, even when they appeared not to be. I glanced once more at each of my friends, wondering which one of them could be the reason, which of them knew more than they were letting on.

"Maybe they just want to hang out," said Harry. "We should ask them."

Tori's face scrunched up into an ugly grimace. "Definitely *not*," she scoffed. "They look like trash."

Harry frowned. "What does trash look like exactly?" He and Sebastian glanced at each other privately, agreeing that she had said something that neither favored. "You're way too judgmental of people, girl."

"Whatever, Harry," Tori snapped back.

I liked Tori—or, maybe I just tolerated her—but the more I got to know her, I realized that I probably never would've befriended her on my own if she wasn't already part of the group I hung out with.

"Have any of you ever talked to them?" I asked. It was my first attempt at obtaining some clues.

"I haven't," said Harry. "But I see the girl near my Art class every day."

Sebastian reached up and rubbed his temples in a circular motion with his thumb and index finger, as if soothing a headache. Tori laid her head in his lap then. Her petite arm, dressed in jingling bracelets, came up to where she gently brushed the side of his face with her fingers. "Baby have a headache?" she mothered.

I think Harry's eyes almost rolled right out of the sockets. Subconsciously, mine did too.

Sebastian braced his hands on the picnic tabletop and leaned his head back farther. Her fingers fell away. Tori stood up, looking slighted, and mumbled something to him. They left together, Tori's mouth constantly moving while Sebastian walked away quietly.

"I told Sebastian that Tori was a handful," Harry spoke up, as we sat on the edge of the skate bowl.

The Jeep was still parked across the lot, and by now all four of the passengers were sitting on or leaning against it. I never really stopped watching them as they watched us.

"Seriously, Harry," I urged, "what did you *really* say about her?"

"Huh?"

"Oh, come on," I said, smirking. "I know guys don't tell other guys a girl is a 'handful'. You're just trying to be polite, which I appreciate, don't get me wrong."

Harry nearly blushed. "Ah, okay, you got me on that one. I told him she was a soulless bitch."

His posture changed uncomfortably. Maybe he'd been brought up in a super-strict family with good morals and all that stuff. A bit different than mine where curse words were integrated into everyday conversation. Except with me and Alex. Really, it was just Mom's boyfriends who brought in the bad habits.

"Hey, it's cool," I said. "I don't get offended easily."

Harry smiled and left it at that.

"Sebastian is my best friend," he said. "He's a smart guy; I don't know what he was thinking when he started dating *her*."

"She's pretty," I admitted.

Harry's expression soured. "If you say so. But I think Sebastian's finally realizing I was right about her."

"What makes you think that?"

"They've been together for like five months, but lately he hasn't been into her as much as he used to be."

I pictured Sebastian and Tori at lunch and around the school; even just minutes ago. "I don't know how they were before," I said, "but now that you mention it, their relationship does seem a little one-sided."

Harry's soured face brightened then. "You see it too?" he asked, eagerly. "I hoped it wasn't just me."

"No, I think you're onto something. Tori definitely seems more into him than he seems into her."

A skater zipped up the side of the bowl and landed heavily right next to me with a *clack*. I jumped and squealed; thankfully my fingers weren't crushed. He smiled apologetically and took off again in a wheeled blaze.

I turned to Harry once the shock wore off. "Is he into Julia? Sebastian, I mean."

"No way," Harry replied, laughing. "Where'd that come from?"

"They just seem…tense around each other."

Harry shook his head. "I dunno, but he would've told me…" His voice trailed, leaving me to wonder if he really believed that himself.

Julia walked up behind us then. "What are you two talking about?"

I felt my cheeks flush with heat, and guilt made me wonder if she had overheard. But that was just the paranoia at work; there was no way she could have.

"I was giving Adria skating pointers," Harry lied.

Julia plopped down on the other side of me. "She needs more than pointers," she joked.

I shook my head, smiling, but not at all embarrassed.

"Hey, no argument here," I agreed with a grin.

Julia reached over and cradled my wrist in her fingers, thumbing one of three braided bracelets I wore, made of colorful thread, woven together in intricate patterns.

"I've tried to make those," she said, "but I'm *way* too impatient."

"My sister made these," I said, fingering them one by one, reminiscing. I had worn them since March, and they were probably going to break off soon. I thought about how ironic that was.

"She used to make all kinds of jewelry," I went on. "I saw the inside of Hobby Lobby enough to point you in the right direction if you ever need beads or glue."

"Hmmm," Julia mumbled absently. "I'll keep that in mind." She jumped up and crossed her arms, looking out across the skate bowl. I thought her comment seemed a little off, and I quickly realized why. Layne, the skater in the *Fight Club* shirt was standing on the other side getting ready to take his turn.

"Whoohoo!" she yelled with her hands cupped into a cylinder around her mouth. "Let's see what you've got, Layne!" It was completely sarcastic.

Layne's eyes barely veered in her direction, though it was obvious he heard her. *Everyone* heard her. Layne rested his board on the edge of the concrete, waited a few seconds and then took off. As he whirred back and forth every which way, I noticed the only spot he didn't cover was anywhere near our current position.

Julia took hold of my wrist and urged me up. Harry followed.

"Come on," she said, heading back toward the parking lot.

"Why don't you just talk to him, Jewels?" Harry suggested.

"No way. I'm totally over him."

I tried not to look quietly at Harry because it felt sort of like talking about Julia behind her back again, but I couldn't help it. Neither could Harry. We shared the same obvious thought about how Julia was still in denial about the whole thing. Whatever it was. It felt like dangerous territory and I refused to probe.

I heard an engine rev. An older model black Bronco with a huge Grille Guard on the front bumper drove nosily into the park. It had a roof rack with four KC Lights and its tires were even bigger than the Jeep's. I knew a thing or two about four-wheel-drive accessories; my step-dad had been a mechanic and a custom auto tech all his life. And my step-brother had followed his lead. Double the unsolicited lessons.

The Bronco rolled toward us slowly.

"Must be a zombie apocalypse nearby," Harry exclaimed, "with *that* tank—sweet!"

As the Bronco drove closer, its size became more distinct; I would need some serious help getting inside that thing. It grumbled its way past us and parked just three spaces over from Harry's car. Two brooding guys, probably in their early twenties, jumped down onto the parking lot, closing the doors behind them. One was tall like Harry and the other had a full sleeve tattoo on his right arm. The tall one reached briefly into his back pocket, maybe to situate his wallet. They spoke to each other for a moment and began walking toward us.

They carried no skateboards, so I knew they weren't here for recreation.

"Wonder who that is?" said Harry.

"Never saw them before," Julia said from behind. She moved away from us then, walking in the direction of the restroom facilities. "I gotta use the bathroom."

I noticed out of the corner of my eye, the four people hanging around the Jeep were all standing in a group, more alert than laid back now. They blatantly stared at what I sensed was about to become a show.

The two approaching held my attention. Why were they looking at me like that? I glanced behind me to see if someone was standing nearby, but no one was around but me and Harry.

They stopped right in front of us; the tall one popping a piece of candy into his mouth—maybe that was what he had been fishing for in his back pocket.

"You and your sister, Alexandra, just moved in up on the hill, right?" he asked me, sucking on the candy.

"Y-yeah, that's right." I hoped I was hiding just how intimidated I was, better than I thought. "How'd you know that?"

He smiled, though I found no comfort in the way he chose to twist it into a faint grin. "We know things," he answered.

Harry leaned against his car next to me, trying to act casual, but I knew he was as suspicious as I was. I could feel he was moving closer in a protective manner.

"Do you live around here?" Harry inquired.

The tattooed one nodded in response, but it seemed more like a dismissal. He was more interested in me than Harry. Both of them were.

I didn't like this at all.

And how did they know Alex? This mystery ate away at my thoughts more than anything. I stood stiffly; my arms bent upwards, hands touching level with my chest. I always grazed the backs of my fingers when I was nervous.

"I'm William," said the tall one. He continued to look at me, waiting for me to respond.

"Adria," I said finally, then gestured to my left, "and this is Harry."

"A pleasure, Adria," he replied, but I detected venom in his closed-lip smile.

He extended a hand, but before I could commit entirely, he made the move to take hold of it anyway, then leaned over to kiss the top, just below my wrist. Instinct told me to pull away, and when I tried, his grip tightened. The virulent smile never left his face; his penetrating gaze never left my own. Dark, beautiful eyes, but more malevolent than beautiful so there could never be an attraction.

Finally, I pulled my hand free, feeling his fingers graze my knuckles.

Harry had moved from the car and stood more rigidly at my side. Nothing about his face was welcoming. The tattooed guy cocked his head to one side, looking at Harry now with a sort of humorous curiosity.

"You must be the boyfriend," he said to Harry.

"No," Harry responded, "I'm not, but maybe you should find another place to hang out."

I winced. The last thing I wanted was for Harry to feel obligated to protect me and end up in the hospital as a result. I could tell, just by the apprehensive tone of his posture that he knew as well as I did these two could end his life.

The tall one, William, smirked.

I heard voices and footfalls behind us on the grass as a small group of Harry's skater friends approached. I felt my palms sweating, and then realized I had been standing the past many seconds with my fists balled at my sides.

Harry's friends stood behind us in the short distance, a just-in-case-distance.

Feeling more confident now that it wasn't just Harry and me, I stepped up and asked with irritation, "What do you want, exactly?"

"No need to be rude," William answered, folding his hands together behind him. "Just came over to get acquainted. That's all." That was lie, and his impish expression wasn't exactly trying to trick me into believing it.

I crossed my arms firmly and just looked at him. Already tired of this stupid game, my nervousness receded quickly. Maybe it was all the practice I had over the years with my step-dad, but whatever it was, it pushed me right up to William daringly. I didn't realize how tall he really was until I was practically standing in the shadow his body cast around me.

William smiled down at me, pleased, and this infuriated me even more.

"Well, I'm not interested in *getting* acquainted," I snapped.

"Why not?" he said, simply.

I stood my ground. I had to. Though all I wanted to do was get away from him.

The tattooed one was staring Harry down now, as if he were just waiting for his chance to jump him. Harry stood with confidence, but I knew on the inside he was as scared as I was.

William licked the dryness from his lips and breathed in deeply. "You were right, Ashe," he said to the tattooed one, but never looked over. "She has the same aggressive scent." He rolled his head around, the veins bulging in his neck as he inhaled the air.

My face crinkled with incomprehension—what was *that* supposed to mean?

I went to leave, taking Harry by the elbow, but was stunned to feel a harsh hand around my bicep that I knew wasn't Harry's. Turning swiftly, I jerked my arm from William, but he pulled me toward him before I could get far enough away from him. Vaguely, I heard the clatter of Harry's friends advancing behind us, and for a split second even caught the four from the Jeep rushing over. But in that next split second, my reflexes took over and my fist went soaring toward William's face. The contact against his nose sent shockwaves through the bones in my hand.

A dozen gasps rose all around me, then everything went silent. No one moved, least of all me. *What did I just do?*

Petrified, I swallowed hard and finally backed away half a step. Harry unfroze and moved over in front of me, probably cursing me in his head for taking it to this level, because being my guy friend, he would be the one who paid the price. He pushed me back with his arm, putting himself defensively between me and William.

William never moved.

A trickle of red emerged from William's left nostril. He reached up slowly and wiped the blood away with the side of his thumb. How in the hell could I have hit him hard enough to bloody his nose? Maybe he's just a bleeder, I thought.

"Interesting," he noted, and then licked the blood clean.

But then, to the surprise of everyone, William and Ashe turned and walked away. I watched as they got back into the black Bronco and drove through the skate park; even the four from the Jeep, who were now standing just feet from me, watched until the Bronco was gone. But their faces held a different intensity, one that I wasn't interested in figuring out. I had had enough with strange, intimidating people for one night.

Suddenly, I was surrounded by a lot of impressed, excited faces, and all I wanted to do was shrink inside myself.

"Damn, girl," said some curly-haired guy, "you got a brick in your hand, or what?"

"That guy was *huge*," one girl said, smiling wide-eyed.

When the excitement wore off a few minutes later and Harry and I were alone again, I was still too bewildered by the whole thing to say much. I was especially surprised by how soon William and Ashe left, and how the entire situation didn't turn into a huge brawl. It didn't make any sense. Nothing about them gave off the impression that they were capable of fear, that anyone around here could intimidate them. How could they let me get away with what I did?

"Looks like they're leaving too," Harry said, watching the Jeep.

All four of them had made it back, and the spiky-haired blond girl was the last to hop inside.

"If those are the type your sister hangs with," Harry said about William and Ashe, "then I feel sorry for you."

That stung a little, but also gave me more to think about. They knew Alex by her given name and they wouldn't have known to call her 'Alexandra' unless Alex was the one who told them.

"What do you think they wanted?" Harry asked. "That was…strange."

I paused, thinking not about the answer to his question, but instead to my own: What *did* my sister have to do with them?

"I have no idea," I answered.

Julia finally came back from a lengthy amount of time in the restroom.

"What happened?" she asked, walking up, dragging her fingers through the ends of her hair. "You two look all depressed."

Harry and I just looked at each other again and shook our heads.

Later, when the streetlights came to life, I decided to head home. Harry offered to give me a ride, but I appreciatively declined. I knew he wasn't ready to leave, and his friend's weren't ready to let him take the stereo with him. Besides, there wasn't a place in his car to put my bike.

I left, feeling a chill in the air as the darkness fell. It was quiet out, and my fears of being alone near any wooded area resurfaced. I rode down one long, winding street instead, and I kept thinking that my next turn was just up ahead, but after many more minutes, I knew I had gone too far. How could I have missed my turn? All sorts of things ran through my mind then: *What if I end up like one of those teenagers they find murdered in the woods? What if those guys find me?* I began to panic, lost on a dark, tree-enveloped gravel road. But worst of all, I felt the eerie sensation of eyes at my back.

Movement transferred in my peripheral vision, an out of place shadow rebelling against the dark. My head jerked sideways and I froze on my bike as a vehicle came slowly around the curve a few yards behind me. I knew somewhere in the back of my mind that I should've taken off right then, but for some inane reason, I didn't. Was stupidity in the face of danger becoming a habit of mine? It sure seemed like it.

The headlights were overly bright so I couldn't make out the vehicle, but I knew that it was larger than average. Higher up…like a souped-up Bronco perhaps? I gasped; the cool air stung my throat as I breathed in too sharply; my heart sped up in two seconds flat.

The gravel under the vehicle's tires grinded loudly as it drove toward me. I pushed the bike pedals down and took off. In seconds, my calves tightened to the point that it hurt worse with every thrust of my feet. But no matter how quickly I rode, the vehicle advanced, and I knew I couldn't outride it. I kept looking back to watch it, hoping it would fall back, or turn down any one of the few roads that it passed, but not keeping my eyes in front of me proved a mistake. I saw the branch out ahead, but not in time to dodge it. It caught tightly in the spokes, sending me flying. I crashed hard onto my hip on the street.

The vehicle slammed on its brakes feet from me and two people jumped out simultaneously.

It was the Jeep.

I wondered if this could get any worse, and then cursed myself for wondering because it usually does once you do.

"Are you all right?" a guy said as he stood over me.

I didn't look at him and refused his help as I stood up on my own, dusting my hands against my legs.

"I'm fine."

I bent over to get my bike, but another guy was already picking it up with one hand and tossing it into the back of the Jeep between the mounted tire and the seat.

"We'll give you a ride home," the first one said. "Come on."

"I'm not getting into your car." I started to walk away quickly, but the quiet one stopped me. "Please," he insisted, with what felt like sincerity. "We won't hurt you." He held out his hand to me, and I just looked at it.

I don't know why, but deep down I believed him.

"Hi Adria." The spiky-haired blond girl waved at me from the front seat. She was smiling hugely.

I swallowed an imaginary lump, and after a long contemplative moment, I—without taking the guy's hand—jumped in the back seat, nearly hitting my head on the cover rail above.

6

"Cool to finally meet you," the girl said. "Officially, anyway. I'm Zia." Her teeth were bright white as if she left a whitening strip on too long. Her eyelashes were thick and black as coal; her skin creamy and flawless. I kind of hated her.

The clear picture of her face blinked out as the driver got in and shut his door, turning off the interior light.

Introductions were important, but I was expecting explanations first. For a long moment, I couldn't speak. I heard Zia's name in the back of my mind, but my awareness hadn't caught up to it yet. I studied the three guys: the driver who looked the oldest and had a short black mohawk; the smallest who sat behind the driver near the door seemed to have a permanent scowl on his face; the one sitting on the other side of me against the passenger door, he was the one who convinced me to get in the Jeep. His skin was lightly tanned, his hair dark, almost black, with a messy short cut; his dark eyes instantly pulled me in to some kind of abyss, which I recognized right away as an inevitable problem.

"Thanks," I said, turning my attention to Zia. "I was afraid you were someone else."

The driver put the Jeep in gear and we pulled away with a jolt; the vehicle's top had been taken off, so it was chilly as we rode away at forty-miles-per-hour.

Zia turned around from the front seat to face me. "William and Ashe, from the skate park?" she confirmed, knowingly.

"Yeah," I admitted. "You know them? Who are they?"

"Brothers," Zia replied flatly. "Don't have any desire to know more than that, really."

"I can see why."

"We're much nicer, despite what the school thinks of me."

I twisted uneasily on the seat, feeling a pang of guilt even though I had never thought badly of her myself. "What does the school think of you?"

Zia laughed. "I'm surprised you haven't heard," she said, turning around again to face forward. "I'm a devil-worshipper and my brothers have been accused of being more than brothers, if you know what I mean."

My face scrunched up in disgust.

"Well, I haven't heard anything like that," I said honestly. "And besides, rumors are just rumors."

"Didn't say I cared what anybody thought," she said. "Well, except maybe for you. If you thought I was a freak you might not have gotten into the Jeep."

She made a valid point. But truthfully, she was only slightly less freaky than the other group I wanted to avoid.

"My brothers are Damien here," she said, nodding toward the driver, "and Joseph back there, who everyone calls Dwarf." She was referring to the little one sitting behind the driver next to me. "And that's Isaac, the quiet one on the other side of you. We live with him and his family—"

"That's enough, Zia," Isaac jumped in.

They were the only words he would say, but the tone said so much more. Instantly, Zia fell silent, though her posture seethed with irritation. I was confused and even a little put off by him.

"Anyway, we'll take you home," she continued. "And some advice? Don't go outside too late around here by yourself."

I slunk back into the seat, pulling my sleeves over my hands and crossing my arms.

Zia added then, "By the way, how's your sister doing?"

How did she know about Alex? Why was Alex mentioned so often by people who didn't even know *me*? This was so strange that I couldn't hold back anymore. "Okay, now I'm a little freaked out," I replied, suspiciously. "How do you know about my sister? And those guys, they mentioned her by name."

"Not sure about William and Ashe," Zia said, "but *I* know because Isaac's oldest brother, Nathan, works at the grocery store with Beverlee. And word spreads fast around here—small town and all. Her name is Alexa, right?"

"No, it's Alexandra, but she goes by Alex."

I *had* to stop being so paranoid about everything all the time. More and more every day I realized just how much what happened in Georgia had affected me, and that I wasn't as over it as I thought I was. I thought about William and Ashe then, wondering if maybe I read too much into them, too. Sure, they were obvious douchebags, but a part of me was so afraid of them that I actually, in a small way, feared for my life. That was ridiculous. Would *every* incident in my life be dictated by *the* incident? And with each new realization, I reminded myself about what I had seen. What I went through.

It was in this unlikely moment, right there in the Jeep with my enigmatic company, that my subconscious finally decided to accept the truth: I saw a werewolf. I witnessed with my own eyes a real, living, breathing, terrifying werewolf much like the ones you saw in the movies and read about in books. And when a person comes to such an unbelievable realization as that, when the human in them can't lie or make up excuses anymore, it changes that person forever. I changed right there. It took me weeks to believe it, but finally the truth caught up with me. I knew then too, that the reason Alex was no longer the sister I once knew was because the truth caught up to her much faster.

The cold of change washed over me in an instant. I heard Zia's voice, and occasionally the voices of Damien and Dwarf, but if they were talking to me, I didn't know it. I absently looked at my company, one by one, and somehow I couldn't see them the way I saw them before. What was being human exactly? It seemed everything around me was nothing but a lie and I would have to start over and relearn everything I had learned since I spoke my first words and took my first steps. *Everything* was a lie and I had been living in this lie for seventeen years. Something as heavy as that was a dangerous burden to carry.

"Stop the car," I demanded.

"What?" Zia asked.

"Please, just stop the car. I appreciate the ride, but I can get home the rest of the way by myself."

"Let us take you home," Isaac urged, laying his warm hand gently on my wrist as I grabbed the back of Zia's seat.

I looked at him and for a moment wanted to listen. His eyes were magnetic; there was a sort of intensity and concern in them that I couldn't place, but there was no time for trying. I wanted to go home and I wanted to do it alone.

"Please..." I said one last time.

Damien stopped the Jeep, and reluctantly Isaac got out. He walked around to get my bike down for me.

"I understand," said Zia. "I'll see you in school if you want. I hope we didn't offend you or anything."

"No, not at all," I said right away. "Thanks again for the ride."

I looked back once before riding away on my bike, and when I did, the only set of eyes I saw looking back at me were Isaac's. The red light from the brakes cast an eerie glow on the street. Finally, the Jeep faded from sight and I could hear the humming of its engine in the distance. I stopped there in the street, one paved rather than covered with gravel, and I held firmly onto this moment. A streetlight burned and hummed gently overhead; a mailbox shaped like an old-timey red barn jutted from the ground at my left, its owners far up the driveway where tiny white lights, glimmered through the darkness.

I was cold, but I didn't care. I was also hungry and had a headache, but none of that mattered either.

Had I become Alex in that moment? I didn't feel angry, or hateful, or capable of treating those who loved me, with contempt. I assumed that if I was in Alex's realm now that I was supposed to feel that way. But I didn't. I just felt different. When I made it home, I went straight up to my room. I searched the internet for anything on werewolves I could find. I searched and read until I could no longer keep my eyes open and sleep took me sometime after four in the morning.

"You fell asleep there?" Beverlee was standing somewhere in my room. "Adria, why don't you get in your bed for an hour; you're going to get a crick in your neck."

I was barely awake, and it took a minute to understand who she was and what she was talking about. I lifted my head from the desk and felt a cool draft of air brush my face where drool had pooled under my cheek. I closed the laptop where there had to be twenty web pages open, which I didn't want Beverlee to see. She probably would've thought nothing of it, but I was momentarily panicked, as if her seeing a simple web page would give everything about my life away.

"Do you want some breakfast? I made pancakes."

I looked over at the clock, and then the window, realizing that the sun was much higher than it usually was—I was late for school. I jerked awake fully then and started to rush around getting ready.

"Adria," Beverlee called out. "Dentist appointment at nine, remember? I'll drop you off at school afterwards."

Oh yeah…

I went through the entire day in a haze. I sat with my regular friends at lunch and they noticed I wasn't myself though I tried not to make it so obvious. It was easy to dodge their questions simply by nodding yes or no, and faking a yawn every now and then to make it seem like I just needed some sleep. But as the days wore on, hiding my issues became more unavoidable. A little more than a month and already rumors were going around about me, which made it to Beverlee's ears at the grocery store. Zia was right about small towns.

"I don't want you to be offended by me asking you this, Adria," Beverlee said kindly as she stood in the doorway of my bedroom one Saturday afternoon, "but it's important that I talk to you about it."

"I'm not on drugs, Beverlee," I mumbled, a step ahead of her. "I'll take a drug test if you want me to."

I sat on my bed with my back pressed against the headboard, a pile of books beside me, the laptop on the other side, and a spiral tablet in my lap.

She walked farther inside and sat on the end of my bed.

"I believe you," she said, "and a drug test isn't necessary to prove it, but will you tell me what's going on with you lately?" She reached out and touched my ankle. "I thought you were warming up to us. You seemed comfortable, and now you're hiding yourself upstairs like your sister." She paused as though waiting for me to look at her while speaking, and I did finally look away from the tablet. "Did something happen at school? Did I do something? Do you miss your mom? I know you must miss her, but I'm here for you if you need someone to talk to. You know that, right?"

I hated her for being so likable. It made me feel guilty for giving her reason to ask such questions and worry about me as much as she was.

Placing the tablet beside me on the bed, I gave her my full attention. The delicate lines around her lips curved subtly as she looked at me, softening the worried expression on her face just a bit. She wore a white long-sleeved button-up shirt with tiny blue flowers sprinkled all over the fabric. Beverlee reminded me of my mom, the way my mom used to look at me before she succumbed to that strange masochist lifestyle.

I did miss my mom. But I had been missing her for at least six years.

"It's nothing you did," I said. "I'm grateful you and Uncle Carl gave us a place to live. I know Alex is too, but she's just taking things harder, and I'm sorry for the way she's treated you." I smiled softly at Beverlee. "I'll be fine. I'm just missing home a little, but I'll be fine. I promise."

It did bother me that my mom hadn't called once to talk to us, but that was something I tried not to think about.

Beverlee returned the smile and then patted my knee. "I do feel better than before I came up here," she said, and rose into a stand. "We're really glad to have you and Alex here; don't forget that."

I spent the entire Saturday in my room, reading and surfing the net, but when I realized I wasn't any closer to finding out anything more about 'real' werewolves than when I started, I put the books away and turned the laptop off completely. I didn't know what I was trying to find, but I was beyond frustrated with it all. What did I expect? Werewolves weren't supposed to be real, and researching them would be like researching UFO's. There would be a book here and there about the possibility of their existence; eyewitness accounts that no one ever took seriously; old village myths from centuries ago;

and random names of some professor or 'expert' who only the crazy truly believed in their research. After all, sane people didn't believe in the supernatural. Normal people believed what the majority believed and everything else was fiction. Right?

It was late, after eleven o'clock when I heard Alex stirring in her room. There wasn't anything unusual about that since she made it a habit to come out of her room after Uncle Carl and Beverlee had gone to bed. Her footsteps faded down the stairs, and I waited, listening. When she never came back up, my interest grew. The routine was usually to rummage the kitchen for something to eat, and sometimes she would turn the TV on for a few minutes before heading back upstairs.

Still nothing.

And then instinct compelled me to look out my bedroom window. I saw Alex, dressed in her robe, walking briskly behind the house and disappearing through the trees.

I slipped on my shoes quickly, grabbed my coat and followed.

I let the back screen door shut softly behind me and I leapt down the back steps, taking two at a time. The moment my shoes hit the frigid ground, I regretted not doubling-up on socks, and grabbing my hat and gloves. I sucked in cold air as I ran, breathing into the warm confines of my coat sleeve. My eyes burned; the layer of moisture coating them, stripped away by the cold October air. Dashing into the woods, I felt swallowed up by the immediate darkness. The wind whipped through the trees and bit the back of my neck and the bare skin above my ankles. I kept running, over brush and limbs and toward a thin stream of water, slowing down only enough to gauge my distance before leaping over it.

Splash! I never saw the second sliver of black water until it was too late. My feet were soaked to my shins, and the bitter cold stung my legs like thousands of needles.

But I kept running.

I knew Alex was just ahead of me because I'd heard the same splash of water before I found it, so I slackened my pace and pressed on slowly. I could still hear Alex's movements out ahead, though they seemed fainter. Her feet shuffled through dead leaves; low tree branches snapped as she pushed her way through them. One snapped under my feet as well and I froze, but Alex never looked back. She continued her strangely graceful trek through the forest as if she knew every downed limb and ankle-spraining crevice without having to mind her footing.

Finally, I could see a small clearing out ahead, bathed by the moonlight. Alex slowed to a walk as she got closer. I stopped and crouched next to a tree, trying to stay warm and failing miserably. The only part of me that felt heat was the skin around my mouth and the tops of my fingers as I continued to breathe deeply into my sleeve.

Alex stepped softly around a maze of young trees. Faintly, I noticed that she was barefoot as she tiptoed over a blanket of leaves and dirt. How in the heck could she be barefoot?! My feet were numb before they got wet, now they were downright frozen. She entered the clearing where there was just enough light to see the outline of her robe and her naked form underneath it—since when did my sister sleep naked? I wondered how it was that she didn't seem cold, though she wore much less than I did.

She reached out her hands in an unusual gesture then. It appeared she was talking to someone; the erotic undertone in her movements was completely odd to me. I tried harder to penetrate the darkness with my eyes, needing proof that this girl was really my sister, Alexandra Dawson—I began to wonder.

I stood carefully and crept farther in, until I noticed another figure, and then I stopped solid, sucking in more bitter air with one unexpected gasp.

He placed his hands on each side of Alex's face, her cheeks gently swallowed up by them. And then his lips covered hers. A boyfriend? No, something about this was different, off. The way he seemed to guide her movements as if controlling her; how she moaned simply by his fingertips brushing against her shoulders. I watched, feeling my insides twist into something hard. Worried about my sister in this place, this weird situation, I intended to step out from my hiding spot and let this guy know she was not alone.

But then a second, and a *third* figure emerged from the darkness, stopping me in a fearful jolt.

The first one grabbed Alex protectively and pulled her closer. The others circled them almost ceremoniously it seemed, their necks craning as they appeared to inhale the air deeply. I heard a few words amidst broken sentences, but nothing made sense to me. I slung the hood off my head and turned a bare ear toward them, hoping to hear something, but I got nothing but a blast of cold air against the side of my face.

The longer I watched the more I began to see that Alex was safe in the arms of this stranger. But it was difficult to see how she touched him, how she reacted to the way he touched her.

Suddenly, the guy picked her up in the cradle of his arms, and all four of them disappeared in an instant. It happened so fast that I staggered from the safety of the trees in a frantic search for any sign of them. I stood there for a moment, freezing and mystified, feeling every bone in my body clack together against my hardened muscles. I could see my breath in front of me, rapidly exhaling in the cold. Finally, I ran through the woods back to our house as fast as I could, surprised I could find my way back so easily in the dark without tripping over the debris on the forest bed.

Alex never came home that night. Or Sunday. And all day at school on Monday, I could think of nothing but her.

"Did you get a good look at them?" asked Julia.

"Not really," I replied, sitting down at our lunch table. "It was too dark."

Julia sat next to me; her soda popped and fizzed as she sprung the tab open. "Has your uncle called the cops?"

"No. He said they won't do anything since she's an adult, and because I saw her willingly leave with them. My aunt and uncle think it's what she wanted. It's what I think, too."

Julia patted my back. "She'll probably show back up in a few days."

"I hope so."

Harry and the rest of our group joined us then. Sebastian looked rough, like he just rolled out of bed. Quiet as usual, though with a girlfriend who did enough talking for both of them.

Lunch was the same as it was every day—except that it was too cold to spend it outside anymore—until Zia walked up, and the table went silent. I never told any of my friends about what happened the night I left the skate park, so they were all a bit shocked that I welcomed Zia as though we had already met and even hung out together before.

"This is Zia," I said, and then introduced everyone else. Tori looked horrified. Harry was more welcoming than I expected, which made me wonder if he liked her. But Julia—she rose to her feet, pushing the chair back harshly across the floor. I sat solidly in my seat, my hands locked to the edge of the table as my mind tried to pick apart her sudden change of mood.

Julia stared bitterly not at Zia, but more toward the wall right past Zia. Four long seconds withered away, and Julia left us all sitting there as she walked out of the cafeteria and in the opposite direction.

Harry and I looked at each other, wondering the same thing.

I noticed Tori smirk, as if proud that at least one of us disapproved of Zia as much as she did.

After a long, awkward moment of silence, Zia looked down at me. "Can I talk to you for a sec?" she said, not even fazed by what just happened, it seemed.

"Sure," I agreed, and stood up slowly.

I glanced back once at my gawking friends as I followed Zia through the cafeteria.

We slipped through the breezeway outside and made our way to the bleachers at the football field. Burying my hands deep in the sleeves of my sweater, I crossed my arms firmly at my chest. I could feel my shoulders stiffening up around my cheeks. I hated the cold. Absolutely hated it.

"I don't know what Julia's deal is," I said. "That was weird."

Zia shook her head. "Never mind about her. I just wanted to tell you I saw your sister yesterday. She's fine I'm sure; hanging out with your buddies, but I need to warn you about something."

"My buddies?" I asked, my teeth chattering. "Warn me about what?" And then it dawned on me. "Wait, you mean William and Ashe? You *can't* be serious." I couldn't believe it. She had to mean somebody else. I mean sure, I couldn't see their faces in the woods, but it *couldn't* have been *them*.

A small group of students walked past us bundled in thick coats, and sat on the bleachers nearby. If I would've known I was going to be outside even for two minutes, I never would've left my coat in my locker.

Zia took hold of my elbow and we walked farther away. What she had to say was for my ears only.

"Listen," she went on, "I know you'll probably want to go look for your sister at their place and all that, but don't. You'll only make things worse for her, and for yourself."

"But why?" I didn't know whether to be confused or offended. "You're telling me that I should ignore that Alex left without telling anyone, or that she's staying with *them*?"

Zia sighed. "No, Adria, I'm saying that…well, it's not safe for you there."

"But it is for Alex? I don't understand."

"They're pricks," she said. "You already know that. You saw that for yourself. And from what I know, the Vargas brothers are pretty territorial."

I think I was trying to take too much in at one time because the more she said the more baffled I became. I had more questions now than when we started. The bleacher next to me looked inviting, so I took that much-needed seat, regretting it instantly after my butt hit the freezing metal.

"I thought you didn't know much about them?"

"Well, I wasn't being completely honest with you when I said that."

"So then why are you now?"

"Come to my house tonight," she said, "and I'll tell you. I wouldn't even consider it if your sister wasn't so deeply involved, so it's kind of inevitable."

"Where do you live?"

"In the hills—we'll pick you up. Around seven, okay?"

"Yeah, that'll work. I guess."

I don't know why I was agreeing to it. Nothing about anything as of late seemed right, and that included going to Zia's house. But she knew things about Alex, or at least about the scum Alex had chosen to associate with…to *live* with by the looks of it.

Uncle Carl and Beverlee couldn't hide their devastation when I told them the news—okay, maybe Beverlee was more obvious about she felt, but I could tell Uncle Carl was just as disappointed.

Zia was late picking me up.

"How long can you stay out?" she asked.

"I don't really have a curfew, but with what Alex has done, I should be home by a decent hour."

She nodded. The Jeep pulled away, thankfully this time with the top on.

Zia wasn't kidding about living in the hills. By the time we got to her house I knew I wouldn't be able to find my way back under any circumstances. I lost my way after the first ten minutes once we passed several dark streets that didn't even have names.

At first glance, the stone house seemed average in size, and evidently old. Then as we came upon it from the side, I realized it was actually two-stories and probably had a deep, creepy stone basement that only old haunted houses in the movies had. There was even an old well out front, stones toppled in heaps on the ground on one side. In addition to the Jeep there were three other vehicles parked out front. I could hear noise funneling from the house: voices and people moving around inside; shadows moved across the downstairs windows behind thin curtains.

As I stood there waiting to be led inside, an uncomfortable feeling washed over me. I turned to look through the black trees and although I couldn't actually see anyone, I felt that someone was watching.

"Ignore the girls," Zia said. "The Mayfairs are cool, but the others, they get wicked jealous of visitors."

I stopped in the driveway, mid-stride. She was talking about those inside, I realized, and not anyone that may have been watching us from the trees.

"What?"

"It's cool," Zia said. "Just stick with me." Her smile widened enough to display her teeth.

"Yeah, they won't cross the line with Zia anymore," Dwarf said as he walked past us.

"You're in good hands," added Damien.

I felt like I was about to be put on an operating table to have a very risky surgery.

"Well…then who are the Mayfairs?" I asked curiously, seeing as how I was about to enter their house full of jealous girls and all.

"Isaac's family," Zia said, as she urged me on. "Don't worry. I'll take you straight to my room, that way you don't have to feel uncomfortable."

I was going to feel uncomfortable whether in her room or at the far end of their driveway.

The front door opened and the warmth from inside engulfed me, like walking into a house that still used gas stoves for heat. Something had been cooking, too. Roast and maybe something with sauerkraut. I hoped I wasn't invited to stay for dinner. I hated sauerkraut.

The moment I entered the enormous people-packed den, all of the voices I had heard earlier, ceased in an uncanny instant.

7

MOST OF THE FACES STARING BACK AT ME WERE NOT WEL-coming ones. One or two smiles could be plucked out of the crowd, and a few with no expressions at all. I could feel my stomach twisting in knots, the saliva evaporating from my mouth. Six. Eight. Eleven. I stopped counting because you had to actually look at people to do it, and by then, I had let my eyes stray downward at the floor instead. Pretty hardwoods. I could almost see my reflection in them.

"Adria," said Zia, standing right next to me, "you've met Isaac."

I raised my head carefully. *She was supposed to take me straight to her room...*

Isaac sat on the center of a giant leather couch with girls on both sides of him, and one lying across the back, behind him. There was another girl sitting on the floor between his legs. These particular girls couldn't have been his sisters. No way. Sisters, at least in my world, didn't sit so closely to their brothers. They didn't lay their heads on their brother's lap and stroke his hair, as two were doing to Isaac. Most of all, a sister in my world would never lick her brother's earlobe. She eyed me from across the room with a threatening glare, and Isaac gently, but bitterly pushed her away from him.

I was repulsed by the whole display, hoping I didn't just walk into some freak cult where everyone in the family engaged in incestuous acts and were trying to recruit me as part of their harem.

As I stood there feeling unwelcome by all and somehow slighted by a guy I hardly knew, he stood and pushed the girls away, asking, "Why did you bring her here, Zia?"

He walked toward us.

"Isaac, stop it," Zia said. "You worry too much."

She lowered her voice to him. "Better watch Rachel though. She don't look too good."

It was obvious which one was Rachel, and why Zia seemed worried as the raven-haired girl sat with clenched fists and a very tight jawline. Surely she wasn't looking at *me* like that; I hadn't done or said anything to cause it.

Isaac never looked me in the eyes. His passed right over me as he turned and walked back toward the couch.

Zia stayed close to my side.

"He'll get over it," she said. "Come on, my room's this way."

The lighting in this place reminded me of our den at home, where only one lamp and the glow of the TV put off a dim light amid the surrounding darkness. It seemed Zia's whole house was just as dark.

We walked up the creaking stairs and passed a few bedrooms on the second floor, which were empty except for odd pieces of missmatched furniture and unpacked boxes piled against the walls. I wondered just how long ago it was Zia and the Mayfairs moved to Hallowell. I vaguely remembered Julia mentioned Zia had only started school a week before I did, but I had long unpacked my things.

Zia's room was at the end of the hall, full of the same stacks of boxes yet still looked like a room that had been lived in.

"I know you're probably wondering about the boxes," she commented, reading my mind perfectly. She walked over to a mound of clothes and tossed them onto the floor, revealing a chair underneath.

"I guess so," I admitted, taking the chair and pushing aside a stray sock she left behind.

"We moved here around the time you did," she said. "Got lucky to find this place—gotta love the seclusion."

A large dresser with a cracked mirror stood directly across from me. In its reflection, I noticed posters on the wall behind me of bands I had never heard of before. Zia liked her punk and metal. A string of multi-colored Christmas tree lights hung sloppily from thumbtacks pressed into the wall.

"Where did you move from?"

She hesitated. "South Carolina."

"All of you…I mean all of *them* moved here?"

Zia shook her head. "Oh no, just me and my brothers and the Mayfairs. The others just hang out here, so to speak."

Zia plopped down amid a fluffy black-and-red bedspread.

"Ummm, how many of them are Mayfairs exactly?"

She looked up in thought for a moment, as if counting in her head. It seemed she started to answer at one point, but then had to recalculate. She used an invisible chalkboard in front of her.

"Including Isaac," she said, "eight—no nine! I forgot about Daisy, Xavier's twin sister. She's usually up in her room and not down there with all the drama."

I looked at her questioningly.

"Isaac isn't the only one who attracts a lot of girls," she began. "His brothers, Nathan, Seth, and Xavier, are chick magnets too." She faked gagging herself with her index finger. "Shannon, Phoebe, Elizabeth, and Camilla, are the sisters."

"Including Daisy?"

Zia nodded. "I get along pretty good with Daisy. Probably because she and I are a lot alike. Now Shannon, she's a real bitch. Phoebe is like her little sidekick, but she can be sweet when Shannon's not around—totally impressionable. Camilla's a slut and Elizabeth is just Elizabeth."

I felt like I should be taking notes or something.

"Large family."

"You could say that," Zia replied with a faint grin.

"And what about you?" I relaxed my back into the engulfing chair, making myself comfortable. "Why do you and your brothers live with the Mayfairs?"

Zia hesitated once more. I noticed these hesitations because they were more obvious than normal. I just couldn't tell whether she was hiding something, or if she was just the type who always thought about her answers before telling them.

"Our parents were killed," she explained quietly with a sort of misplaced pause. "In a fire a few years ago. Isaac and my brothers had been good friends, and we didn't have any other family except back in Michigan—Dad's second cousin, I think. He was a train wreck. No big deal though; we wouldn't want to live with any other family anyway. Trajan is…well he takes care of us."

"Trajan? Is he Isaac's dad?"

"Yeah," she revealed. "They're all half brothers and sisters; three different mothers, but let's not get into that. If Isaac knew I was telling you this stuff, he'd kill me."

I scoffed quietly. "I believe you," I said. "Why is he such—"

"An ass?"

Sort of. Kind of. "Yes."

"Don't be fooled by the exterior, Adria. Isaac isn't that bad. He's just got a lot on his plate."

"Yeah, I could see that downstairs," I grumbled under my breath, not quite sure why I really cared. The guy was attractive, but he seemed a little too…I don't know—something *un*attractive.

Zia smiled. "Oh, the girls." Then she laughed a little. "More exterior. Isaac doesn't really give any of them the time of day."

Was she serious? I knew what I saw. He might not have been returning their 'affections', but he looked cozy through my lens.

"They're not his type," Zia told me, intruding upon my thoughts it seemed. "He just…well, he has a hard time getting rid of them."

There was another one of those hesitations again.

"So, about your sister," Zia said.

I sighed, grateful to have the subject changed. I didn't like that my mind was becoming entirely too curious about Isaac Mayfair.

"Yeah, about Alex."

Zia crossed her legs on the bed. A gust of wind rattled the window; wind chimes outside rang erratically. 8:02p.m. glowed red on the bedside clock. A pyramid of empty soda cans stood next to the clock, the top of which had an incense stick poking out of it. I could still smell the incense lingering in the room from the last time it had burned. A stack of CD's lay strewn on the floor next to one wall, a pile of paperback books next to another. Zia was not a very organized person.

She looked my way, her gaze severe, yet somehow gentle at the same time.

"The Vargas family," she began. "They're like a cult."

Oh great, so my whole freak cult theory couldn't be thrown out entirely, after all.

"And it looks like Alex is their newest recruit," she went on. "They won't hurt her though. They're protective of their family, if you want to call her that."

"I'd rather not."

"Well, my point is that you and your aunt and uncle can go to bed at night knowing that Alex will be all right with them protecting her, but..."

"I was waiting for the 'but'," I interrupted.

"*But* if you or anyone else tries to force her back home, or goes onto their grounds, I can't promise that you won't be hurt, maybe even killed."

The scariest part of her comment was that I didn't think she was kidding.

I couldn't believe what I was hearing. I knew this was bad; I knew my sister was wrapped up with the worst crowd ever, but I never expected to hear something so harsh.

"And I know you might think you should call the police," she added, "but don't. That'll only make things worse."

I stood up then and began to pace.

"I don't get it. I don't even understand what you're telling me. What kind of cult? What do they do? Is it some religious thing, or what?"

"Definitely not religious."

"Well then what? And why would they kill me? Wait—how do you know that?" I stopped in front of the door and stared across at her. I knew I must've looked desperate, because I was.

Zia stared me straight in the eye. "Look, just don't go after her. Let her do what she wants. Let her figure out what she's doing on her own time." She sighed. "Your sister needs them for about a week more. After that, when her head is clear, we'll all be able to tell what side she's on, and so will she."

I was officially baffled by this conversation.

"Are you insane? What do you mean she *needs* them? I—"

"Please, just trust me on this."

Trust her? I just *met* her.

Unfortunately, I had nothing better in the idea department to offer up. Reluctantly, I asked, "So what do I do until then?"

I collapsed back into the chair. Any other time and I would've already been out the door and dragging Alex back home, but something about Zia's sincerity was frightening. This wasn't like a teenager running away from home to live with her boyfriend or anything. This was a hundred times worse. I could feel it in my bones.

8

MY BODY WAS STIFF; MY HANDS WERE PRESSED FIRMLY BEtween my knees; I realized that the colorful specks swirling in my line of vision were from staring at a mosaic lamp too intensely.

I didn't notice that Zia never answered my question. I think I had forgotten that I asked one.

There was a knock at the bedroom door, which instantly pulled me out of my reverie.

"You may enter," Zia commanded very regally. I would have laughed at that if my body hadn't been so numb at the moment.

In walked Isaac. "She thinks she's royalty," he said, then turned to Zia. "He needs you to stay with Aramei for a while."

I could feel Isaac's secret glance pass over me without actually having to see it, and I struggled to keep from looking up at him.

"Where's he going?" Zia asked, as she stood from the bed.

Isaac shrugged. "No idea. He just asked me to tell you." He turned to me then, looking straight at me, which shocked me a little inside. "Did she tell you to stay away from the Vargas Family?"

I nodded.

"And do you believe her enough to listen?"

I wanted to throw him a contemptuous glare just for thinking he had the right to talk to me like I was a child, but for some reason I simply nodded again.

"And did she explain to you that if your sister shows back at home that you should call us before you do anything else? And that you and the rest of your family shouldn't do anything to anger her?"

"Ummm…no. And *what?*" I looked to Zia for answers.

"I didn't get that far," Zia said. "But thanks for covering that part for me." Her smile was cheerily sarcastic.

I stood beside Zia and crossed my arms tight against my body. "Why don't you two tell me what's *really* going on with my sister. I don't appreciate the weird hesitations and the little covert glances between you." I meant for it to sound as harsh as it did, no longer caring if it came off insulting.

When they exchanged yet another questionable glance, I went on, "You can't expect me to just ignore that my sister has run off to live with some…*cult* who, according to Zia, could *kill* me if I tried to get her to come home. And then to listen to you guys who—no offense—I hardly know, and who seems to be hiding things from me." I paused. "Look at it from my perspective, okay?" I put my back to them and gazed out the window. The trees looked cold; naked, frightening branches stood stiffly all around the house.

"You told her they would *kill* her?" Isaac remarked with reprimand.

I swung around, hands moving straight to my hips. "Hey, don't slam her for that," I snapped. "I think that's pretty important information, *thank-you-very-much*. What the hell have you offered so far? Nothing! And aren't you missing your female leaches? You seemed to be missing like five at the moment."

Honestly, I didn't know what set me off. Maybe because Zia, in her strange way, was the only person actually trying to help me help

Alex, and him putting her down for it just ticked me off. But for some reason, Isaac smiled faintly after my impromptu outburst, which threw me completely off guard. Zia too, was amused, trying to hide her smile by biting down on the inside of her cheek.

"You're right," he said smoothly, and with a sly smile. "I just think you should be careful; stay away from all of them, and keep your family away from them, too."

It didn't escape me that he avoided calling me out on my other accusations. And for the moment, I was grateful for that. Why should I care how many girls threw themselves at him?

Oh, hell—did he catch that? Yeah, he definitely did. My heartbeat quickened the moment I locked eyes with him. His half smile hitched farther up, like he knew I had an insane amount of butterflies floating around in my stomach all of a sudden. Hell, hell, hell. *Please tell me—out of all the guys I've met since I moved to Maine—that Isaac Mayfair isn't the one my hormones are going to go all stupid on me for.*

I wanted to take the time to yell at myself for the absurdity, but I knew I had more important matters to confront than my emotions. So instead, I focused all my energy on Alex, where it was supposed to be. She was in trouble, and I needed to figure out how I could get her out of it. And there Zia and Isaac were, telling me that I couldn't do *anything* about it?!

"None of this makes any sense," I said. "In fact, it sounds crazy. I should just go to the police."

"Their dad's…a criminal," Zia said, though it kind of felt made up. "A convicted felon who was also suspected of being involved in the murders of three people. They threw it out of court because there wasn't enough evidence. And his *kids*, they're just as bad as he is."

My eyes naturally tapered downward. I didn't really believe her, but I ignored my doubts for now. It was obvious she wasn't going to give me the whole story, no matter how much I asked, or demanded.

Defiantly, I replied, "All right, one more reason to go against everything you asked me to do and get Alex away from them right now."

I went toward the door, pushing my way past Isaac. He took hold of my arm and stopped me just as I stepped into the hall.

"Adria," he said, trying to make me listen, but I refused to fall for it this time.

Isaac sighed heavily and let go of my arm. "All right, then at least let us be with you when you confront her. And wait until tomorrow night where you can see her at The Cove; that way there will be others around."

I looked at each of them, back and forth. "The Cove?"

"It's a hang-out near the river," Zia explained. "Alex has been going up there with Ashe a lot, but others go there too, so we won't be alone with them."

"If we take you," Isaac began, "just know that your sister won't be the sister you knew—prepare yourself for it. Don't expect her to treat you very nicely."

"She hasn't exactly been the sister I knew for a while now, so what do I have to lose?" Then I asked nervously, "William and Ashe will be there?" I only wanted to have heard them wrong the first time. I never really wanted to see either of those guys again.

"Yep," Zia answered. "You can say Ashe is your sister's very territorial boyfriend."

It was funny how referring to him as Alex's boyfriend triggered an immediate rage in me, but everything else Isaac and Zia told me, didn't come close to having the same effect.

"Well, the guy doesn't know the meaning of territorial yet," I threatened. The room went silent as I thought about it a second longer. "Fine. It's a deal. I'll wait for you and The Cove."

Isaac nodded once in acknowledgement. Having no problem ending the discussion there, he turned to Zia. "What do you want me to tell my father?"

Zia looked over at me, and then at Isaac, suspiciously. I somehow got the distinct impression that the gears in her head were working overtime, probably coming up with ideas they shouldn't. *Don't you dare leave me alone with him*, my eyes threatened her.

"I can go sit with Aramei now," she said, a little too coolly, "if you'll keep Adria company."

Isaac looked slightly perturbed. Me? I just wanted to wipe that smirk off Zia's face. She knew she was my ride back, which I was ninety-percent sure she was about to flake on.

"Zia, that's not a good idea right now," Isaac rebutted.

I didn't think it was, either. I'd already made a fool of myself tonight; I didn't need a repeat performance. Yet part of me did want to stay, and that only made me want to leave even faster.

"Of course it is," Zia insisted, harmoniously. "Besides, maybe if Rachel sees you hanging around some other girl, she'll get the hint."

"Xavier took care of her for me."

"Oh?" cooed Zia with an inquisitive raised brow.

Isaac smirked, apparently ending that conversation.

"I'll be back in a few," Zia said to me, already heading down the hallway.

"Wait! Hello?" I actually held my hand up like we were in class. "Curfew—I can't stay here."

"Your curfew is self-imposed," Zia shouted down the hallway. "And I'm just going to help put Aramei to sleep. It won't take long."

Obviously, Aramei was a child. I thought to myself how Trajan must be a busy man in the sack to have yet another child so young. But since it was to take care of a baby, I could hardly argue against it. I shook my head; I never should have told her I didn't have a curfew.

Zia left us alone in her room, and while I stood there for what seemed like an eternity, I altogether refused to look his way. No way was I giving my insides the opportunity to leap for joy again.

"Come on," Isaac said, with the gesture of his hand. "I'll take you down to meet everybody."

Quietly, I wondered which would be worse: going downstairs to be stared at like something filthy and threatening, or staying up in Zia's room alone with Isaac.

Not even up for discussion.

"Yeah, let's go."

To my relief, there weren't as many people downstairs as before, and the crazy-looking one, Rachel, was gone. But the looks I got were all the same, except for the curly-haired slender girl sitting on the end of the couch who wasn't present earlier. Her smile made me a little more comfortable. "Don't go into the back room," she said, grinning up at Isaac. "Xavier's in there with Rachel." She had a heavy English accent.

She stood and extended her hand to me then. "Daisy Mayfair," she introduced herself so cordially.

"Adria Dawson." I happily shook her hand.

Isaac turned my attention to others sitting on the couch, and introduced them, too.

"And you already know Damien and Dwarf," he said, when he got around to them.

I smiled in response.

"And here comes my brother, Nathan," Isaac added, looking toward the foyer.

Nathan was tall, with short, dark hair and dark eyes to match. He looked familiar, but I couldn't place where I'd seen him before.

"I'd be next in line to inherit the throne if *he* wasn't in the way," Isaac teased about Nathan.

At least I *thought* it was a joke. Who had thrones in their family that didn't involve the porcelain variety?

Nathan balled his huge fists, and jokingly punched at the air toward Isaac's face.

"Don't be so harsh, little brother," Nathan said, tossing his arm around Isaac's shoulder. "You know the second oldest is where all the action's at. Not too high up on the scale to be intimidating to everyone, and not too low on it to be dismissed."

He added looking right at me, "Adria, right?" He smiled wide. "I've seen you at Finch's Grocery a couple of times. I work in the back. I'm the stocker."

"Oh yeah!" I said, but the reply was really for me. That was where I had seen him before. "Yeah, my aunt practically runs the place now with Mrs. Finch being sick and all."

Nathan moved from Isaac and tossed his arm around the back of my neck. "Be careful," he whispered, leaning toward my ear. "My brother has this problem, you see."

"Nate," said Isaac, glaring, but then he looked at me instead. "Don't listen to him. Really."

Nathan pulled me closer. I could feel the humor in his pose, the huge, mischievous smile plastered all over his face.

"No, seriously," Nathan went on. "Isaac is what your folks might call a Ladies' Man."

I saw Isaac's expression out of the corner of my eye; it shrank into something less solid, and more humiliated. I laughed. Inside, of course.

"I've noticed," I replied quietly, watching the girls on the couch eyeing Isaac.

"He even has his own cologne," Nathan added. "It's called Dark Allure, or some cheesy shit like that." He swirled the hand that hung over my shoulder melodiously at the wrist.

"Nathan is a complete liar," Isaac said, shaking his head, gaining his confidence back. Catching my gaze, he lightly admitted, "I don't wear cologne."

His eyes abandoned mine to latch onto Nathan's for a telepathic moment. "You haven't tortured Xavier in a while. Why don't you go see what *he's* up to?"

"Yeah, Nate," Daisy said from the side; a crooked smile lay faint on her lips. "You should find Xavier. I think he's in the back room with the lot."

She and Isaac shared a knowing look, and even I began to wonder if they were setting Nate up to find the couple in a compromising situation.

Nathan seemed suspicious. After all, neither Isaac nor Daisy exactly hid the fact that there was some plotting going on between them. I felt his arm slip from around my neck.

"All right, all right," he said, giving in to their suggestion, though not falling for their obvious tricks. "Tell the big boss, Beverlee, I said hi."

"I will." Totally wouldn't, because that would mean admitting to being here.

Nate walked past Isaac and slugged him playfully in the stomach. Isaac waited until Nathan was out of sight. "Sorry about him," he said. "He doesn't get out much."

I couldn't be sure, but I sensed that maybe Isaac really was embarrassed by what his brother said to me. But why would he care? It wasn't like Nate exposed the mother of all secrets—Isaac laid it out for everyone to see. And apparently, even seeing it for myself wasn't enough to completely shut down these impish feelings trying to rise inside me. There was something about him that was drawing me in—albeit very slowly.

I doubt I hung out with Isaac and Daisy for more than thirty minutes when Zia rejoined us. But when she came back, she seemed stressed, and told Isaac something about needing Trajan home ASAP because Aramei was sick. It must've been pretty bad, because the next thing I knew I was being politely rushed out, and driven home by Isaac, Damien and Dwarf. Because apparently I required three escorts.

"Tomorrow around eight," Isaac said. "We'll pick you up if that's a good time for you."

We were sitting at the farthest end of my dirt and gravel driveway. The hot amber of a cigarette glowed brightly and then faded from the front porch. No one smoked in our house, but I was certain it was a cigarette.

"Eight o'clock is good," I said, and then opened the door and stepped down from the Jeep. "Thanks for the ride…again."

"Not a problem." Isaac's lips never smiled, but his eyes seemed to have a brightness about them. Amused, I just huffed and slammed the door.

I didn't know what was happening to me. Yeah, Isaac had a strange family dynamic, and a plethora of girls—which I agreed with Zia he didn't seem nearly as interested in as all of them were—but still, I was into him. And it didn't help that he was also gorgeous beneath that rough exterior.

Isaac Mayfair had somehow become my type—whatever that was. Yes, *he* was my type. Screw killing the infatuation. I was completely over that.

I heard the Jeep pull away, but my focus was on the smoker. As I approached, the glow of the cigarette disappeared, but I could smell the smoke lingering in the air.

It was Aunt Beverlee.

"I didn't know you smoked," I said, standing at the end of the steps.

I could see her waving furiously in the dark at the puffs around her head. "I don't," she replied. "Well, I used to. I've been smoke-free for five years, but every once in a while…"

I knew the story without her having to finish. My mom had lived by the same story for years; smoking only when totally stressed out, until she picked the habit up again full-time.

"Well, it's disgusting," I said. "Don't let me see it again."

Beverlee laughed. "You're right, I know."

"Alex came by," she said then. Nothing about her tone suggested that my sister's visit was a good one, but I was surprised and hopeful. I went up the steps quickly and sat in the empty chair next to Beverlee. Here I had gone to talk to people who might tell me about Alex, and she ended up coming home at the exact same time.

"What happened?" I asked, already feeling impatient. "What did she say? Why did she leave? Is she coming back?" I always tended to ask a ton of questions when I was stressed out.

Beverlee hardly looked at me; instead she stared out in front of her.

"I don't know," she said with a sigh.

"You don't know if she'll be coming home?"

"Or why she left," Beverlee added.

I wished she would just tell me what happened and get it over with, but I knew I had to be patient. Clearly, she was still working the meeting out in her mind, and maybe even whether she wanted to tell me anything or not. Finally, she turned to face me. A shadow covered most of her face, but I could tell her expression was downcast with worry. My eyes strayed for a second to notice a stinking ashtray on the little round table between us, which had at least two cigarette butts in it.

"At first," she began, "she seemed interested in us and in you, asking questions about how you were doing. At one point she even seemed concerned for *my* feelings." Beverlee shook her head then, confirming Alex's concern might've only been Beverlee's hopeful fantasy. "But then she snapped at me. I mean, all I did was comment about her boyfriend." She sighed and confessed, "I probably shouldn't have said anything in front of him, I admit."

"What did you say?"

"Just that any respectable boy wouldn't fondle her the way he was doing right in front of me."

"What?" I was shocked and repulsed. "He was here? He did that, really?"

She nodded. "If Carl had been here…"

"For the record," I said sternly, "you said exactly what I would've said. I can't believe Alex let him do that. That's gross."

"She didn't try to stop him, either," said Beverlee. "In fact, she was enjoying it. I just don't get it. I don't get *her*. I can understand rebellion, but I think Alex is beyond that. She's…*cruel*."

"Did she say anything else?"

"I think she was really just here for you. You were the first and last person she asked about. Wanted to know where you were and told me to tell you to stay away from the Mayfers, I think."

"The Mayfairs," I said, though aloud to myself rather than correcting her.

"Yes, that was it," she said. "Wait—you mean Nathan's family?"

Absently, I nodded.

"Adria, don't tell Carl that she came by. I'm going to tell him so he'll know she's all right, but I don't want him knowing the rest."

I agreed with that entirely. Alex coming here was actually helping us all to do what Zia and Isaac wanted us to do. I didn't like it, and I still couldn't get past the part about leaving Alex with these people and not doing anything to help her see reason. But maybe tomorrow night would be what made *me* see reason.

9

Geometry was quieter than usual. Mrs. Schvolsky was out sick and we had the harshest substitute ever employed by any schoolboard. Everyone was afraid of her, even Lance Becker, the class show-off who always had something sarcastic to say.

Harry sat behind me. "*Psst!* You won't believe this," he whispered, leaning into the back of my head; I felt the heat from his breath on my scalp. The substitute looked up from her desk momentarily. When she looked back down into her paperwork, Harry went on, "I saw Julia in Augusta last night."

I acknowledged him by slightly turning my head, but not enough I was looking at him.

"So?"

Obviously, there was more to it, and I waited impatiently for him to get to the point; the substitute made me nervous.

"She was hanging out with those losers from the skate park."

I couldn't help but swing around so that I could look Harry in the eyes. "What!" I whispered harshly.

Harry was nervous now, too, and so was every student in our vicinity: Lance Becker buried his blond head further into his paper, scribbling furiously; Michelle Lancaster put her hand to the side of her face so that maybe it would rule her out as being one of the listeners.; Criminally beautiful Genna Bishop, sat up straight and pretended to be thinking.

"I'm serious," whispered Harry. "They came to the skate park last night—where were you anyway?"

I turned back around quickly as I heard the substitute's chair creak under her movements. I watched her, barely moving my head and pretended to be studying until I thought it was safe to inch around again.

"I was at Zia's house."

Harry leaned in even closer. "Really?" he asked, with a suspicious eagerness that I recognized right away, confirming my suspicion that he had a crush on Zia.

"You like Zia, don't you?"

Harry gritted his teeth. "Shhh! Not so loud."

I laughed inside. It wasn't that he was ashamed that anyone knew he had a thing for Zia; when it came to girls, he just embarrassed easily.

"Think you could drag me along next time you go? Or, maybe bring her to the skate park when I'm there? I'll be there tonight, but then I guess I'm there every night, huh?"

Yeah, Harry definitely had a thing for Zia—the babbling was kind of cute.

I glanced back at the substitute once more, just to be sure. "You can go with me tonight," I whispered. "Isaac's taking me to the river to meet up with Alex. I'm sure Zia will be there too." Only after I offered did I realize it probably wasn't the best time to bring anyone else along, but it was too late to take it back.

"Awesome, The Cove," he said, just above a whisper, and then dropped his voice again. "I'll come to your house then? My car's still in the shop."

"Yeah, just be there by seven."

I was just about to tell him we'd be riding with Isaac when the substitute looked right at me. "Miss…" she glanced down at her seating arrangement list, "Dawson—anymore whispering and you may leave the class."

I felt like I was back in Jr. High. I lowered my head into my book.

Why would Julia be hanging around Alex's group? Around *Alex*? As I thought about it further, I realized that Julia *had* been acting a little standoffish lately. No big deal though. It wasn't like she and I had enough time to get close, so I didn't feel like she'd stabbed me in the back or anything. Too much.

By midday, I was in Art class when the intercom interrupted the school.

"I have a very important announcement to make," said Principal Davis' voice, "so please let me have everyone's attention."

Everything about her voice was solemn, and every student seemed to share the same eager look.

"Last night," Principal Davis began, "Sebastian Reeves was allegedly abducted from his home. His family has reason to believe he may have been hurt. You'll be able to learn more details on the news tonight, but we want every student to be careful when you're off school property, especially in the evening hours." She took a deep breath and continued. "And if anyone has any information on Sebastian Reeves, any at all, call the police right away, or you can come to the office and speak with myself, or Mrs. Chesney."

I heard the speaker squeal once before it went dead.

The entire school was in shock. The atmosphere changed in an instant. I don't know how long I sat there, glued to my desk, or how I was capable of eventually pulling myself out of my swimming thoughts. Sebastian was my friend, one who hardly ever spoke to me, but my friend, nonetheless. How could this be happening? I had to know more about the kidnapping. The lack of information was driving me insane.

"His bedroom window was broken," Lori Avery said, as Harry and I walked beside her through the hall, "and they said his room was, like, destroyed."

"Tori's mom checked her out of school," said another girl. "I bet she's totally freaked out. Sebastian was gorgeous. If he was *my* boyfriend, I'd be wicked freaked out." It annoyed me how she was referring to Sebastian in past tense. He wasn't dead. God, when I thought about it, my stomach did flips. I hoped he was okay.

So many strange things were happening lately. By the end of the day, I managed to create a mental list:

1. Alex joined a cult.
2. Julia seemed to be joining Alex and the cult.
3. Sebastian was abducted (what if by the cult?)
4. I met a strange family much like a cult.
5. I had a crush (not so weird? Very weird!)
6.

I left number six blank, but ready just in case, because at the rate things were going…

Harry arrived early and watched the news with Beverlee and Uncle Carl and I. As expected, Beverlee was worried about me going out anywhere. Uncle Carl agreed. But with Harry there, and since I wasn't going to be out riding my bike, they didn't hold me prisoner for the night.

"Keep your cell with you and don't lose it," Beverlee demanded.

Channel 8 said the same things Lori Avery had told us in the hall earlier at school.

But there was more.

Apparently, there was also blood in Sebastian's room and on the windowsill and glass. His wallet was left undisturbed on the nightstand (this, Beverlee heard from Mrs. Finch, who knew the Reeves' family well). The police unofficially ruled out robbery based on that. It was just all so horrible. I *was* afraid. Even if I was allowed to go out alone, I wouldn't have, that was for sure.

What happened to Sebastian weighed heavily on Harry. They had been friends for a long time. This was hard for him, and he tried his best not to let it ruin the rest of the night. He wanted Zia to like him, and I think he was less confident now about hanging out with her. I played the little sister (he was only two months older than me) and gave him my sisterly advice: "Don't think the worst, Harry. I know it'll be hard. And if you let yourself feel guilty, I'll smack you myself."

He thanked me by thumping me on the back of the head.

Isaac was fifteen minutes late. Dwarf, Damien, and Zia were with him, and as usual, Damien was driving.

"Mind if Harry rides with us?"

Isaac looked at Zia and then at me in that harsh, secretive way he always did. I had to say though, it made me feel good he actually looked at me too this time, rather than at Zia *about* me. I suddenly felt like a part of them. And bringing Harry with me worked out in ways I never expected.

"It's a little tight in here," Damien said to me. "I guess your skinny butt will fit between them back there."

"Or, she could just sit on Isaac's lap," Zia said from the front with that obvious hidden meaning she was becoming famous for.

Isaac glared at Zia from behind. He probably would've kneed the back of her seat if it wouldn't have drawn more attention to him.

"Well, she can sit on *my* lap," Dwarf offered with a huge, sly smile.

Isaac leaned over and possessively took hold of my elbow. Next thing I knew I was hoisted onto his lap and he was motioning for

Harry to get in next to Dwarf. Isaac's arms slipped around my waist, holding me tightly like a seat belt, and a few shivers rose goose bumps on my skin.

Great. I barely knew the guy and already his touch was making my insides come alive. Worse? I was pretty sure I liked it. I took a calming breath and introduced Harry to everyone he hadn't met yet.

"I would ask if you were Adria's guy," Dwarf said to Harry, "but I guess that'd be a stupid question, huh?"

They looked at each other and sort of laughed under their breath. I thought I might feel Isaac tense up at that, but he didn't do or say anything. Not that he probably wasn't thinking about squeezing Dwarf's small head with his big hands. *Hands*. I glanced down at Isaac's then, noticing how they were resting on opposite elbows, so close to each of my hipbones. I tried to will them with my super mental powers to grasp my hips instead, but apparently, I had no super mental powers.

Zia surprised me by turning around fully to see Harry. Maybe I won't have to work as hard as I anticipated at playing matchmaker, I thought. Then again, Zia was friendly by nature, and I was probably reading too far into it, too fast.

"I've seen you skate," she told Harry. "You've got some wicked talent."

I think Harry lost his mojo right then. He was slow to respond, and when it came, he sounded unsure of himself. "Ummm, thanks. I guess seven years of practice helps."

"Well, it's definitely paid off," she replied, both her smile and eyes beaming.

I wanted to nudge Harry, to urge him to continue the conversation. If anything, to distract me from the arms wrapped tightly around me. If I trembled just once, he was so going to know. And part of me was willing to let Henry continuing bombing his conversation just to keep my mind busy on something else.

Luckily, I came up with door number two before I threw him under the bus for my own sake. "So what do you think happened to Sebastian?" I asked anyone in the jeep willing to take the bait.

"Don't know," Dwarf answered.

"This might sound harsh," Zia said, "but I think we shouldn't worry about Sebastian right now. You have enough to worry about with your sister."

Zia was right about that, but it didn't make me feel any better. I probably shouldn't have even brought Sebastian up, especially with Harry there. I was doing exactly what I told Harry not to do: feeling guilty about going out while Sebastian was out there somewhere, hurt and maybe even dead.

I forced myself to think about him less. Unsuccessfully.

When we made it to The Cove there were a lot of people hanging out, but I couldn't spot Alex among them. Isaac helped me climb out of the Jeep.

The Cove was nothing like hanging out at the skate park. There was a lot of drinking and smoking here. Beer cans littered the parking lot and I could smell weed all around me. There were two cars blaring different kinds of music, and a lot of harmless shouting. I saw a few people from school, even Genna Bishop from Geometry class, but no one I really knew. I could hear the river nearby, just beyond a few trees, and there was an old abandoned building in the distance that looked creepy against the black sky.

And the nights were getting colder. I was just glad I was learning to better prepare myself for the weather in Maine.

"This place has changed since I was here last," Harry remarked.

I waited for him to go on.

He looked around, investigating. "A bunch of us used to come out here and just hang, but it looks like the loser crowd took over."

Nothing was ever going to make me feel any better about Alex. Everything just seemed to get worse.

"I don't see Alex," I said. "Maybe we should just go." I was lying to myself, as if not finding her in less than five minutes meant she didn't come anymore and things would be okay.

And then I heard her voice.

I froze. Alex emerged from the trees near the river with Ashe and William. Others were with them, including Julia. I was so mad that as Isaac took my arm into his hand there was no euphoric electricity this time. I could think of nothing but Alex as she walked toward us boastfully; a proud, sinister smile etched on her face. She was completely willing to be with them and nothing I could do or say was ever going to change that.

I felt Isaac's grip tighten around my arm. I wasn't tempted to go anywhere, so it was more protective on his part than containing me to this spot. Zia and her brothers crowded closer behind us.

Ashe, standing in front of Alex, grinned and said, "You surprise me, Isaac. Never thought you'd bring her here."

"Hi Dria," Alex said with a grin I didn't recognize. "How's that bitch Beverlee doing these days?"

I felt my face tighten with anger. "What's *wrong* with you? Beverlee's so worried about you she mopes around all day, and even started smoking again."

"Gotta die from something," Alex scoffed.

Julia, hanging all over the shortest, stockiest of their group, said with a smirk, "Are you and Harry a thing now?"

"Ummm, no," Harry replied, making a show of looking at the way Isaac was latched onto me, silently begging the question of how Julia came up with that assessment. If he wondered if there was something more going on between us than Isaac holding me back from my sister and her new messed-up playmates, he didn't let on. "What's up with you anyway, Jewels? Not like you."

"Oh, shut up, Harry," Julia snapped. "You never knew me well enough to know what I'm like."

"Glad for that," Harry mumbled under his breath.

"Remember me?" William added, looking at me now while rubbing his chin with his fingertips as if to bring to memory what I had done to him. I was ready to punch him again…just waiting for the word.

"Yeah, I do," I answered hatefully. "And I have nothing to say to you."

"If your aim was better," William said, "I would've—"

"You would've *what*?" Isaac growled, stepping forward.

William smiled bitterly. "Oh, please," he said. "Spare me the cocky, protective display. I was going to say I would've fallen in love with her."

"The day William falls in love I'll kiss you on the mouth," Ashe, standing next to Alex, said to another.

"Shut up, Ashe," William bit.

I hated them both, especially Ashe, who had such a spell on my sister that it was sickening. I hated how he touched her and how she seemed to love it. I knew exactly how Beverlee felt last night when they came to our house. I was ready to tear into Ashe right then.

"Why are you letting him grope you like that?" I blurted. "It's disgusting."

"Have to grow up sometime," Alex replied, just before turning her chin and letting her tongue snake out to trace Ashe's lips.

They couldn't keep their hands off each other. My palms were sweating, my fists clenched. And then I felt Isaac's hand move down and interlock with my fingers. My heart lurched in my chest. The anger going on inside me was so overwhelming I couldn't take the time to acknowledge it much though.

Alex broke away slowly from Ashe and stepped closer to me. Isaac's hand tightened around mine.

"Dria, can I talk to you alone?"

"No," Isaac answered immediately, "you can't."

I looked at him reassuringly. "It's okay, I'll be all right. I need to talk to my sister."

Hesitantly, Isaac let go of my hand. I saw Alex mock him from the side, but there was no time to defend him. This was my chance, and somehow it felt like my last chance to talk some sense into her and make her come home.

"Don't leave the parking lot, Adria," Zia said. "Seriously."

I nodded, agreeing.

The tension between the two groups as Alex and I walked away was nerve-racking. I was so afraid a fight would break out. We walked several feet and then I stopped, wasting no time.

"*What* is your problem?!"

"Oh, stop it," Alex mumbled, waving me off. "We're not little girls anymore. I tried to make you understand that before we were shipped off to this shithole of a town. I planned to move out of Jeff's; wanted you to go with me."

"That was different. You weren't"—I tried to find the phrase—"you weren't like you are now. You were normal. My sister. Now you're…you're someone I don't know."

Alex dropped her voice and looked at me with a serious face. "You're right," she said. "I'm nothing like I used to be. But Dria, my change is for the better. I've never felt so independent, so protected, so alive! I feel strong—you can't imagine."

"Well, make me understand," I pleaded. My anger subsided and was quickly replaced by sadness. "Look," I said, placing my hand on hers, "I admit living with Beverlee and Uncle Carl isn't living in Georgia, or being out on your own, but they're great. I actually like living there and I don't get why you just left, or why you'd bring Ashe to our house and openly disrespect Beverlee like that. She never did anything to you to deserve that."

Alex moved her hand from mine.

"This isn't about Beverlee and Carl," she replied. "This is about you and me. You're my sister and you should be with me, not with family members who only took us out of obligation, and definitely not with scum like *that*."

I took immediate offense.

"You're calling *my* friends scum?" I snarled. "*My* friends didn't try to attack me. *My* friends have been there for me while *you* haven't been. *My* friends aren't part of some freakish cult that lure girls and turn them into hateful *sluts*." I regretted that a bit, but it needed to be said.

Alex took it better than I expected. She scoffed and said with that eerie smile again, "Say whatever you want, but just know that you'll have to make up your mind soon. And if you can't, I'll have to do it for you."

I drew my chin back in surprise. "What's that supposed to mean?" I demanded. "And besides, my mind *is* made up. I would never follow you so long as you're with *them*."

Alex leaned her head toward me, practically touching my ear with her lips. Her breath smelled rancid. "You know too much, Dria. And I have no control over what they have to do to protect what you know." She paused. I could've sworn she actually *sniffed* me. "I'll tell them you agreed to at least think about it, but it'll only buy you a very short time. After that, you're on your own."

I couldn't believe my own sister was threatening me, that she would side with anyone who *had* threatened me. I was reeling inside, but the situation had changed from a sibling disagreement, to what felt like nothing less than a life or death ultimatum. I thought about what Isaac and Zia told me about the Vargas family. It was true, after all.

Tears swelled in my eyes, but I managed to hold them back. "How could you do this? That family is dangerous. How could you stand by and let them threaten me?" I wouldn't let her speak. "And how do I know too much? I don't know *anything* about them!"

Isaac was approaching from the side; his shadow advanced largely out ahead of him.

"I can't say anything else. Just remember what I told you. Drop the dead weight and come stay with your flesh and blood where you belong."

Alex left me standing there.

I hated her in that moment. Part of me wanted to cry, the other part wanted to jump on her from behind and beat the sense into her that obviously wasn't getting in there any other way.

"Adria," said Isaac, "we need to go."

Julia and Harry were shouting at each other. She was in his face, urging him on, taunting him.

"You're a stupid, wannabe skater," Julia shrieked. "I never liked you anyway. Always wondered why Sebastian did."

"Don't bring him into this," Harry shouted. "I bet you don't even know what happened to him. You've been too busy with *them*."

Harry was doing his best to hold back saying the things he really wanted to say. I rushed toward them and took Harry by the arm. "Come on, let's get out of here."

Just then, Julia's boyfriend stepped between Harry and me and grabbed Harry by the front of his shirt. In less than two seconds, I was eating asphalt and heard fighting all around me. As I tried to crawl away and get to my feet, my hand was stepped on, and then one body fell right on top of me. My ribs hurt and I could feel my face burning where the asphalt had scraped my chin. People in the crowd who weren't even involved in the brawl were shouting on the sidelines.

"Fight! Fight!"

"Oh, shit," said another voice, "did you see that!"

I heard a girl screaming, "Someone do something!"

"Kick his ass!" shouted another voice. "This is going on YouTube!"

I stumbled out of the center of the chaos and tried to pull my senses together. I could barely tell who was fighting whom, or who was winning what; everything was a blur. But I did see Alex and Dwarf fighting.

Dwarf fighting Alex? Why would he be hitting my sister?

I was going to jump in and help her—I was on Dwarf's side, but this was not a fair fight—but to my shock, Alex dropkicked Dwarf square in the stomach and sent him soaring across the parking lot. He rolled once, and then with such grace, sprung back up from the ground and landed on his hands and feet like a cat.

Shock beset me, but I didn't have much time to try understanding it.

Isaac was fighting William. Zia was fighting Julia and had Julia on the ground. Damien and Harry teamed up against Ashe and Julia's boyfriend.

I just stood there, paralyzed.

Then a man emerged from the darkness as if he were part of the shadows, and with his presence, it was surreal how everything just stopped: the fighting, the shouting, the excitement of the onlookers, it all at once ceased in an instant. It felt like I was the only one among them who breathed.

The man walked slowly onto the blacktop, his hands folded together and resting on his backside. He walked with such dominance and authority; his black hair was pulled into a ponytail behind him. Both arms were canvases for tattoos, even along the tops of his fingers, which I noticed as he unfolded his hands and let them rest at his sides.

Suddenly, the spectators broke the calm, all running for their cars. Some dashed away on foot; tires squealed and headlights bounced through the darkness until they were too far away to see anymore.

It was quiet again. It seemed like minutes had passed before the man spoke calmly.

"In public is not the place," he said.

Somehow, I knew this man was not here to break up the fight for the sake of doing the right thing. That cold and calculated look on his face suggested a man of power, not of morals.

"That law has never stopped them before," Isaac said in response.

A faint, yet sinister grin crept up on the man's face, but he dismissed Isaac altogether and looked at me.

"You must be Alexandra's sister," he said. "You favor her." The man then said to Alex without looking at her, "We have much to discuss later."

"You don't have anything to say to my sister," I snapped, stepping up. "I don't know how you did it, but I'm not going to stand by and let you brainwash her!"

Isaac grabbed me by the waist and pulled my back against his chest. "Don't say anything else," he whispered harshly in my ear. "Keep your mouth shut." At first, I tried to break away from him, but his grip was firm.

"You should not have come here," the man told Isaac. "Any of you. You should have stayed where you were and out of our affairs."

I thought he was talking about The Cove. That would have made sense, but as the man continued talking, I became more confused.

"Virginia, South Carolina, Georgia," he went on. "Trajan should pick a spot and mind his own business."

"Everything you *do* is Trajan's business," Isaac said. "Especially when it comes to Innocents."

Isaac passed me to Zia as if I was a possession and they were trading watch over me.

"You and Harry get in the Jeep," Zia said.

I looked at her argumentatively.

"Go. Now," she demanded.

I felt like a child, but as much as I hated it, I knew I had better do what she said.

As Harry and I walked quickly toward the Jeep, I heard the man say, "You know it'll happen—"

"If you have anything to say," Isaac interrupted, "say it to Trajan."

"I do so plan on it," the man replied.

10

With a heavy heart, I watched Alex leave. It was over. I lost my sister for good, and that was something I never could've prepared myself for.

Damien drove me home a route I had never gone before and it seemed to take forever. I was lost in a trance while Isaac held out his hand to help me down from the Jeep in my driveway.

"If your sister comes here tonight," Isaac began, "alone or with anyone, you call me." He slipped a piece of paper into my hand with his phone number scribbled on it.

"Will you?" he said.

Numbly, I replied, "Uh, yeah, no problem." I put the paper in the back pocket of my jeans.

"Look at me," Isaac said. He tipped my chin his way. I saw how his dark eyes regarded me; how he seemed so thoughtful beneath such a hard visage. For the first time since I'd met him I was beginning to believe that maybe he was feeling a little something between us, too.

"We'll be watching out for you and your family," he said.

Listlessly, mechanically, I replied, "Thanks."

Isaac sighed. "Don't worry about your sister. As much as you hate where she's at and who she's with, I promise they won't hurt her."

I found no comfort in his words, but I didn't want him to know that.

Harry followed me up the dirt driveway and toward the porch, but I stopped before I got too far and said to Zia, "Thanks for taking me, even if it didn't turn out like I had hoped."

Zia waved apologetically and they drove off.

"Do you think they'll mind if I come in for a while?" Harry asked.

I didn't even think to ask Zia if they could give Harry a ride home. He had walked to my house earlier, but it was still daylight then. His car had been in the shop for two days.

"They won't mind. I'll see if Uncle Carl can give you a ride later."

Beverlee and Uncle Carl welcomed Harry and even told him to help himself to the kitchen if he was hungry. I needed someone to talk to, someone who had been there during the fight. Harry was better than any other, especially since he had become my closest friend. Uncle Carl agreed to give him a ride home in a few hours even though it would be late. And Beverlee knew right away that Harry and I were just friends and that there was nothing more between us. It was fine that I had a 'boy' up in my room alone with me, late at night. Somehow, I knew if it had been Isaac instead, Beverlee wouldn't have let him past the den.

"I really screwed that up," Harry told me, plopping down on the chair next to my window.

"What do you mean?"

"I made an idiot of myself in front of Zia." He put his elbows on his legs and leaned forward. "She probably thinks I'm a joke."

I smiled. "Harry, she doesn't think that at all."

"How do you know? You haven't had time to talk to her since it happened."

"No, but a girl knows when another girl is totally not interested in someone."

Harry straightened his back some, looking over at me. "You think she's interested in me?"

"Well, I'm not sure about that," I said, sitting on the end of my bed. "I just know she's not *dis*interested."

"Well, that doesn't make any sense."

"Look," I said, "if Zia was repulsed by you, you'd know it. Really though, I think you might've impressed her tonight."

Harry's brows wrinkled. "Impressed her? I got into a shouting match with another girl and then got my ass kicked by her boyfriend; I doubt that impressed anyone."

I shook my head, smiling and then kicked off my shoes. "From what I saw, Julia got what she deserved. You did good by not punching her in the face, even *if* she's a girl. Secondly, you were holding your own in that fight. I admit *I* was a little impressed."

"Really?" he asked, the smallest of smiles inching upward.

"Yeah, really," I answered. "But me, on the other hand? I got knocked to the ground, stepped on, and then crushed by no telling who, and I didn't even get a punch in." I laughed, adding, "If anyone looked like an idiot, it was definitely me." I didn't even care that that was true.

"Well," Harry said with a grin, "a guy knows when another guy is interested in a girl, and you could've puked in Isaac's lap and he would still have a thing for you."

My smile was warm and thankful. I needed to hear that. I wasn't sure what was going on between Isaac and me, or if anything was actually going on, but it was nice to hear it wasn't just me picking up on possible signs.

"That man," Harry added darkly, "he must be their dad or something." He shook his head and shuddered. "Glad he's not *my* dad—dude has some issues."

Harry was right about that, but he didn't know half of what I knew. That wasn't saying much though, because I was pretty clueless and still in the dark too.

Harry and I stayed up all night talking. I felt like I could tell him anything, and I pretty much did. It was like having my sister back, when we would talk for hours about Sam Winchester and school and everything in-between. Since before Alex and I left Georgia, I hadn't been able to confide freely in anyone until Harry came along. And he was a guy, so our gossip wasn't one-sided: he offered a guy's perspective and I offered the opposite. And I knew he wasn't going to go to school the next day and talk about me behind my back to someone else in our group.

I told Harry about my mom and her drunk, abusive husband. He told me about his older brother who was in prison for breaking and entering. Harry admitted he never liked to talk about that and that he was ashamed of it. I told Harry about my first kiss and that I was still a virgin. He confessed he was not a virgin, but had only been with one girl, who dumped him for one of his friends shortly afterwards.

There was so much to talk about, so much that both of us needed to get out. Even Sebastian, who we spent all of six minutes on. Harry veered off the subject, needing to fill that conversational space with something less depressing.

Only one thing was left in secret, and I didn't want it to be a secret any longer.

"If I tell you something," I said, sitting up cross-legged on the center of my bed, "do you promise not to think I'm crazy?"

Harry laughed. "I can't promise you that, but I can promise not to tell anyone else why I think you're crazy, if I do."

I crinkled my nose at him.

"Okay, I promise I won't think you're crazy," he agreed. "What is it?" He moved toward my bed and sat on the edge.

I started to back out, but I needed someone to talk to about it. It should've been Alex, but that was never going to happen. It couldn't be Beverlee because although I loved her and could trust her with my life, some things you just couldn't tell the adult who was taking care of you.

I sat there for a moment, absently twisting the corner of my pillowcase in-between my fingers.

"Do you believe in—" I paused, regretting not rehearsing this beforehand. "I mean, have you ever wondered if there are really things out there that exist other than humans?"

"What, like aliens?" he offered.

He was totally interested.

"Yeah I guess so," I replied, but still beating around the bush. "But what about other things…things like—"

"You mean like vampires, or ghosts?"

He was getting closer, a little too close. I was already backing out. This *was* crazy. Why was I being so stupid? I finally had a friend close enough I could confide in and gossip with and who wouldn't two-face me and I was about to ruin it all with insanity.

So I decided to approach the question differently.

"Yeah," I said, "ghosts, vampires, aliens…werewolves."

Harry chuckled and lay across my bed, his shoes dangling off the edge. He brought his hands up and interlocked them behind his head.

"Nah," he said. "Not really. Well, aliens maybe, because let's face it, the universe is just too big for us to be the only ones in it." He turned his head to see me rather than continue looking up at the ceiling. "All that other stuff—old myths twisted into something fantastical over time."

I sighed.

"Like that whole thing with Vlad the Impaler," he went on, looking up at the ceiling again. "Sure, all that brutal stuff he did was pretty heavy, but every bit of it totally believable. People just passed the stories down through time, adding this and that, which eventually created Dracula."

I sat cross-legged and rested my hands in the hollow of my lap. Maybe I should take it up a notch, I thought.

"What's your theory on ghosts then?" I asked, curiously.

Harry fell into a pensive moment, twisting his bottom lip in his teeth. "Maybe I saw a ghost once," he revealed, and I leaned forward, hopeful. "I was visiting Waverly Hills Sanatorium with my parents for Halloween one year—not sure if it was really a ghost, but I saw *something*."

"So you really think it might've been a ghost?"

Harry shook his head. "Nah," he decided, and the hopeful interest drained from me quickly. "When you go to places like that you're already expecting to see something. I think it's all in the mind."

If Harry didn't even believe in ghosts, I knew there was no way he would believe in something as preposterous as a werewolf—I wasn't even sure I believed it one hundred percent, and I actually saw one.

"Why do you ask?" He looked over at me once more.

"Just curious." I tossed the pillow from my lap onto the bed, and got up. "I'll be back in a second. Do you want a soda or anything?"

Although disappointed, he didn't push the issue.

"Sure. Thanks."

And that was the end of that.

I woke up with Harry's smelly sock practically straight up my nose. Shocked, and still half-asleep, I freaked that there was a guy in my bed, so I shoved him as hard as I could onto the floor. Right when I heard the loud *thump!* I realized what I had done.

"Harry! I'm *so* sorry!"

He stumbled into a standing position, his hand pressed against his ribs. "It's all right," he grumbled.

"I wonder why Uncle Carl didn't take you home last night," I said, looking around the room, still in somewhat of a daze.

Beverlee stood in the doorway of my bedroom. I don't know how long she had been there.

"Because we fell asleep on the couch," she said. "And I'm terribly sorry. I feel like a horrible parent, adult…whatever you want to call me." Beverlee was clearly beside herself over this; she was practically stuttering. "Carl is going to call Harry's parents and apologize. I just hope people don't start talking. Oh God, Sandy and Marla at the store will have a field day with this kind of gossip." She was getting Harry's shoes for him.

"Beverlee," I said, "calm down, no one is going to say anything."

"Nothing happened, I swear it," Harry quickly added, taking his shoes from her.

"Honestly, Aunt Bev, Harry and I don't like each other that way. We're just friends."

After a moment, Beverlee sighed. "Oh, I guess you're right. I mean there's nothing romantic about his feet being up your nostrils, or you halfway off the bed with drool hanging off your chin."

I couldn't help but laugh, and I absently checked my chin.

Harry and I talked with Uncle Carl before Beverlee drove us to school, and convinced him that calling Harry's parents was unnecessary. If Harry's parents had noticed he was gone last night, they would've called his cell wondering where he was. I was just glad Uncle Carl believed us, and there weren't any lingering suspicions about our relationship.

The night at The Cove changed more than just Alex, or mine and Harry's friendship. Things at school also changed drastically. In just a week, my group of friends went from Julia, Sebastian, Tori, and Harry, to just Harry and Zia. Julia was officially a 'drop out', and Sebastian was officially 'deceased'. But only by the school gossip—thankfully, there was no proof of that. Tori decided there were people at school better worth her time, and so she dropped us like last month's fashion trends. She was a total witch, even to me when I had never done anything to her, but I didn't care.

The way I saw it though, things were now how they were supposed to be, all except for Sebastian, of course. Zia, Harry, I were the perfect trio. We hung out everywhere. School. My house. Harry's house. The skate park. But never Zia's house. It seemed intentional, and that was frustrating. I wanted to go there, not just for Zia, but because I wanted to see Isaac. Zia dodged my suggestion whenever I'd bring it up. After another week and still not one trip up the winding, dark roads, I was fed up with the secrecy and the games.

I was going to go to the Mayfair house on Saturday, uninvited if that was what it took. If he didn't actually like me, then fine. I just needed to know one way or the other, because it was driving me insane how we left it. Even now, I was too nervous to call him, because he didn't technically give me his number for *that* reason. And besides, trying to figure him seemed harder over the phone than in person.

Saturday morning I agreed to go with Beverlee and help her at the store. Apparently, Sandy and Marla took vacation time together, and Mrs. Finch, the owner, was sick again. Poor Mrs. Finch; she suffered from diabetes and a host of other illnesses, which kept her sick most of the time. Sandy and Marla were Mrs. Finch's evil daughters. The whole thing reminded me of some twisted *Cinderella* story, except Mrs. Finch always treated Beverlee like the daughter she wished Sandy and Marla were. Nathan Mayfair also worked at Finch's Grocery, but only nights as a stocker.

Lucky me, I was nominated to be a fill-in cashier today. I had never worked a cash register in my life, but thankfully, Beverlee was never too far away if I needed her.

The bell above the front door rang as a customer entered the store. "Good morning, Mrs. Perry," Beverlee greeted; she was on the bread aisle at the front of the store, straightening the snack cake boxes.

"Mornin' Beverlee," answered Mrs. Perry. "Ran out of coffee last night, right when I was in the middle of my soaps."

She was a plump old lady with white-gray hair, and she carried a big black handbag pressed gently against her rounded stomach.

"Oh," she said in a perky, interested sort of way while looking straight at me, "this must be one of your nieces; the good one, I'm sure."

Beverlee grimaced as she came out of the aisle.

"They're both good girls," Beverlee said, hoping I'd believe she never spoke badly of Alex. Really though, I wasn't upset by it.

"Adria, this is Mrs. Perry. She's been shopping at this store for twenty years."

Mrs. Perry smiled, causing the cavernous lines around her mouth to stretch and deepen. "Twenty-one years next month. Little places like this are the best," she said. "Those big chains lose sight of people, and the people are what matters. Can't shop at a Driscoll's and talk to the owner whenever you want. Don't even know who the owner is. Probably doesn't even live in the same state." She added, "How is Mrs. Finch anyway?"

"She's not well," Beverlee replied. She lowered her voice a bit and added, "I think she's getting worse."

"I was afraid you'd tell me that," Mrs. Perry said, sadly. "Well, do give her my well-wishes. Tell her I'll bring her over a Lemon Meringue pie."

Beverlee had started to say something, but Mrs. Perry put up her wrinkled hand decorated by gaudy rings and said, "Sugar-free, of course."

Beverlee smiled and nodded.

It was pretty much the same kind of people and the same sort of conversations in the store for the next two hours. I probably met half the town, with the exception of anyone my age. And in a small town like Hallowell when most of the residents came into a small store like Finch's Grocery, one can safely expect the gossip to be rampant. And I thought school was bad. The townspeople—the *adults*—had us beat in the gossip department. I learned that Marlene Higginbotham was cheating on her husband with some hot construction worker (Beverlee's words, not mine) who was only here for a few weeks on a job in Augusta. I heard all about Penny Fairweather's secret night job as a stripper; and how Lenny Parsons was gay and had been hitting on Mark Schultz. Then there was 'Fat-ass Felicia' (again, Beverlee's words), who apparently tried to steal my uncle away from Beverlee.

I didn't know any of these people, and I was so glad.

Just before lunch, Nathan Mayfair walked into the store, and my interest perked immediately.

"Hey, Adria," he said, as he walked past the candy stand near the front door. "Beverlee around?"

"Yeah, she's in the back. You're here early, aren't you?"

"I didn't pick up my check last night," he said. "How have you been?"

A customer walked in and I greeted her with a smile. She picked up a handheld basket and disappeared down the meat aisle.

"I've been all right. Nothing new, nothing bad. Things have been pretty normal."

Nathan looked a lot like Isaac, I noticed. I never had much opportunity to compare their resemblance before.

"Beverlee hooked you into working, I see."

"I don't mind so much," I admitted quietly. "I get to hear all the juicy town secrets, and learn before it's too late, exactly how I *don't* want to be when I get old."

Nathan chuckled. "I hear yah. I'm lucky that way—working nights keeps my virgin ears from being molested by all that stuff."

Where have I seen him before? Suddenly, I couldn't stop thinking about it. I had seen Nathan somewhere else other than at the store. I was *sure* of it.

"Hey," I said, "is something going on with Isaac lately?"

"Not that I know of. Why?"

I felt stupid, and maybe even a little obsessive.

"It's nothing," I lied. "I just wondered."

Beverlee came through the bread aisle waving an envelope. "I've got your check right here," she said, placing it into Nathan's hand. "I guess I'll see you Monday night then."

"Yes, ma'am," he answered respectfully.

Nathan said goodbye and left with the bell ringing behind him.

"Don't worry," said Beverlee, "I'm not going to keep you in here all day. If you want, you can leave around one. I've got a few more things to do and then I'll be free to run the register for the rest of night."

I couldn't contain the smile as much as I wanted, but Beverlee understood. "Thanks. I mean it's not that I don't want to help, I just wanted to go to Zia's later."

"You've been a wonderful help," Beverlee said. "I can give you a ride there later if you want."

"That's okay. Harry finally got his transmission fixed and I'll be catching a ride with him."

"He's a nice boy." (I wasn't sure if I liked where this was heading.) "You two still just friends?"

My throat suddenly felt dry. "Definitely," I answered, "best friends actually, so don't get any ideas."

She winked and left it alone.

My last hour at the store felt the longest. I was too anxious to get to Zia's, so I made sure to bring what I needed with me to the store so that I could freshen up there. Just before I left, I brushed out my hair, changed my clothes and put on some tinted Chap Stick. I had forgotten to bring my deodorant, so I took some off the shelf in the Health & Beauty aisle and told Beverlee to subtract it from my day's pay.

"Have you talked to Zia at all?" I asked Harry later, in the passenger's side of his car.

"Not since school yesterday," he replied, and then looked over at me. "She doesn't know we're coming?"

"No, but that's all right."

"What if no one's home?"

"As many people that live in that house, *someone's* sure to be there."

Not that Harry cared much; he was still trying to win Zia over, and any chance to go to her house and blame an unexpected visit on me, he was not going to pass that up.

When we pulled in Zia's driveway, there were no other vehicles in it. We sat in the car for a moment, contemplating, neither of us wanting to be the one who got out to knock on the door. In the end, we decided to go together.

No answer.

"Come on, Harry," I said, stopping him from leaving the porch. "Someone has to be here."

He waited on the second step and I knocked again, louder. Finally, I heard movement inside. The door clicked and then opened slowly; a face peeked out between it and the frame.

"What do you want?" a girl asked, tiredly.

I couldn't tell at first, but then recognized her as Daisy Mayfair, the sister of Isaac who Zia actually liked.

"Is Zia or Isaac home?"

She didn't answer right away, but she stood there looking at us. "This is a bad time," she said, firmly. "I'll tell Zia—"

The door swung open and a taller girl pushed Daisy out of the way. "Adria, right?" She was grinning.

I hesitated. "Yeah…I'm Adria, and this is Harry; we're friends of Zia."

"And Isaac?" Her grin deepened.

"Uhhh, yeah, I guess so."

Harry came back up the steps to stand next to me; I got the feeling he was as uncomfortable as I was now. The tall girl stepped aside and waved us in. "Please, come in and make yourself at home. I'll get Zia for you."

Daisy stood with her back against the wall, looking as though she wanted to say something. Warning lights were flashing like crazy in my mind, but I stupidly ignored them. The den wasn't full of people this time, just the tall girl, who went toward the stairs, and now Daisy as she made her way to the couch.

I heard muttering in the stairwell above.

"You should leave," Daisy whispered. "This is a *really* bad time."

"Why? What's going on?" I whispered back.

Daisy kept looking at the stairs, as if watching for anyone who might be listening, or coming down. The worry on her face set me on edge, made me question if we really did need to go.

The tall girl came back down the stairs and stopped in the middle; she waved at Harry and me. "Come on up."

We both looked at Daisy once more before following the tall girl. "Zia's in the third room on the right," she said, in a low voice.

Harry started to follow me, but the tall girl stopped him. "Can you wait here?" she said. "I think Zia's getting dressed."

"Ummm, sure," he agreed.

I left him with her and headed toward the room, my steps much slower the closer I got—I don't know why I was so nervous. I heard strange noises coming from out ahead. Whimpering? Whispers? I wasn't sure, and I could hardly make anything out. The door in question was cracked just barely, and at first, I knocked on it lightly. "Hello?" I said, but there was no answer. "Zia?"

I carefully pushed open the door.

My heart dropped into my feet. Isaac lay across his bed with Rachel curled up beside him; her head was pressed against his bare chest; her long, graceful fingernails traced the contours of the muscles over his ribcage. She slowly rose up in the bed, grinning. It didn't matter that Isaac was fully clothed from the waist down—just seeing her half-naked in a pair of pajama shorts and nothing but a bra, told me all I needed to know.

I finally had my answer: Isaac definitely wasn't on the same page as me.

"What?" Rachel gaffed. "You thought he was going to be yours, didn't you?"

Isaac seemed to be asleep, but his eyes cracked open just barely, enough to look at me. They were full of nothing warm, his eyes; they seemed dark, cold.

"He would never want you," Rachel went on, mocking me, making me feel like the total idiot I knew I was.

Rachel leaned down and started kissing him—and I saw him kiss her back.

Disgusted, I let the bedroom door slam behind me when I left, and I took the stairs faster than necessary; I was so blinded by humiliation that I didn't even see Zia coming, and we practically slammed into each other.

"What are you doing here?" she asked, seemingly concerned. Or maybe it was disappointment, I couldn't tell. But it was plain that Zia knew I had seen something I shouldn't have.

"Don't worry," I said. "I won't be stopping by here again. Message received." I pushed my way past her. "Harry! Let's go!" I was practically choking on the embarrassment as I reached the bottom of the stairs.

Harry had already risen off the sofa. I didn't have time to ease the confused look on his face yet. I just wanted to get out of there and as far away from the Mayfairs as I could.

"Adria," Zia shouted, "you don't understand!"

"You should've just told me, Zia!" No wonder she didn't want me coming around.

I hurried toward the front door, hearing Isaac shouting my name from the top of the stairwell. "Wait, Adria!" he said, his voice hoarse, probably because he just had Rachel's tongue down his throat. "It's not what you think! Please wait!"

How *dare* he give me that clichéd line.

I rushed right out the door and jumped into Harry's car.

"Please, just take me home."

Without another word, my best friend lived up to his title and we drove away.

11

I KNEW I HAD OVERREACTED; I KNEW THAT I SHOULD'VE just kept a cool head and left without making a scene—I knew it. But if there's one thing I've never taken well, it was being humiliated.

It took me thirty minutes to work up the courage to admit what happened—I felt so stupid.

"That's harsh," Harry said. "But you have to see it from Isaac's perspective."

My lips parted in disbelief. What happened to my best friend whom I could confide in and trust to be on my side? And then I realized, he was the 'guy perspective' and that I *could* confide in and trust him more than anyone. Harry was not telling me what I wanted to hear, he was telling me what I *needed* to hear.

"You're not his girlfriend," Harry said plainly. We were sitting on the hood of his car in my driveway. "I admit, he could've been a little more clear about his intentions, but you two weren't together, so technically he didn't do anything wrong."

The truth stung.

"Maybe not. But it doesn't mean it hasn't hurt my feelings," I said simply. Scorched my feelings, more like it.

Harry nodded, agreeing. "True, but you did go to his house uninvited, and you did go into his room, uninvited. I'm sure he didn't mean for you to catch them."

"Wow, Harry—got any salt you can rub into my wounds? Maybe a nice torch to cauterize the rip in my chest?"

He threw his hands up. I shook my head and rolled my eyes, then buried my head in my hands and groaned. I knew he was right, and that technically, I couldn't be mad.

But couldn't I? I hadn't imagined everything, had I? Was I so off-base to think he liked me? If he hadn't, why the hell did he chase me down the stairs trying to convince me otherwise?

My head hurt. So did my pride. And I didn't even want to think about facing Zia again in school. Why didn't she just tell me he lost interest in me, and started liking Rachel? Yeah, it would've stung, but not nearly as bad as seeing them in bed together.

Harry and I looked up at the star-filled sky, and it reminded me of Georgia. I used to sit out in that barren field around our house and gaze up at the stars for hours. To think, if I had only done that instead the night Alex and I saw what we saw, none of this would have ever happened.

"I hate to say this," Harry went on, "but it's your own fault for being into someone who made a bad first impression to begin with." From the corner of my eye, I could see him shaking his head. Harry was blunt, but I one hundred percent respected him for it. "If I saw Zia in a situation like you saw Isaac, there's no way I could ever be attracted to her."

I looked over at him with annoyance. I never said it was *smart* for me to like him. But it didn't matter that it was my fault for letting down my guard, that I got my hopes up too quickly, or that I read too far into a situation and twisted the events to make them something in my mind that they weren't; Isaac Mayfair still led me on. Subtly I knew, but sometimes subtle can be more powerful than straightforward flirting.

I fell for it, but I was definitely not going to let it happen again.

When I was alone in my room that night after Harry had gone home, I had time to reflect. I didn't know how I was going to show my face at school for the next day or two, or at Finch's Grocery when Nathan could show up there. I was sure the whole Mayfair house was buzzing with rumors about how I was such a dumb girl to just randomly show up like that uninvited. I couldn't think of anything more embarrassing than that.

All day Sunday, I dreaded Monday. Still mad at Zia, the last thing I wanted to deal with was having to avoid her at school.

To my relief, Zia was absent on Monday.

And she was absent on Tuesday.

Wednesday.

Thursday.

I was getting worried, and the school was starting to talk.

"I bet she dropped out like Julia Morrow," said a girl in the hall between classes.

"What if she was kidnapped like Sebastian?" Harry asked, his voice laced with concern. We were in Geometry and Harry was whispering into the back of my head like he always did.

"I'm really worried," he said. "I haven't heard from her at all. I even tried calling her landline last night, but no one answered the phone."

That was strange. There were like two hundred people living in that house and for not one person to answer just didn't seem right. *And who has a landline anymore?*

By the time I got home from school, I was prepared to dismiss everything. No one had reported Zia abducted like they had Sebastian, and it was true that Zia had a problem with keeping school hours before I ever met her. Things weren't so strange after all, I thought. Until Beverlee came home from work and I overheard her talking to Uncle Carl about how Nathan hadn't been back to work since Friday night.

I lay in bed staring at my cell phone that contained Isaac's number, which I had never called. I thought about calling a hundred times, but all I had were a bunch of lame excuses I knew anyone would see right through.

But I didn't want to talk to him anyway.

I tossed the phone on the end of the bed a little too hard and it bounced off and clunked against the hardwood floor. I curled up on my side with my pillow and fell asleep crying and angry. Only crying *because* I was angry. Mostly at myself.

The knock at my bedroom door woke me sometime later.

"Sorry, I didn't mean to wake you," Beverlee said, as she peeked around the door. "Zia's downstairs."

I lifted quickly, my mind still trying to catch up to being awake, and I looked over at the clock on the nightstand. I thought it would be much later than nine. I felt like I had slept for hours.

I forced myself the rest of the way awake, but with incentive. I could only wonder why Zia would be at my house. Now I just had a few seconds to decide how I wanted to act toward her: still angry about the Isaac thing; over the Isaac thing completely; or just glad she was okay and full of questions about where she had been.

"Thanks. Can you send her up?"

Soon, Zia was knocking lightly against my opened door. She came inside, smiling cautiously. Apologetically?

"Hey girl," she said.

"Hey."

She came over and stood near the bed, picking my cell phone up from the floor on her way.

"I really hope you don't mind I'm here."

I looked down at the swirly colors on my bedspread.

"No, I don't mind," I said, and then I looked up at her. "Where have you been? Harry and I have been worried."

"Yeah, sorry about that." She looked away briefly. "Isaac was really freakin' sick with pneumonia, and then Nathan got it, along with Dwarf and me. It sucked hardcore."

"Pneumonia?" I scoffed. Please don't tell me a fever made Isaac get naked with that girl.

Zia smiled softly as if there was some kind of hidden meaning behind it that I should know. "I'll have tons of homework to catch up on."

"Well, I'm glad you're okay," I said. "And Harry'll be relieved to know. I'll have to call him later. Soon. Soon, but later; I mean after you leave."

Zia stopped my babbling. "I just don't want you to be mad at me."

The more embarrassing subject was inevitable. I just wished it held off a bit longer.

I sat up the rest of the way. "Look, I know what Isaac does isn't your fault, and since you're living with his family, you can't necessarily go around telling his secrets or he'd probably kick you out. I'm not mad at you, Zia, but a little heads-up would've been nice, since you were obviously trying to hook us up."

Zia shook her head. For a second, it seemed she wanted to say something, and I guessed I was kind of expecting her to explain herself, but she looked away instead.

I sighed.

"I would've done the same thing though," she said finally, "if I were in your shoes." I got the feeling those weren't the words she'd really wanted to say; they felt more like a tradeoff.

"So what happened then?" I asked.

Zia went over to my vanity and ran her fingers through her short, spiky bangs. Her reflection looked back at me through the mirror. "I told you why we've been M.I.A for so long."

"Yeah…" I waited a moment longer, just in case she wasn't finished. "And what about Isaac?"

She put one last piece of hair into place and turned to face me again. I couldn't figure out her expression, and it bugged me.

"I never speak for Isaac," she replied. "But he wants to talk to you and tell you himself."

"What?"

"Yeah." She nodded. "He sent me over here to pick you up. Damien is outside waiting."

"He sent someone to *collect* me?" I scoffed. "You've gotta be kidding me."

"If you don't want to talk to him, I understand, but I really think you should go and hear what he has to say."

I really didn't want to deal with this. It was bad enough I let myself be into a guy who completely humiliated me; honestly, I'd never been so humiliated before by *anyone*.

"If he wanted to talk to me, why didn't he come over here himself?"

Zia grabbed my sweater from the ottoman by the window and threw it into my lap. "You'll have to let him tell you that," she said. "Coming or not?"

I just stared at her.

I had nothing to say to Isaac Mayfair. I accepted he was never my boyfriend to begin with, but I was still bitter.

For a long moment I just sat there, fingering the sweater in my lap. Finally, I looked straight at Zia, this time with resolve. "I'll pass," I sang. "Go tell him to snuggle up with one of his other five girls."

Her expression failed under a shroud of defeat.

I stood from the bed and began picking things up from the floor: A pair of gently worn socks; a stack of paper which I had scrawled random notes and doodles on when Harry had spent the night; I tossed my dirty clothes into the laundry basket, and lined my shoes against the wall.

"Adria," Zia said, pleadingly, "come on."

"Are you serious right now?" I said, stopping in the center of the room. "Do you understand how humiliating that was? And now to be *summoned* back?" My voice trailed.

Zia's perfectly manicured hands dropped lightly at her sides. She wore a form-fitting gray coat that tied stylishly around her hourglass waist and stopped just past her hips. I don't know how she always pulled it off, but every time I looked at her, I had to swallow a tiny dose of envy. I was the girl-next-door compared to her, who always, with powder-white skin and black bewitching eyes, looked like a walking Photoshop ad.

I went over to the mirror and pretended to be cleaning off the vanity, when really I was looking at myself. I could see Zia behind me, finally deciding to sit down on the wooden chair near the bed. Absently, she poked her finger at the soft wax in the heart shaped candle holder beside the clock.

It never bothered me before this night, as I looked at myself in that brusque and spiteful piece of glass, that maybe I just wasn't hitting the mark. Maybe that was why guys always chose Alex over me. Maybe that was why I spent every weekend reading a book, or staring up at the stars alone, instead of going out like every other girl I knew.

Maybe that was why Rachel was with Isaac and I wasn't.

But enough about Isaac Mayfair—Zia was my friend, and I was glad to have her back. So was Harry when I called him later that night after she had gone home. And like before, the three of us at school were inseparable. Zia and Harry had so much in common, I thought there was no way they wouldn't end up together. But despite the amount of attention she gave Harry, I noticed too that she seemed to keep it at a certain level. She never made a move forward, or indicated directly, or indirectly, that she might've been interested in Harry for anything more than friendship. I could see it, but thankfully Harry could not. He continued to walk around the school with a beaming smile on his face even when he wasn't actually smiling.

I couldn't break it to him, that Zia seemed to have a lot on her mind, and that Harry probably wasn't part of it. At least not in the way he hoped. I figured it was best to just let him believe there was still a chance. After all, I wasn't even sure myself if my suspicions were right.

On Thursday, Harry and I waited out front on our usual bench for Damien and Dwarf to pick Zia up from school. It had been only her brothers lately; Isaac was nowhere to be seen, and honestly, I was thankful for that. I thought. But on this day, Isaac was in the backseat of the Jeep, and the second I saw his dark hair and eyes peering carefully at me through the window, my heart trembled and hardened simultaneously.

"There's my ride," Zia said, slinging her bag over one shoulder. I could tell right away she was trying to be nonchalant, knowing my comfort-level went down about a dozen notches upon seeing Isaac for the first time since I saw him with Rachel.

"Want a ride?" Damien asked, waving at me from the driver's seat.

"No, but thanks," I replied, trying not to look at Isaac.

It was the same thing on Friday: Isaac was with Zia's brothers when they picked her up in the afternoon. And also like the day before, Isaac looked at me at least once, and I looked back just before walking away without saying a word to him.

If Isaac had something to say to me—and it sure seemed like he did—he had opportunities, but instead he kept to himself. It frustrated me that he didn't just speak up, that he didn't tell Damien to wait while he dragged me off to the side to explain himself. Isaac was way too controlled, so much so that it made him unreadable. But what I started to get from it was that maybe he had lost interest in me altogether.

Fine. I didn't really care much by this time.

Much.

"Hurry up!" Harry waved at me from his car window, and I picked up the pace, gliding down the front porch steps. The sun was blazing, which made it feel about five degrees warmer. I took what I could get when it came to the tiny notches on that rooster temperature reader Beverlee had nailed near the front door. I was relieved I could get away with wearing my dark red jacket and just a sweater underneath. Winter clothes always made me somewhat claustrophobic.

I hopped in the passenger's seat and shut the door fast as if trying to dodge a downpour. It wasn't frigid out, but it was still cold and my Georgia blood wasn't used to it.

Harry nudged me while I was preoccupied by adjusting the seatbelt. I looked over and saw Uncle Carl standing on the porch. I took a deep breath then, preparing myself to open the car door again and get hit with a cold blast of air. Really I was exaggerating the situation—the wind was hardly blowing at all.

"What time will you be back?" Uncle Carl asked from the porch as I looked over the roof of the car at him. He held a magazine low at his side, two fingers keeping his place.

"Before dinner," I said, waving. "I told Aunt Bev."

"Oh," he said. "Well then you have a good time."

I smiled brightly, hoping to make him feel less awkward about always being the last to know things.

"I'm a little nervous," Harry admitted, as I shrank back inside the warm car.

He had the heat blazing inside now, and it only took a few seconds before I felt suffocated by it. "Whoa, Harry," I said, reaching over to turn it off, "way too hot even for me."

I took off my jacket and set it on the seat between us, adjusting the seatbelt again.

"What's there to be nervous about? You're awesome at skateboarding. A pro."

Harry glanced over at me squeamishly.

I pursed my lips. "Come on, you know you are."

We drove away, hitting the pothole at the end of the driveway at just the right angle. My whole body jerked sideways and against the car door. Instinctively, my hand went up for the handgrip. Few people had ever missed that pothole, except Beverlee and Uncle Carl, who were so used to it that they never cared to get it filled in.

"But this is different," Harry said, pulling onto the main road. "There'll be sponsors."

"Guess you better suck it up and get it together then, huh?" Like Harry, I was blunt when it came to telling him the truth. Except when it came to Zia, of course—I just didn't have the heart to tell him.

When we arrived at the skate park minutes later, even I was a little nervous for him. The parking lots were packed full, and we had to find a place on the grass, which clearly displayed a sign that read: NO PARKING ON GRASS. But we weren't the only ones with the same idea, so I thought it was good Harry's car wouldn't be singled out for a ticket.

I got out, leaving the door open while I slipped my jacket back on and zipped it practically right up to my chin. I buried my hands deep in the pockets and bumped the car door with my butt to close it. My head was spinning there were so many people. I wouldn't have chosen to come here on my own, but I wanted to be supportive to Harry, who had been waiting for this opportunity for two years. He said the last time they had a sponsorship skateboarding event in Hallowell, Harry was bedridden with the flu.

Harry popped the trunk and pulled out his skateboard.

"There's Zia," Harry said, waving at her as she walked up with Damien, Dwarf, and two girls I saw once in passing at the Mayfair House.

"What a turnout," Zia said, stepping up. She wore a leather antique bomber jacket.

Secretly, I began to look for Isaac, hoping he didn't show up, too.

"I'm going to head over," Harry said, nodding in the direction of the action, and then smiling at Zia. Then he looked at me. "If I break any bones," he said, "you're driving me to the ER. I don't do ambulances. Got it?" He dropped his car keys in my hand and I just stared at him.

"What if I can't drive?" I joked. "Did you ever think of that?"

Harry laughed. "Well, then I hope you're a fast learner." He smiled once more at Zia and then walked away into the crowd.

Of course, I knew perfectly well how to drive.

Damien and Dwarf went off somewhere with their girlfriends, leaving Zia and me alone.

We huddled together on the dead grass watching the event. Many of Harry's skater friends were there, all showing off for the crowd, but especially for the three men standing off to the side who everyone knew as some big-shot scouts from California. When it was Harry's turn, I felt my body tense up with apprehension. All I could think about was how I hoped he wouldn't fall, or be so nervous that it got in the way of his talent. I hated this. My stomach swirled around so much that the back of my neck began to sweat.

I knew nothing about skateboarding. Absolutely nothing. But when Harry was finished, I could tell by the blushed smile on his face (and the fact that he didn't fall) that he was happy with his performance.

"Can you see their faces?" Zia said about the scouts. She stood up. "Y'think they were impressed?"

I stood up with her, clutching onto the sleeve of her coat and trying to stay warm. "I don't know," I said, peering through the crowd. "I can't see them at all." There were just too many people.

Harry left the skate bowl and stood off to the side with two of his friends. Zia grabbed me by the wrist. "Let's go talk to him," she said.

Just when I started to follow, I noticed something that stopped me dead in my tracks.

Zia stopped too and looked at me, searching for a reason for the resistance.

"Go ahead," I said, looking away from Isaac across the lot so Zia wouldn't know. "I need to get something out of the car. I'll be there in a minute."

Zia nodded and slipped into the crowd.

I chewed on my bottom lip as I turned around again to see Isaac; two sickeningly beautiful dark-haired girls were with him. I just stood there, my feet anchored to the ground. I was *angry*.

And this was the moment in which I began to panic inside. I looked away from Isaac, lost in an unforgiving bubble of realization. "I've become my mom…" I said, lowly under my breath. I clenched my fists inside the pockets of my jacket.

On the ride home, Harry talked so much about the event, and about Zia, that I could get away with hardly saying anything at all. He wasn't chosen by the scouts, but he was ecstatic that two out of three of them complimented his skill personally. "Two more years," one scout had said to Harry, "and we might be asking you to come to California."

Harry couldn't get over it; not that it bothered me. I was totally happy for him, and proud that he didn't let this year's rejection get him down. His face was bright with dreams of California and professional skateboarding events and trophies and probably having Zia at his side. It made me smile to see him so happy.

"What's on your mind?" Harry wondered aloud, looking across at me from the driver's seat.

I guess I wasn't hiding my misery as much as I tried to.

We pulled onto my street and finally over the pothole and into the driveway. Harry put the car in park and turned around on the seat to face me.

"Spit it out," he demanded.

I couldn't look at him at first, not only because I worried what he would think when I fessed up, but I was also ashamed that I let this get in the way of his happy moment. This was supposed to be Harry's day, not a day for my ridiculous feelings to get all of the attention.

But I knew Harry, and there was no point holding it in.

"I saw Isaac today," I said, looking out the windshield.

Harry's left hand slid off the steering wheel and he pressed his back firmly against the leather seat.

"You're gonna have to go over there," he said.

Perplexed, I turned to see him.

"Confront him," he said. "If it's bothering you this much then you should do something about it."

I sighed deeply.

"Harry," I began, "I'm really sorry. You were awesome out there today. I—."

Harry grinned wide and placed both wrists on the steering wheel, letting his fingers dangle. "You don't have to tell me something I already know," he joked, trying to brighten my mood.

I couldn't help but laugh; I felt my miserable, taut face break into a smile.

Then he got serious again. "Thing is," he went on, "what you should really do is just forget about it and go on with your life"—he pointed at me briefly—"that's what you'd easily be able to do if you didn't care. But obviously, you care."

"I don't care," I cut in. "Not really about Isaac anyway; what makes it so hard to put it all behind me is not knowing."

"Not knowing what?" Harry said. "That he's not into you? You already know that." *Damn, Harry, you don't always have to be* that *blunt!*

"No," I came back. But then I paused, because I was still working everything out in my head.

Harry's left brow inched higher than the other; he just looked at me, waiting.

Then finally I said, "Not knowing if what I saw was really what happened." I paused again, looking out the windshield, lost in my thoughts. "I don't know, Harry, but something about all this just doesn't…fit. You know what I mean?"

Harry laughed. "No. Really I don't."

I couldn't explain it to Harry—I couldn't explain any of it to myself yet, really—but something in my gut wouldn't let me just forget about it and move on. Not yet. I just needed to know the truth. If the truth turned out to be exactly what I saw, then I could live with that, and at least I'd know—the not knowing was driving me crazy.

"Thanks Harry," I said, and leaned over to hug him tightly. "If only you weren't so skinny, I'd be into you."

Harry roared with laughter, and then reached out, rummaging his hand destructively through my hair. "And if you weren't so brunette, I might be into you."

It was no secret, Harry loved blonds.

"All right," I said, "I'll talk to you later. And I mean it—you were awesome today."

He smiled his thanks and I got out of the car and ran to the front porch so the cold wouldn't kill me. By the time I got into the den, I heard his car scrape over the pothole.

For the next two hours, I stayed in my room, thinking about everything, and I came to one conclusion: Harry was right. I looked across the room at my cell phone sitting on the dresser, taunting me. But rather than calling Isaac, I decided to do exactly what Harry said, and confront him personally.

"Hello?" Zia said on the other end of the phone.

"Hey, Zia. Got a minute."

"Sure, what's up?"

I paused and took a deep breath, trying to word it all right in my head in the few seconds that I had.

"Hello?" Zia said, as if our call had dropped.

"I'm still here."

"Is something wrong?"

I took one more deep breath.

"Do you think Isaac still wants to talk?" Instantly I hated how the question came out; it made me sound desperate, and clingy. Gah! I hated that!

I don't know how, but I got the feeling Zia was smiling on the other end.

"We can come over right now and pick you up," she said, eagerly.

I didn't expect it to be so soon. It took a moment for me to agree.

"Ummm, sure," I said, nervously. "Now would be good, I guess."

Zia and Damien were at my house within the hour.

"Zia," I said, from the back seat, "maybe this is a mistake."

She turned to see me, smiling. "Hey, I've got your back."

I had only been thinking of confronting Isaac; Rachel failed to cross my mind, until now. Even more reason not to go through with this. "No really, Zia," I begged, "I don't want to do this. Everybody in that house looks at me like I'm a disease."

Truly, that fact didn't bother me so much; I was just looking for other excuses.

"If you're worried about Rachel," she said, "then don't, because she's been dealt with. *Be-lieve* me."

"How—"

Zia put up her hand. "Nope. I'm not going to say anything else. I don't speak for Isaac, remember?"

"Yeah, yeah," I mocked, "I remember. Well, I still don't feel comfortable in your house though."

"That hurts my feelings," she said, smiling.

"Can you blame her?" Damien jumped in, steering the Jeep onto another dark street.

"I guess you're right," Zia agreed. "But they only look at you that way because they're jealous of you."

"Jealous? Why would anyone in that house be jealous of *me*?"

I saw Damien's dark eyes gazing at me from the rear-view mirror. "Because you have something every one of them want," he answered.

"I do?" Trying to figure out what that might've been was a severely wasted effort. "What could I possibly have that they don't? Humility? Self-respect? I can't imagine they favor either."

"Isaac Mayfair's interest, of course," Damien replied.

I swallowed, hard.

12

WHEN YOU WANT TIME TO DRAG BY SLOWLY, IT WILL BE SURE to disappoint you. We were at the Mayfair house in minutes after Damien's absurd response. I couldn't speak the rest of the drive. I wanted to. I had wanted to tell Damien that I didn't appreciate his asinine jokes. I wanted to tell Zia that that was twice now she didn't take up for me.

I was prepared only to sit outside in the Jeep and nothing else, but Zia and her trademark persistence wouldn't allow it.

"Girl, come on," she said, beaming, as she looped her arm through mine and walked me into the house.

The den was as empty as it was the last time I had been here; I didn't even see Daisy, or the tall girl who I knew, deep down, had it out for me all along. A flame burned in the fireplace. It was quiet. It seemed darker and more vacant than usual, yet the chills down the back of my neck made me feel like eyes were watching from every corner, every shadow. A part of me thought that ridiculous, but the other part was convinced.

I went farther into the dim, spacious den and stood near the burning fireplace. Above the mantle, high on the wall, an antique painting of a man and woman hung; the man was someone of great importance and power; handsome and dominant with flowing dark hair and scars peeking from the neck of his military coat. There were scars on his unshaven face; scars were probably all over his body, I thought. But he was still attractive, even though he looked to be in his forties and that wasn't exactly my thing. The woman with him seemed much younger; she was so frail; so gentle and innocent, with the softest cinnamon-colored hair.

A shadow moved in the kitchen near the stairs. Daisy and two more faces were watching from the darkness. Why? Creepy much? I half-raised my hand to wave at Daisy, but then just put it back down when I noticed more faces here and there, watching me from rooms to my left and right, and from upstairs. I felt like a spectacle, but that was nothing out of the ordinary in the Mayfair house. It was the only thing I *was* used to.

"Where are you going?" I said to Zia.

She stopped near the kitchen entrance. "To make something to eat," she said. "Isaac's coming."

My heart sped up in half a second.

Before I could respond, Zia disappeared around the corner, and at the same time, there were footsteps moving down the stairs.

Isaac was coming…but so was Rachel.

The moisture evaporated from my mouth; revulsion and fear, the only two things I felt for Rachel, devoured me.

"You've got to be kidding me," I mumbled over heated breath.

This was not at all funny; I thought that Isaac wanted to talk to me, maybe to apologize and 'explain', but with Rachel in the mix, it could only mean one thing: they were going to apologize *together*.

Damien was an idiot, and I couldn't wait to tell him.

Rachel descended the last step first with Isaac not far behind. She approached with a withdrawn, hateful reluctance, almost as if every one of her steps were forced.

Since they were clearly a couple, I did the only respectable thing to do.

"I'm sorry," I said, as she moved forward.

She turned to glance at Isaac standing behind her; that hateful glare in her eyes, and the way her mouth stayed tight and angry, kept me on edge.

Isaac nodded at her, and she looked back at me.

"You're not the one who should be apologizing," she said. "That's what I came down here for, even though you—"

Isaac stepped right up behind Rachel then, interrupting something she apparently wasn't supposed to say. The tension in the room suddenly thickened; Isaac growled—*growled?*—low and guttural, and Rachel's hateful expression failed under a more controlled one.

"What you saw that day," Rachel went on, "was a lie."

I listened intently, trying to not to let the shock show on my face just yet.

"Isaac was sick and messed up on meds and I took advantage of it."

Already I felt the Idiot of the Year label attaching itself to me as the picture of what really happened began to clear up in my mind. My shoulders were stiff with every uncomfortable emotion imaginable. "You set me up?" I asked slowly for confirmation, bitterness in my words.

Rachel hesitated. It was obvious that she didn't want to tell me any of this; she would rather walk barefoot across broken glass.

"Yes, I set you up and I'm sorry."

Though I knew her apology was as sincere as Jeff telling my mom he'd never drink again, that didn't matter to me; knowing the truth trumped sincerity.

My gaze met Isaac's. I wasn't sure what to say at this point. I felt stupid standing there. I believed Rachel; nothing could take that away from me, but I was unsure of everything else: whether Rachel was going to jump me, or if Isaac was ever going to speak.

And then he did.

"Rachel, and every other girl here," he said, stepping past her and toward me, "know I'm not the one for them." He seemed to choose those words carefully; I could see it on his face.

He came closer.

"And I never want you to feel again, the way she made you feel," he added.

The faces watching from the shadows moved as if disturbed by Isaac's words. From the corner of my eye though, I saw Daisy smile at me.

Isaac turned to Rachel then. She nodded once as if quietly acknowledging some secret demand, and then she left the room. I had expected her to glare at me one last time, to threaten me with secret gestures, but she didn't even look in my direction.

"But...I saw you kiss her," I said in a soft whisper. It felt awkward having a discussion like this with others listening. "I know what I saw."

"I'm not denying that happened," Isaac said sullenly, "but I don't remember it if I did. Oldest excuse ever, I know, but it's the truth."

I still wasn't sure if I believed him. "You ran after me," I challenged. "Told me it wasn't what I thought it was."

"I vaguely recall that happening. I saw you leaving. I didn't understand why you were there or why you were leaving so upset, I just knew the reason for it couldn't have been right."

"But what about the girls I saw you with today?" I let my expression become slightly less defensive and accusing.

A slim, knowing smile spread carefully across Isaac's face as if my obvious jealousy pleased him in some way.

"My sisters," he revealed. "Shannon and Elizabeth."

Crap. I had forgotten he had more of those stashed somewhere. Seriously with the procreation. Their father needed to be stopped.

I felt so stupid; for a second, I couldn't bear to look him in the eyes.

"Adria," he said to me, "you did nothing wrong."

I literally huffed loudly at the absurdity of his comment.

"Look at me," he added, after a pause.

I raised my eyes.

Isaac started to explain further, but then took hold of my hand. "Let's go somewhere more private."

I looked to our joined hands. There wasn't electricity this time, but I could feel the urge wanting to build inside of me; if only I'd let it; it was simply waiting for the okay.

It was a relief to step outside and get away from everyone listening. I pulled hand from his, and then my sweater tight in the front, and then covered my hands with the sleeves. I think Isaac started to put his arm around me, maybe to help keep me warm, but he backed off at the last second.

"Where are we going?"

"Harvey's Coffee," he said. "We'll take my car this time." We walked to a standalone garage on the other side of the house. He opened the car door for me and I got inside quickly. A couple of beaded black necklaces hung from the rearview mirror; his car smelled strongly of cherry air freshener; and there were a few empty water bottles in the floorboard.

"Sorry about the mess," he said, hopping into the driver's seat. "Blame Zia, she drove it last."

"At least you have a car," I said. "I'm still riding a bike."

We pulled out of the garage and away from the Mayfair house. I secretly looked over at him, glimpsing the delicate yet strong set of his jaw, the intensity of his eyes. A million thoughts were swimming around inside my head, but most of all, I tried—unsuccessfully—to tame a dozen new emotions.

Harvey's was a cozy coffee shop with booth seats pressed against the large windows, and a couple of small round tables placed throughout. Other than Isaac and me, there were two other customers inside, both of them sitting with their noses buried inside a newspaper and a laptop. Only one barista was behind the counter and she greeted us along with an offer to try the newest iced coffee blend. I never liked coffee much, but had always loved the smell of it. Isaac ordered one black for himself.

"Come on," he urged, "you should try something. I'll get you a small one if you want."

"Ummm, sure, thanks. I'll have whatever that was she said." I couldn't remember what it was, but it wouldn't have mattered; I knew nothing of coffee lingo. Alex had been the Starbucks lover of the two of us.

We took our drinks to an empty booth and Isaac sat across from me. He was even more striking in the light. I tried not to look at him directly too much, but in my glimpses, I began to notice more about him. He was unlike any teenager I had ever met: reserved and mysterious, dangerous, and dare I say, gorgeous. All those qualities combined often made a person pretty irresistible. But there was more to his rough exterior than I had noticed before. Scars. Like in the painting over the fireplace mantle, Isaac had more scars than the average teenager: one noticeable on his throat—which I'd seen before but never thought much of—several on his hands and wrists; I wondered about his chest and back, and instinct told me there were probably scars there too.

Then I noticed one thing that should've been questionable all along: was he really a teenager? He didn't go to school and was apparently older than Zia, but I really had no idea.

"Did you graduate already?" I asked, taking a sip through my straw. The drink was surprisingly good.

"Graduated last year," he answered.

"So, you're like eighteen now?"

"Turned nineteen in July."

Two years older than me; that was good. Older, which was kind of mandatory in my book, but close enough to my age I didn't feel like I was infatuated by a pervert. I began wondering how Beverlee and Uncle Carl would take this, since he was officially an adult.

Isaac raised the coffee mug to his lips and blew away the steam rising from the rim before taking a sip. When he placed the mug back onto the table I reached out and touched his hand. "Where did you get this scar?" I turned his hand over, palm down. The scar had been deep, cut straight along the top of his hand between two knuckles. But then all of the visible scars he had seemed to be deep.

"That one, and these here," he said as he pulled the neck of his shirt down, "I got from falling through a sliding glass door."

I winced. "Oh God, I can't imagine what that was like."

"Excruciating."

He pulled up the sleeve of his left arm. "And this one I got in a motorcycle accident."

"One of *those*," I said, grinning foolishly.

He smiled right back at me, which was quite charming. I had never really seen him smile before. Not like that.

"One of what?"

I played around with him first, taking a longer than usual sip from my drink, fingering the straw, even sloshing it around in the blended ice.

"Come on," he urged, laughing impatiently, "one of what?"

"A scar junkie."

"Never heard that before."

"Some guys think scars are their battle wounds. They sit around in circles comparing size with other guys and showing them off to girls." I really didn't think of Isaac that way, but it was fun to tease him about it.

Isaac laughed again. "Well, you asked *me* about *my* scars, so that label doesn't fit me, does it?"

"Nah, I guess you're safe."

A quiet moment passed between us. I think maybe we both knew that getting the obvious out of the way first would be the best way to go about things.

I sloshed the straw around in my drink some more.

Finally, Isaac spoke up.

"The girls who live in my house," he began, looking right at me, "they aren't all that bad, just…young."

If you say so, I thought.

"My sisters would never treat you the way Rachel did, but the rest of them, they'll get over it."

"Get over what exactly?"

I pulled my legs up and sat cross-legged in the booth, my hands folded together atop the table.

"You," he said.

I glanced up at him, feeling a sudden nervous sensation swimming around in my chest. And I'm pretty sure every line in my forehead wrinkled in that moment.

"They could just sense it," he went on. "Even before I could… well, they could sense the attraction."

It was my turn to speak, but I didn't want to say the wrong thing. If I misunderstood what he was trying to say, I wanted to be the only one of us who knew it.

I needed a quick diversion.

"I'm not trying to be nosey," I said, taking the topic slightly off course, "but why do so many people live in your house anyway?"

"We're a large family," he said. "I have five blood sisters and three blood brothers. Each of us has a friend, or girlfriend, or whatever, who my father has allowed to stay with us."

"And who does Rachel belong to?" I asked, as if she were a stray pet.

Isaac laughed a little and sipped his coffee. "Definitely not me," he clarified. "I think my sister Shannon brought her in."

"Then who did you bring?" I regretted the inquiry, fearing it would be a girl.

"Zia," he answered.

That definitely caught me off guard. If it had to be a girl, it made me feel good that it was Zia. On the other hand, it worried me more. The last admission I wanted from Isaac was that he and Zia used to have a thing. Zia was my best friend, next to Harry, and I wouldn't know how to deal with that.

"We met in New Hampshire," he began. "She was homeless, and I talked my father into letting her stay with us."

"So, you two weren't…"

"No," he said right away, laughing. "We've always just been friends. Anyway, she brought Dwarf and Damien in and Dwarf and Damien brought others in. You get the idea."

"Well, your dad must be a really caring person to take on so many people like that."

Isaac rolled my straw wrapper into a tiny ball between his index finger and thumb. "Truth is," he said, "my father could do without so many being around all the time, but…well, it's just the way of things."

"The type that can't say no."

Isaac shrugged.

"Hey," I continued, shifting my body to sit more upright instead of so slouched, "where is your dad, anyway? I don't think I've ever seen him around."

Isaac slowly took another sip of his steaming coffee, and then set the mug softly onto the table.

"Very busy man," he replied. "He's in and out, but has too much to deal with to be hanging around here."

I didn't sense any animosity for his father's constant absence, but that didn't mean it wasn't there.

"Does he even live here?"

"Oh, yeah he lives with us," Isaac said. "But even when he's here he keeps to himself. Aramei needs a lot of care, and he's the only one she fully trusts. Or, I should say, he doesn't trust many to take care of her."

Aramei. I remembered that name from my first visit. Zia had left me with Isaac to help take care of her.

"Is she…" I paused, hoping to find the way to ask without offending Isaac, "…sick, or handicapped? Is she your sister?"

"No, no she's—well, we really shouldn't talk about her."

I left it at that, as curious as I was about it.

I was surprised how easily the conversations came, and how natural it felt to be around Isaac. Customers came and went, but we hardly noticed. I loved the way he smiled, the way he laughed, the way his dark gaze met mine, which made me feel like a little girl all over again. I kind of felt on air with Isaac, like I could do anything and he'd never judge me, and he'd be right there with me to do it too.

"So where's your mom?" I asked.

His charming smile faded, and the mood grew dark. He wasn't going to answer at first; I sensed a major urge to withdraw completely.

"I don't have a mother," he said flatly.

I should've let it go right then, but I was too slow to realize such things.

"But everyone has a mom," I said, urging him.

Only after I said it, did I understand how much Isaac did *not* want to talk about this.

But he did, anyway.

"Her name is Sibyl—haven't spoken to that woman in years."

That woman?

"Sorry I brought it up," I apologized. I put my lips to my straw this time only to look as though I was doing something.

"No, it's okay," he assured me. "Sibyl made her own choices."

I heard him say then, "Traitor," under his breath.

Like the subject of Aramei, I knew it was best to leave the one of his mother alone too. I was learning about Isaac Mayfair, but raising even more questions. But I figured if he wanted me to know more about his personal life, then he'd tell me.

So, I focused on us, instead.

"Isaac, why didn't you talk to me before? I mean, about what happened with Rachel?"

Another customer entered, letting a cool blast of air fill the space around us.

Isaac shook his head, smiling very faintly at me. And then his eyes met mine, making my heart lock up in my chest. "I tried, remember? But you didn't want to talk to me, and I respected that."

"But you could've come over, instead of sending Zia."

He slid the half empty mug away from him and crossed his hands on the table in its place. "I could have, yes," he said, and I looked back up at his face. "But Rachel would've put up a fight, and I thought it was better she didn't know where you lived."

Isaac sighed and reached his hands across the table then, palms up. Gently, he slipped them underneath mine, uncurling my fingers with his own, and brushed his thumbs across the sensitive skin above my knuckles. I looked down at them; the warm blush in my face forcing my eyes to stray from his gaze.

"I never expected this when I came here," he admitted. "That I would meet you." He was still looking right at me, but it was difficult for me to see his eyes, as if I were nervous about the unfamiliar world they would surely pull me in to. But I wanted to be in that world, no matter how nervous the thought of it made me.

I tried to find a worthy response, one that would make me seem more confident than breakable, but I could think of nothing.

"Tell me about your family," he said suddenly, and finally I could look at him for a longer length of time. "Tell me about you." He was beaming, eager for me to begin.

I smiled softly, and felt his fingers slip away from my palms as he leaned back into the booth seat again.

"Not much to know about me, really," I began. "But what do you want to know?"

"Everything." His eyes became brighter. "Where were you born? Where have you been? What makes you tick?" He laughed. "I don't care—anything you tell me I know will be interesting."

I couldn't imagine how anything about my average, dull life could be conversation-worthy. Sadly, the most exciting thing was my masochistic mother and her idiot husband and that wasn't a topic I cared to bring up.

"Well," I began, "I was born in Atlanta, Georgia—moved to Athens when I was about five and lived there until recently."

"Why did you move?" He sipped his coffee once more, but never took his eyes off me even to set the mug down.

I didn't want to lie to him. It was different than with friends at school who I had just met and didn't feel comfortable telling the truth to. With Isaac, I felt like I could tell him anything. I didn't want talk about anything negative, but more than that, I just wanted to be truthful.

I hesitated at first, taking one last sip of my drink before deciding that if I drank anymore I might feel sick.

"Bad home environment, I guess." I shrugged. "My mom married a guy who thinks she's a punching bag when he gets too drunk."

He frowned, and I could detect a hidden spark of anger behind his eyes.

"Did he beat you?" he said.

"No," I admitted. "He pushed Alex and me around several years ago, but he never actually hit either of us."

I saw his jaw tighten subtly, and I could tell right away that the next sip of coffee was merely to conceal his expression.

"Push around, hit, verbal abuse," he said, "it's all the same."

"I guess so," I said, "but my mom needed me, and I personally wasn't affected by any of it much."

I suppose that wasn't entirely the truth; I wouldn't be the already grown-up seventeen-year-old that I was, who had never been into relationships much, otherwise.

"Let's see," I went on, looking upward at the orange-glowing light above our table, "what makes me tick?"

He grinned then, waiting readily.

"Can't stand reality TV," I said. "And when someone uses my bar of soap—it's gross to think you're washing yourself with something someone else has rubbed all over their private parts." I visibly shuddered, and noticed Isaac quietly laughing at me. "Hmmm," I contemplated, surprised by how difficult it was to remember these things. "Oh! Litterbugs. And smokers who flick their ashes out the car window—got some in my mouth once; if you think my soap phobia is funny, you should've seen me flailing around in the front seat trying to spit the ashes out. The people in the car next to us probably thought I was mental."

Isaac laughed. "I think I would've been thoroughly amused."

I smiled back at him.

"What about travel?" he said. "Other than Maine, have you ever been anywhere outside of Georgia?"

I nodded. "Went on a field trip my freshman year to Gulf Shores, Alabama. Dug for diamonds in Arkansas once." I thought about it further, until I realized I hadn't really seen much outside of Georgia. "I guess that's it."

"Did you find any?"

"Find what?" And then I realized. "Oh, diamonds? No. I found a bunch of rocks that I *thought* were diamonds until the park employees looked them over and shattered my dreams." I chuckled and took another drink, regardless of the caffeine overload.

"What about you? Surely you're more interesting than I am."

"I doubt that," he said with a soft smile. Once again he managed to make me blush.

"Come on. Indulge me."

He smiled and breathed in deeply. "I love the smell of rain and the sound of silence," he said. "Nature. The ocean. The universe."

I laughed. "You and my Uncle Carl would definitely get along."

I let him go on.

"I've travelled a lot, but I'd really like to get in one place and stay there."

I pulled forward some, folding my hands on the table in front of me. I thought back to the night at The Cove, remembering what that man said about the Mayfair's travel expeditions.

"You must've been everywhere. Kind of hard to choose a favorite place among so many, I bet."

"No," he replied. "Without thinking about it, I can say that Maine beats them all." His smile was warm and unquestionable.

As a car pulled into the tiny parking lot, Isaac turned his attention to it. Oddly, he seemed to be smelling the air as he inhaled a deep breath. He glared out the frost-covered window next to us, watching the car with a curious intensity.

"Someone you know?"

"Yes, and I think we should leave."

He didn't wait for me to say anything in response, but stood from the booth seat, slipped on his coat and took me by the hand.

"Who is it?" I asked, as he walked me to the door.

He never took his eyes off the parking lot. The car was still running, its headlights shining brightly through the dimly lit lot. I heard the engine rev when Isaac opened the glass doors and we stepped outside.

"Bad company," Isaac answered, practically dragging me to his car. "Looks like your sister is never going to give up."

I swung my head around to see into the car, but the windows were tinted too dark to see anything.

Isaac ushered me into the passenger's seat and then shut the door behind me.

"Alex is in that car?"

"Don't get any ideas," he warned. "She's not your sister anymore."

Isaac threw the car into gear and we sped away. The car didn't follow, which surprised me. I kept looking back over the seat and through the frosted window, but all I saw was blackness.

"Why didn't they follow us?"

"No need to," he said. "They already know where to find you. That was just their way of warning me. Your sister has an agenda, one the Vargas family won't let her forget." He looked over at me harshly. "What did she say to you the night at The Cove? I need to know everything."

I just wished he would keep his eyes on the road. It seemed they were on me a little too much and I wondered how he could continue to drive without swerving.

Telling Isaac 'everything' was out of the question, at least in this particular instance. I couldn't bring myself to put him or Alex in anymore conflict. Bringing up the part about them threatening my life was a seriously bad idea. There was no telling what he might do.

"Alex just wants me to stop hanging around you and Zia."

"She said more than that—I know it."

"How would you know?" I asked, accusingly. "Are you calling me a liar?" I *was* a liar, but that was beside the point. I pretended to be offended, but was impressed by his ability to read right through me.

"Adria," he said, softening his eyes, "the Vargas family wouldn't go through this much trouble if it were that simple." He finally put his eyes on the road for a longer time, though I doubted he really saw it much. "And Viktor wouldn't get involved if it was just a simple sisterly disagreement."

"Viktor?"

"He's their leader…well, their father, the one you saw at The Cove—but don't change the subject."

"Okay," I gave in. "The only other thing she said was that she wanted me to move out and live with her and those jerks. She threatened me and tried to guilt-trip me, but that was all, I swear."

I could tell right away that Isaac didn't believe me, but he didn't pressure me for anymore answers.

"Oh no!" I said, noticing the time in blue numbers on the dashboard. "Beverlee is gonna freak! It's so late." I reached in my coat for my cell phone, but realized I had left it at home, which explained why I hadn't received a call long ago.

"I'll take you home now," said Isaac.

I hated how focused and apprehensive he'd become; his interest in me drained, the turn of events and our time together cut short.

Isaac dropped me off at home, and insisted on walking me to the door. "You shouldn't be out at night by yourself," he said. It wasn't necessarily a decent gesture as it was a concerned one.

"I think I can manage the distance between your car and the front porch," I said, grinning.

He still went along, finding nothing funny about it.

"Remember what I said about calling me if your sister comes here."

"Yes, I remember."

Finally, Isaac loosened up some and relaxed the serious expression in his eyes. He reached out and brushed my cheek with his fingertips. "But that doesn't have to be the only reason you call me. You know that too, right?"

I could feel the blush in my cheeks, hot like fire.

The front door opened and Uncle Carl and Beverlee stepped out together; light from the living room spilled out onto the porch

Isaac dropped his hand to his side.

"Sorry I'm so late," I said, smiling squeamishly.

Isaac was very charming, and much less intimidated by my aunt and uncle than I thought he would be. He reached out to shake Uncle Carl's hand, who hesitantly accepted. He seemed suspicious of Isaac, and against the gesture entirely, but his hand had a customary mind of its own.

Isaac nodded and smiled at Beverlee.

"Damien's Jeep was having some trouble," Isaac lied, "and they were waiting for me to get back so I could give her a ride home."

Uncle Carl and Beverlee looked over at me simultaneously. "Yeah, and I forgot my cell, or I would've called."

"You couldn't call from their house?" Beverlee accused.

I hadn't thought of that, but apparently Isaac had. On the other hand, maybe he was just good at lying—not a good trait, but then again, it was necessary in certain situations.

"They were broke down about two miles from our house," Isaac said. "I saw them as I drove past on my way home."

"Really sorry, Aunt Bev, Uncle Carl. Didn't mean to worry you."

They lightened up then and Beverlee urged me inside.

Uncle Carl reached into his wallet and took out a twenty. "Some gas money for bringing her home. We appreciate it."

Isaac respectfully waved the money away. "No, but thanks," he said. "It really wasn't out of my way; I'm heading out to pick up one of my sisters not far from here."

I thought that was a lie, too.

"All right then," said Uncle Carl.

It was obvious Uncle Carl and Beverlee had their doubts about leaving Isaac and me together alone on the porch, so that didn't happen. There was a split second when all four of us stood in awkward silence, until Isaac decided it was time for him to leave. He stepped off the porch. "Have a good night, Adria. I'll tell Zia you want her to call you in the morning."

Our minds were synched almost perfectly already. I never told Isaac that, so I knew it was his way of telling me to call *him* in the morning.

I watched Isaac walk toward his car and I couldn't resist making a mental note of every step he made, how gorgeous he was even when most of his features were obscured by the night. He glanced back at me once after he opened the door, and he smiled at me before he slid inside.

And to think, I almost walked away from him without knowing the truth.

Maybe Harry was right about something else, too—I *did* care.

13

Up before ten in the morning, I decided that as much as I wanted to call Isaac, I would just let him sleep. At least that was the plan to tell him if he later asked why I waited so long. Really, I just didn't want to seem so eager.

Beverlee and Uncle Carl left early for work and I was alone in the house. I watched television and then tried reading a book, but I wasn't much in the reading mood. I cleaned—seemed to be doing a lot of that lately—swept off the giant front porch and even watered Beverlee's poor, dehydrated plants.

I eventually did try calling Isaac before noon, but his cell didn't ring and went straight to voicemail—a sure sign his phone had been turned off. "Hey, it's me," I said into the phone. "I know you're probably still asleep; just wanted to call. Not necessarily the morning anymore, but you can't say much now can you?" I laughed. "I'm cleaning the house for my aunt, so I'll talk to you later."

It was nice having the house to myself, but after a while, I was so bored I was going out of my mind.

I ended up in the barn, checking stuff out that looked like it hadn't seen sunlight in fifty years: a couple of old rusted bikes lay against the barn wall; a wooden baby bed was tossed on a pile of other unknown junk; a desk covered in sawdust; lots of hay, though I wasn't sure of its purpose since there were no animals. The only thing that looked as though it had been taken care of was the bright red riding lawnmower parked near the front door. There were spider webs everywhere, and the air stank of mildew. The roof probably had a year left in it; the far corner looked close to falling through.

When I stepped out and back into the sunlight, I could've sworn I saw a figure move past the kitchen window inside the house.

Approaching with caution, I almost scared myself enough not to go any farther. But it was the middle of the day, the sun was high in the sky, birds were singing, and I could hear a plane passing by somewhere. Bad things didn't happen to people when the weather was nice; definitely not in broad daylight while birds were chirping.

It probably wasn't anything at all, I thought.

I walked onto the porch, tiptoed to the living room window, and peeked inside.

Nothing.

Ditching the paranoia, I walked right in and went to the kitchen to make a glass of iced tea. As I squeezed a lemon into it, I heard a creaking sound coming from upstairs. I had heard that distinct sound before, but only when Uncle Carl was walking out of his office and into the hallway restroom.

Someone was definitely inside the house.

Quietly, I set the glass of tea on the counter and opened the drawer closest to me. Great—it was the drawer where Beverlee kept her collection of harmless wooden cutlery. The big, sharp knives were on the far side of the kitchen sitting securely in a knife block. I would have to walk around the enormous bar to get to it, and I was so scared that the distance seemed like a mile.

Footsteps came down the stairs; I could see the shadow of a figure accompanying them.

I dashed across the kitchen and reached for the knives, but instead, knocked the whole block onto the floor, and even still the knives didn't come out of it.

"Adria," said Alex, "what are you doing!"

Shocked to see that it was my sister, I didn't notice that I had managed to get one of the knives into my hand. I clutched it close to me.

"Put down the knife."

When my heartrate slowed and I could think clearly, I placed the knife beside me on the bar.

"What are you doing here?" I said. "You scared the *crap* out of me!"

Alex was slow to answer, or maybe I was just so scatterbrained that I absently refused to let her get a word in.

"Seriously," I went on, "what are you doing back here?"

"Am I not welcome?"

Alex opened the refrigerator and began drinking straight out of the orange juice carton.

"Well, after what you've put Beverlee and Uncle Carl through, I'm not sure anymore."

Alex sat down at the bar, sadness in her face. I watched her as she played with the ends of her fingertips, head lowered, quiet and clearly poignant. I knew then I had to drop the mad act with her and become her loving sister again. I sat down on the empty stool next to her. "Alex, what's wrong? Look, I was just messing with you. Beverlee and Uncle Carl will let you come back; I know they will."

Alex sighed and looked over at me.

"That's good to know," she said. "And I know I screwed up bigtime, but I'll talk to them."

"Good," I said, smiling, "then that's settled. I'm so glad you're home." I went to hug her, but something about her demeanor stopped me.

"That's not the only reason I came here," she said.

I looked at her probingly.

"I have some bad news; but don't worry, it isn't about me."

I waited impatiently, but at the same time I wasn't sure I even wanted to know.

"Julia's dead."

I think the world stopped moving for a second, at least my world did. When a person hears news like that, it can play tricks on the mind. What did she say? Did I hear her right? Seriously, is this some cruel joke? Death? I had forgotten all about its existence. No…It can't be true.

After an extremely long pause I asked, "How?"

"She got really sick," Alex began, "and refused to go to the hospital. She just *died*. Her dad found her. It was awful."

To speak was an effort for me. I couldn't see anything in front of me, either; just blurs of faces and random objects. "What kind of sickness?"

"Not sure. The flu, pneumonia; I don't know. The coroner picked her body up early this morning."

Hearing that Julia had died was enough; I didn't really want to know about the coroner and that whole dismal process. But it hit me then; Isaac and Zia had been sick recently, too. Could Julia have died from the same illness? I was panicking inside all over again.

"Have you been sick?" I asked, worriedly. "You don't think you have it, do you?"

"No," she answered. "I feel great."

It was odd how she said that. In a time like this, one didn't usually feel great, or nice, or anything above okay. I was having a hard time reading her.

I was supposed to call Isaac if Alex ever came home, but so far, I found no reason to. Alex was being civil, definitely more herself without Ashe and the rest of them around.

My sister wanted to come home. She had finally admitted to herself that she'd made a huge mistake. Maybe Julia's death helped her to see it; but whatever it was, my sister was seeking forgiveness and change and I could find nothing wrong with that.

My cell phone almost vibrated right off the counter; Isaac's name displayed on the screen

"I'll be right back," I told Alex, and I waited until I was outside on the front porch before I answered.

"I slept late," he said on the other end. "Should've left my phone on, but I'm so used to turning it off at night before I go to bed."

"It's all right," I said. "So, what's up?"

Our conversation was awkward before it began. Unlike Isaac, I wasn't a good liar, and it was difficult for me to talk to him with the whole guilt-thing hanging over my head.

"Not much," he said. "Zia and I wanted to stop by later on, if you're up to it."

"Ummm, I don't know if I have time today," I said, almost stuttering. "I think Beverlee and Uncle Carl wanted me to go somewhere with them tonight and right now…well, I'm still doing stuff around the house."

I paused for a moment and said, "Did—." Julia never left my thoughts, and I had started to tell Isaac what happened, but caught myself just in time. He would want to know how I knew about it, and that was a lie I knew I couldn't pull off on such short notice. I needed the rest of the day to figure out how I would go about the horrible news of my ex-friend. Besides, I had many more questions to ask Alex about Julia and the Vargas family and everything in between.

I hated lying so much I wanted to just spill it and tell Isaac that Alex was home. The only thing I wanted more than spending time with him was having my sister back. You never really expected to have to challenge the two best things ever. People were usually lucky just to get one.

"Okay," he said with a leery pause, "then I'll just talk to you tomorrow then—is everything all right over there?"

"Yeah, everything's fine," I said, faking a smile in my voice. "I'm just exhausted from all the cleaning."

I was confident he believed me. I was more worried about Isaac thinking I didn't want to see him than I was worried about him finding out that Alex was in the house.

After hanging up, I went back inside to find Alex in the den, kicked back with her feet on the coffee table. She had not one, but three large glasses of iced tea lined in a perfect row next to her feet. A bag of chips sat next to her on the couch. If Alex was going to win back the respect of Beverlee and Uncle Carl, she was going to need a lot of work.

I had less than five hours to help her.

"Alex," I said, as I approached, "you know Beverlee doesn't even let Uncle Carl put his feet on the coffee table."

She looked at me, smirked, and then slid her feet onto the floor. A few seconds later and she was gulping down one glass of tea without taking a breath.

I sat next to her.

"Thirsty?"

The empty glass pinged against the coffee table as she set it down. "Definitely."

"So," I went on, "what made you decide to come home?"

"I missed my little sister." The chip bag rattled as she dug around inside it.

Okay, this was ridiculous, and I was already on the verge of saying something to Alex I might regret. It was hard to take her seriously when her attitude flip-flopped from promising to impolite from one second to the next. She just needed time, I thought. At least she was home and making an effort—I couldn't expect a miracle.

"What about your boyfriend?" I inquired, as I reached into the chip bag too.

"He's awesome," she answered. "You two should start over and get to know each other."

The news that she and Ashe were still together wilted all my hopes about her reasons for coming home. Even if she had said something more like how they were fighting and might break up, I could've worked with that. But 'awesome' and anything about me giving him another chance was like being punched in the stomach.

Still, I held my tongue.

Alex continued with a mouth full of bright orange. "He was the one who brought it up, about starting over with you and getting to know you and stuff." She stopped long enough to swallow. "I told him I'd talk to you, but not to expect anything."

Yeah, the sun will extinguish before that happens. I moved around unnervingly on the couch.

"But really, sis," she said, finally with eye contact and no food in her mouth, "I missed you. No guy can come between blood, and I'm really sorry for letting it even just a little."

I was screaming inside. *A little?*

"It's all right," I said, calmly. "I missed you too."

We sat there for several long and silent seconds, but I was the only one who seemed bothered by it. Alex continued to stuff her face, and gulped down more tea, her gaze fixed across the room, seemingly on nothing in particular. I wondered what she was thinking about, whose faces were looking back at her in her thoughts. Somehow I got the feeling none of them were mine.

"Are you going to go to school?" I asked.

Alex laughed. "Coming home is good deed enough. I won't be going to school, that's for sure."

"Why not? You graduate this year."

Alex sprung off the couch and went back into the kitchen. "It's just not for me, Dria. I'd rather just get a job."

I heard the refrigerator door open, and then the tea pitcher slide off the top rack.

"Hard to get a decent job if you're a drop-out," I muttered from the living room.

"Oh well," she said, "it's not like I want to be a psychiatrist or anything."

"You *need* a psychiatrist," I mumbled under my breath.

Alex came back into the living room with a glass of water this time. "And you don't need a diploma to be an actress or a model—I think I could do either one."

Wow. Rude, inconsiderate, and now conceited, too.

"Yeah, I guess you could do that…"

"Enough about me," Alex cut in. "What's with you and that Mayfair guy?"

Something told me this was a risky topic, but I ignored the instinct. It was nice that Alex wanted to know about me; I had started to wonder if she cared at all.

I brought my feet onto the couch, my legs bent beneath me. "I know you'd like Isaac," I said, with a smile I couldn't contain. "I've never met anyone like him."

"Have you slept with him yet?"

I think I stopped blinking. "No…"

"Good," Alex said, "and don't because that wouldn't be too smart."

I stood from the couch and looked down on her with a tight, angry jaw. "That's really not any of your business. But you could be a little less blunt." I was tired of this, and went toward the stairs. "I'm going to take a shower," I said, bitterly, looking back at her. "Beverlee usually gets home around five, and Uncle Carl around five-thirty. I'll be up in my room if you decide you really want to talk to me."

I left Alex sitting there.

My shower was much longer than usual, and I made it a point to spend more time brushing my teeth, combing out my hair and washing my face so I could avoid Alex. I kept telling myself that she just needed time and that progress wouldn't happen as quickly as I wanted it to. It was a dream to see Alex home. As much as I hated it though, I had to accept that she would probably never be the sweet, caring, Alexandra Dawson she used to be, and that I was going to have to adjust.

Excuses. That's what they were. In my heart something ominous lingered, but like every other obvious warning, I ignored it too.

Beverlee wasn't as welcoming as I was when I first saw Alex. It seemed she was more in tune with the warnings I so recklessly disregarded. But, thankfully, she didn't kick Alex out.

I listened from the top of the stairs to Alex apologize and explain how she had made some bad decisions and such. It all sounded fake to me, so I know Beverlee probably wasn't buying it, either. But being the kindhearted person that Beverlee was, she retained a calm and accepting attitude. Uncle Carl reacted the same way as Beverlee had when he made it home from work.

Trying to show Alex that she was welcomed home and that people here loved her, Beverlee made a huge dinner and asked that we all eat together at the table. It went as well as it could, considering. I had been holding my breath the entire time, just waiting for Alex to say or do something to completely ruin the evening. But it turned out that Alex's weird obsession with water, tea, milk, orange juice and even V8, was the biggest concern.

"Alexandra," said Uncle Carl, "maybe we should set you a doctor's appointment."

"I agree," said Beverlee. "You could have Diabetes."

Alex's brows wrinkled; she moved her fork around in her peas. "There's nothing wrong with me," she said. "No need to waste money on a doctor."

"It wouldn't be a waste," said Uncle Carl, more verbal than I had heard him in a while. "We'll take you anyway, just to play it safe."

Alex shrugged. "Whatever."

By the time dinner was over, there was nothing left in the kitchen to drink except water from the tap and a few beers Uncle Carl kept hidden in the crisper behind the shredded cheese.

"We're going to see the late showing of *A Secret Soldier*," said Beverlee. "Want to come?"

"Nah, go ahead," Alex said from the couch in the den.

It would have been nice if she had turned around to see Beverlee and Uncle Carl, but she just waved her hand, dismissing them. I thought it would be good for all of us to go out, but since Alex clearly was not interested, I knew I should stay home too. I didn't trust her alone in the house. I was finally beginning to listen to those warnings. Though still not enough to call Isaac.

Upstairs in my room, I sat at my desk surfing the net. Like my extra lengthy time in the bathroom earlier in the day, I did whatever I could to keep busy and out of Alex's sight. Just having her in the house made me uncomfortable. I started to wonder if that was why Beverlee and Uncle Carl decided to go see a movie—they were uncomfortable. They had never gone out like that since we moved in.

After checking my email, I ran out of things to do. There wasn't anything to clean, that was for sure. I thought about calling Isaac. I wanted to call him more than anything, but I worried Alex would waltz into my room and give herself away while he was on the other end of the phone.

But then something just clicked in mind.

"What am I doing?" I said aloud. "I can't let her do this to me." I was a prisoner in my own home all over again, just like in Georgia when Jeff was drunk. I was hiding out in my room, afraid to venture too far out into the open—Alex pushed me too far this time.

I practically flew off the chair and swung open the bedroom door, rushing out of the room with retribution in my steps—telling her exactly what I thought of her was long overdue. I passed Uncle Carl and Beverlee's open room, feeling ashamed that someone with the same blood as me would treat them so badly. Pressing on to the end of the hall, I barely stopped to watch my footing as I glided down the carpeted steps. But when I got to the end, I froze.

Alex stood at the bar with her back to me, her petite shoulders hunched over the countertop so unnaturally that I could hardly make out where her neck started and her back began. Her elbows peeked out from the sides, moving furiously back and forth as if she were eating something ravenously with her hands. I glimpsed a meat packaging tray and ripped Saran-wrap hanging over its edges; blood dripped from the bar and oozed over the side and onto the floor in a red, slimy mess; frightening grunts reverberated from Alex's chest.

Against everything my instincts were telling me, I crept up closer from behind to get a better view. Blood smeared the side of her face and dripped down her wrists; the sound of raw meat stretching and ripping was stomach-turning as she shredded a raw roast with her teeth.

My fingers found my lips, and I felt like I was going to vomit. "My God…" I gasped, but I didn't mean to say it out loud.

Alex's bloody, ravenous face swung around to see me; her eyes were black like marbles, her teeth…her face…

Something was very wrong with this, something so much more than Alex standing there eating raw meat.

My cell phone. My hand jerked from my mouth and went to my pocket, but I had left my phone upstairs on the bed. I began to back my way toward the front door.

"Stop," Alex demanded. "You have to help me."

I was screaming inside. The sound of her voice was not…it wasn't human. It was familiar—demonic.

Running for the door, I almost made it when I felt my body lift into the air, and then I soared through the room. I flew past the lamp, clipping it with my head, and crashed into the wall; pictures of my extended family came falling down all around me. Alex stood over me; her black eyes wider and more deadly; her breathing was rapid; I could see her chest rising and falling so fast, so desperate that I thought her heart would stop beating any second and kill her in an instant. I started crawling past her, my palms moving over picture frames and broken glass, but I didn't get far.

Alex grabbed the front of my shirt and lifted me off my feet. I heard the fabric ripping, and the weight of my body dropped slightly, but Alex gripped tighter to hold me in place. I hovered inches from the floor; I couldn't breathe and I was choking; black and orange flashes of light attacked my vision.

I began to cry. "Alex—stop. P-Please. Alex!"

She dropped me. I gasped and coughed, desperately searching for air until it found my lungs again.

Alex gripped her head suddenly with both hands and screamed out. Her cries pierced my ears so intensely that it made me cry harder. Her flesh began stretching over her face and neck and arms, as if she were growing too fast inside for the flesh to keep up. Long, black, gnarled hair grew from her skin; her head tilted back as her face began to grow outward, a snout penetrating through her skull. Alex roared— *roared*—and it felt like the whole house shook around me. Her body grew taller, the hair longer; her feet had become deformed, her long legs, hind-like and grotesque.

She drew her clawed hands behind her, lifted her chin and howled.

I lost it.

I totally lost it.

A part of me could still see her, but my senses were disconnected from it all. I wanted to scream, but I couldn't. I tried desperately to jump out of my skin, out of this restrained comatose state, but I couldn't do that, either. Only when I heard yet another howl, and the sound of the large window in the den shatter, did I come out of that coma.

Counting Alex, four werewolves stood in my house.

Werewolves.

Alex ran with a chilling ease at the other three; the floor shook beneath me. She and one other clashed in mid-air, Alex's head-start propelling them back out through the broken window. The others followed.

I got to my feet and ran out the front door. It didn't matter that I should've tried to hide, or run away from them; hypnotized by the event, all I could force myself to do was watch.

14

FOUR WEREWOLVES QUICKLY TURNED INTO FIVE, AND THEN six. My heart thundered behind my ribs and in my ears; fascination and fear working together to keep me conscious. I had lost sight of which one was Alex, as they all looked the same to me.

Amid the chaos, I thought of Beverlee and Uncle Carl, hoping they wouldn't come home early. If I was going to die like this, I didn't want to bring those I loved down with me.

The porch rumbled and shook beneath me; the dead plants hanging above, swinging back and forth. A pungent stench filled my nostrils, and slowly I turned around to see the seventh beast coming toward me on the porch. I took off in the opposite direction, leaping over the porch railing, and landing in the wide open where the others caught in the bloody brawl could clearly see me. I didn't know where I was running, or why I thought running anywhere was going to help, but I ran. I ran and ran. I could feel the hot, rancid breath of the one chasing me, moistening the flesh on my back.

Don't run into the barn, I thought to myself. But there was nowhere else to go.

I ran right into the barn and fell to the ground, backing my way against the nearest pile of rusted junk. The enormous beast bore down on me, walking slow and methodically in my direction as though wanting me to look it in the eyes before it ripped me to pieces. And I did look it in the eyes. They stared back at me so cold and predatory. I thought to myself: Please God, just don't let that one be my sister. I didn't want to be killed by Alex. Anyone but Alex.

It happened in a blink; but the beast soaring at me was not of its own accord. Another werewolf had entered the barn and dove at it, sending it crashing violently into the wall right past my head. I rolled out of the way seconds before debris could crush me. They fought so fiercely they almost brought the barn down. The weak roof in the corner fell, exposing the darkness to the moonlight. Anything mounted along those rotting walls came falling down in every direction.

The force of their feral blows was supernatural; no human could have survived even the weakest one. Blood glistened in their long, mangy fur, and deep gashes as long as my arm were cut into their massive bodies.

I started to run out of the barn, but fell over an old tire obscured beneath the hay.

One last violent blow struck one of the beasts down. I didn't know which was which. Thinking that one of them had actually been there to save me was not in my thoughts. All I knew was that they were both werewolves and I was a human girl. I looked at them, wondering which one was going to win me as the prize…the meal.

Those outside howled; the one still standing, glared at me, but it didn't advance. Blood and thick saliva dripped from its massive teeth; its dark gaze going back and forth between me, the barn exit, and the werewolf lying wounded on the floor.

One last howl from outside and the werewolf took off for the exit and disappeared; the barn door ripped from its hinges and splintered into a million pieces.

I was paralyzed. It felt like the breath keeping me alive had become something thicker, more toxic in my lungs. I choked several times before I could breathe steadily.

It had become utterly silent outside; the howling and gnashing of teeth, the clash of their lycanthrope bodies—everything stopped.

I was too afraid to move to see if they were still out there. Hot breath emitted from my barely-open lips in rapid puffs of freezing air. My breath was the only sound.

One werewolf still lay wounded just feet from me—a small sense of relief short-lived.

It stirred.

My heart jumped, and I saw the rusty machete next to me on the barn floor, covered by even rustier saw blades. I grabbed it and stood up. I knew that no matter how wounded it was, that this would still probably end badly for me, but by this time I wasn't going down without putting up a fight.

And if it was Alex, then I had to help her by ending this savage, murderous life.

From a deceptively safe distance, I gazed down at the beast. It panted and moved its massive head around in a circular motion. My whole body tensed; I felt my courage quickly dripping out of me. Before I lost it all, I took two steps closer and raised the machete above my head. I felt my legs tremble, barely holding up my weight; I could scarcely hold the weight of the machete as if my arms were as frail as paper.

I should've killed it right then; I had the opportunity, but the beast opened its eyes and looked right into mine. The eyes staring back at me seemed to bore into my soul, stripping from me everything that made me vengeful. A conflict tore my mind apart. I told myself that if I didn't kill it that it would kill me, but my heart dictated those thoughts. Something was in its eyes, so true and sincere, so absolutely pleading.

The beast's form then began to shift as the body lay there on the blood-soaked hay. I watched, every one of my senses pulling me in every direction. I still had the machete. I still had one last chance to strike the blow and take off its head.

Only fate kept me from using it.

The hair began to disappear into the flesh; the snout fading behind the skull; its skin slowly turning from grey-black to a more human-like complexion. The sound of bones cracking was horrific in my ears as they set themselves back into place. The gnarled hands and hind-like legs distorted and shrank to normal size.

Not realizing I had ever moved, I saw that I was pressed into the wall behind me. I backed away, but could go no farther.

Isaac Mayfair lay naked and bloody on the floor of my barn.

Tears began burning my eyes and throat. I wasn't sure about what I was seeing—*who* I was seeing. I wasn't sure of anything: not the bitter taste of blood in my mouth, or the ground I stood on, or the light wind rattling the hole in the roof. Nothing.

I heard the machete hit the ground, pinging against something else old and rusted as it dropped from my hand. I went with it, falling to my knees.

And I wept.

I put my face in my hands and let it all out; my whole body shuddering in a tumultuous display, and I cried and cried until I couldn't anymore.

I could look up slowly.

Isaac carefully sat upright; I heard his neck crack as he rolled his head to both sides; he moaned through gritted teeth until the pain of resetting his shoulder passed.

He stood, facing sideways to shield his nakedness from me, and he walked to the lawnmower, took a filthy, tattered blanket that had been used to cover it, and wrapped it around his lower body.

Sebastian, my missing friend from school, ran naked into the barn and stopped at the entrance.

I couldn't handle this, seeing Sebastian alive, seeing Isaac who had just shifted from a werewolf into Isaac again. My eyes darted back and forth between them, and then I was even more shocked when Nathan Mayfair stood next to Sebastian. He too was completely naked.

The pieces of this puzzle were all fitting together at once, overwhelming me. It took seeing Nathan naked, and in partial darkness, to realize where I had truly seen him before. He was the one who fell onto the path in Georgia and told Alex and me to run away. He was the one who turned into a werewolf and fought the one after him.

No words exchanged between the three of them, only nods of acknowledgment as Isaac assured them that they could leave.

Isaac and I were alone again.

He approached me, and instinctively, I recoiled. "Have you been hurt?" he asked, as he carefully knelt down in front of me.

Tears streamed down my cheeks; my body shook all over.

Carefully, I gazed up into his face, and he reached out his hand and touched my lips softly, wiping away a trickle of blood. How amazing a touch so gentle could come from such a violent beast, I thought. When finally Isaac sensed my fear of him began to diminish, he took me into his arms and held me pressed against his naked chest. My posture only rejected him for seconds before the warmth of his embrace eased my trembling body.

"Adria," he said, very carefully, "where else are you bleeding?"

I hurt all over, but none of my wounds stung as they usually do when the skin has been seared. I pulled away from Isaac slowly and looked at myself. "I-I think I'm just sore." Absently, I touched my lips where the blood had been, where his fingers had so gently grazed me.

I wasn't sure how to answer his question; everything was surreal to me. "I busted my lip—not sure how—I'm okay though…"

Isaac inspected both of my arms, and then carefully turned my body at the waist and pulled up my shirt to see my back.

"Are your jeans ripped anywhere?" He eagerly helped me straighten my legs out onto the floor. He also inspected my back and front and then put his hand on the end of the front of my shirt. He waited, looking to me first for permission. I let him pull my shirt up enough so he could see my stomach. He was respectful and went no further.

Isaac leaned in and kissed me long and hard on the forehead. I could feel the emotion in his touch, the undeniable need to protect me from everything. The warmth from his mouth spread all throughout my body.

"If you had been Turned by one of them," he said, solemnly, "it would have…"

I wanted to know the rest, but I said nothing.

Isaac drew me toward him again and held me there, pressed against his warm body.

"I admit," Isaac finally said, "I expected more of an *un*conscious reaction." He didn't laugh, but I heard the faintest hint of humor in his voice.

"This isn't my first time," I revealed.

He pulled my head carefully away from his chest and stared at me. "Explain that."

"In Georgia," I began right away, "Alex and I were, well not necessarily attacked, but caught in the middle of a fight between"—I stopped and pictured Nathan's face—"well, your brother was there; I know that now." My voice became distant.

Isaac's embrace tightened.

"He told us there was only one girl," he said, more to himself, it seemed.

"The worst part about all of this," I said, also more to myself than to Isaac, "is that somehow, hidden in the deepest part of me, I knew Alex was one of them. It crossed my mind, but I couldn't get past how ridiculous that was. It was hard believing what I saw that night."

Isaac remained quiet, giving me my moment of realization.

When I had had enough time to go over that understanding in my mind, I turned my attention to him again, dismissing Alex altogether.

"But *you're* hurt," I said, rising up to examine his wounds. "There's blood *everywhere*." It was true, about the blood; but as I examined him more closely, I saw that his wounds were not as bad as they should've been. The gash on his chest I knew had been deeper just seconds ago. I looked at him interrogatively.

"I heal fast," he said. "It won't completely disappear, but most of it will."

"Guess that explains your scars, doesn't it?"

He nodded.

I reached up and grazed the skin around the fresh wound; to see any part of him mangled like that, it broke my heart.

"You don't have to tell me what the Vargas family is," I said, "but which one of them was that? The one I saw in here."

He couldn't look at me then. "That was Sibyl."

His mother. She attacked her own son? I felt so awful for him, and so much hatred for her.

"You saved my life."

"I didn't save anything," he said. I could hear the shame in his voice. "She would've killed you if Viktor hadn't called her off."

He added, "I'm really sorry, Adria, for what Sibyl did."

"Don't apologize to me," I said. "I just hate that your mother would be so cruel. I don't understand why…"

"Nothing much to understand," he said, while still looking at my arms for wounds. "Sibyl betrayed my father with Viktor when I was eight."

I said nothing more about that.

"How did you know then?" I asked, after a quiet pause. "About Alex being home? I don't buy that you all just happened to be in the neighborhood at the right time."

"I could sense it in your voice on the phone earlier," he revealed.

So, I sucked as a liar, after all.

"But you still saved my life."

Sibyl was his mother and bound to be somewhat stronger than him. And as far as I saw, they both seemed neck and neck up until that last second. And I thought it was my fault. I remembered how just before the last blow that took Isaac down, that I had started to run for the exit.

"You were distracted by me, weren't you?"

He tilted his head slightly to one side. "No, I was too preoccupied to be distracted."

"And here I thought you were an excellent liar," I said. "You saw me try to run out of the barn, didn't you?"

Reluctantly, he gave up just to appease me. "I did see you, but Sibyl is much more powerful than me—not to mention *older*, and probably would've still won."

"How much older?" I asked. "And really, what does age have to do with it?" The way he said 'older' piqued my curiosity.

"By at least one hundred twenty years," he said. "So it has *a lot* to do with it."

My buzzing mind came to a sudden stop. Not that I knew a thing about real werewolves to begin with, but I least expected them to be immortal. I thought they could be killed by silver bullets and fire. I thought they could be killed by rusty machetes.

"I couldn't have killed you if I tried," I said, realizing.

Isaac laughed and stood me up with him, his free hand holding the blanket tight around his waist.

"No, that would've killed me so long as it wasn't dull and your aim was perfect."

"So, you're not immortal?"

"Not technically," he clarified. "We can be killed by anything that can kill you except sickness and disease—we're immune to everything. And it's not as easy to kill one of us—better have something bigger than a shotgun."

"Wait a minute," I interrupted. "So you didn't really have pneumonia? None of you were sick? Then where—"

Isaac curved his big fingers gently around my wrist. "We can talk about this later," he said. "I think your aunt and uncle are home."

"Oh no…" I looked toward the broken barn window; Headlights shone brightly up the driveway, bouncing in the darkness as the car went around the pothole.

"Just tell them you went for a walk and someone broke in while you were gone."

That was one excuse down, but I knew it wasn't going to cover everything. Alex was gone, and my shirt was covered in blood; I was going to have to hone my story-telling skills in less than two minutes.

"But what about you?" I didn't want Isaac to leave. I had so many questions, but more than anything, I didn't want to be apart from him right now. "Where will you go? What about your clothes? What if they come after you?" I was a bit frantic.

Isaac took me possessively into a kiss, stealing all the words from my mouth, and the frantic thoughts from my mind in an instant. He enveloped me in his arms; his lips pressing against mine so firmly that it made me feel weak in the legs. The warmth of his arms, the smell of his skin, the taste of him; combined, it sent me over the edge. His kiss was like a dream and I never wanted to wake up from it.

He pulled away reluctantly, staring into my eyes. "Adria," he said, "I won't let anything happen to you, ever."

If he wanted me to walk away from him and do what I needed to do, he was not making it easy for me. But I knew I had to go. Uncle Carl and Beverlee were getting out of the car, ripping my eternal moment with Isaac Mayfair right out from under me

We looked at each other, and words unspoken that said so many things we both had wanted to say passed between us. I left him in the barn, feeling like the next day just couldn't come fast enough.

How I came up with such a perfect story to tell Uncle Carl and Beverlee in such a short time, was fueled by betrayal. I knew without a doubt that Alex would never be coming home. She nearly killed me. Alexandra Dawson was no longer my sister. She and the Vargas family were, just as Zia and Isaac had tried to warn me, a danger to me and my family. Doing whatever I possibly could to keep her away from them was priority.

The story I gave them was that I suspected Alex was on drugs and I confronted her. Alex, angry and defensive, went into a rage and attacked me. We fought inside the house and she pushed me through the den window. Because of everything she had done, it was easy for them to accept drugs as the cause. The raw meat on the bar? Drugs could be blamed on many things.

I convinced them after an hour that I was physically okay, and that a trip to the hospital was completely unnecessary.

Uncle Carl was about to call the police after I told them my story, but I begged him otherwise. The police—no one—could get involved in this. I explained how it would only make things worse and that I couldn't handle it emotionally. They worried about me, but they agreed to leave it alone. But Alex was not allowed back. She was eighteen and responsible for herself now.

It hurt me to have to do that to Alex, to lie about her and get her banned from coming home. It was not in my character to smear someone's reputation the way I did hers. I knew that Beverlee would innocently talk to her customers at Finch's Grocery. Rumors would begin to spread. Alex wouldn't be able to go into any public place in 'small town' Hallowell without suspicious and hateful glares from the town's residents.

Something told me that Alex wouldn't care.

Sure, everything seemed resolved, but there was still one thing I couldn't resolve myself: The Vargas family wanted me dead in order to protect what I knew about them.

A part of Alex was still my sister at one time, when she convinced them to give her a chance to talk me into living with her. That was what her threats were about at The Cove that night. But I knew then that all of the chances Alex had been given were used up and that time had run out.

Isaac was at my house before seven a.m.

"You should've told me what Alex really said to you at The Cove," Isaac argued from the driver's seat. "I had no idea you knew about our kind."

"Why didn't Nathan tell you?"

I sat quietly on the passenger's side.

"He didn't see both of you that night; said that it was dark and he was shifting—you sort of lose sight of everything in that moment."

Isaac insisted that only he should take me to and from school from now on. He even spoke with Beverlee and Uncle Carl, and surprisingly, they had no objections.

It was difficult hanging out with Harry only because he was the one out of the three of us who didn't know anything. He could sense that something between Zia and I had changed. He knew something was wrong and that I was perfectly aware of it. Of course, I was, but what he suspected was far from Zia being a werewolf. By the next class, Harry felt snubbed and withdrawn. He probably thought I told her all about his crush and that she wasn't interested. He assumed neither of us knew how to break it to him.

I hated that feeling. It wasn't even the truth, but I felt like I betrayed Harry. In a way, I *was* betraying Harry by not telling him that his best friend, Sebastian, was alive and well. It didn't matter that I had no choice; I was a horrible friend because of it.

Zia and I had to make up a quick excuse about why Harry couldn't join us at Zia's house after school that day. He wasn't supposed to hear us talking, but he did as I stood at Zia's locker.

"Uhhh, sorry Harry, but we've got plans," I tried to explain.

Zia interrupted, "We're having a girl's night."

Lamest excuse ever, especially since it was obvious it wasn't true. If anything helped Harry to confirm his suspicions then, that was surely what did it. We couldn't talk at all with him around, and talking about 'it' was what I wanted to do more than anything. Having normal conversations just seemed so pointless anymore. How could a person sit next to a werewolf at lunch and act normal?

Harry didn't talk to either of us for the rest of the day. It hurt me to see him that way, feeling ousted by me *and* the girl he liked. As much as I wanted to put his feelings first, I knew there wasn't anything I could actually tell him that would fix it.

The day dragged by in a blur. I couldn't remember anything that we went over in any class, and my next teacher made sure to point out that I looked 'awful' and needed 'some serious sleep'. I quietly thanked her for those observations and laid my head down on my desk.

I just wanted the day to end. The whole thing was an act; school was the last place I wanted to be. Unfortunately, going to school and pretending that nothing as preposterous as, I don't know, *werewolves*, had attacked me the night before, was a necessity for Uncle Carl and Beverlee's sake.

I just never imagined a seven hour day could truly feel like seventeen.

After school, I would be going back to the Mayfair house. But this time I knew the experience would be much different from every other time before.

15

"I'M NOT READY," I SAID, STANDING AT THE DOOR OF THE Mayfair house with Isaac. "I never felt welcome here before; now things are just—"

Isaac cupped my face in his hands, gently parting my lips with his own. "No one here will ever hurt you," he said, slowly breaking the kiss. "And things are different now. In a good way; you'll see." He pulled away just inches from my face; the sweet smell of his breath only made me want to taste it longer.

I knew things would be different all right, but I couldn't imagine how they would be any better. I knew their secrets. My sister was their enemy. I was with Isaac, whom many of the girls were a little more than fond of.

If anything, I was a threat.

When we stepped inside, Isaac interlaced his fingers through mine and held my hand tight. Walking through the foyer, it was like going down a dark tunnel where at the end I would meet my doom. I heard voices in the den like a wave of whispers. The fireplace crackled from afar, and the sound of footsteps in the rooms upstairs all shuffled to the same section of the house at once. I noticed right away when I stood at the den entrance that people were above me at the top of the stairs, looking down at us.

There were more faces in the den than I ever witnessed previously. So many people. So many…werewolves. I squeezed Isaac's hand so tightly I thought I could crush it, if that weren't completely absurd.

"Hello," said some random girl carrying a tray lined artistically with crackers and cheese. She held it out to me with a bright smile. "Cheese cracker? I made them for you."

Mentally, I was scratching my head. I turned my eyes slightly to see Isaac on my right. He just smiled.

The last thing my body could handle right now was food, but this was one of those times where courtesy was an uncomfortable necessity.

"Thank you."

I held the cracker in my hand. Dozens of silent faces were staring back at me. I then ate the cracker because that cracker felt like the line between acceptance and something much worse. I resented Isaac a little for not saving me, but just a little. At least it wasn't a full course meal.

"Come with me," Isaac said, pulling me along.

As we came to the couch, those sitting on it moved immediately, and with Isaac's guide, I took the center cushion.

Why is everyone staring at me like that?

If something didn't happen soon to shift the nerve-racking atmosphere in this place, I was going to die of anxiety.

Just then, Daisy Mayfair waltzed through the crowd and sat next to me; her long curly, blond hair fixed neatly over her shoulders. Nathan followed and stood in front of me.

"I could never be sure if you were there that night," Nathan said about the Georgia incident. "Sorry you had to see that."

"I have one question about that night," I said, looking up at him.

"Shoot."

"How was it you were naked *before* you shifted?"

Mild laughter erupted throughout the room.

"Nathan can't keep his clothes on," Isaac joked.

Daisy chuckled and added, "He walks around naked a lot. You'll see him from time to time, everything hanging in the breeze."

I felt my face scrunch up.

"Don't listen to them," Nathan said, plopping down on the other side of me. "Isaac's just jealous, and Daisy was born an English smart-ass, so she can't help it." He put his arm around me. "Really though, to answer your question: I had shifted once before you saw me. Had been running through the Appalachians all evening." He dropped the casual tone a notch and added, "It was a long night."

"Of all the things she could be asking," said Rachel from the crowd, "she chooses Nathan in the nude."

I tensed immediately and my insides turned to stone.

"That should tell you all you need to know about her, Isaac," she added.

Rachel glowered at me from across the room with that same devilish smirk she always seemed to wear. She would never like me. That shouldn't have mattered, but it did. I wanted to feel welcome by everyone in the Mayfair house. Even one enemy would always make me feel as though I shouldn't be here. But worse than anything, this was not a high school bully; Rachel was a werewolf, and capable of much more than rumors and after school beatings.

Nathan stood from the couch; I could see the veins throbbing in the side of his neck. The whole room went from whispers and quiet laughter to disciplined silence.

"A wise decision," he threatened, "would be to leave Adria alone. She outranks you, Rachel."

I cringed. Nathan didn't know how to let someone else's enemy down lightly, that was for sure.

Wait. I *outranked* her? I couldn't grasp that at all.

Rachel lowered her head obediently to Nathan. "Forgive my disrespect." She raised her dark eyes, and I could see them boring into mine; her posture giving Nathan one thing and her gaze giving me another.

Isaac stood in front of Nathan. "This is my problem, brother," he said, "and I'll deal with it accordingly."

They spoke so different when speaking to each other—so proper. I felt like I went back in time about two hundred years.

Isaac guided me to stand. He looked out then at everyone. "Adria is my girl," he announced, and I felt my insides melt, "and she will be treated as you would treat me, by *all* of you."

"But she isn't *one* of us," argued Rachel, pushing the emphasized word forcibly through her teeth. "And Trajan will not allow it. You know this, Isaac."

As much as she was defiant, Rachel was still maintaining a great amount of respect for Isaac.

But I didn't like where this was going.

"Trajan is my father, not yours," Isaac said. "And I know more about what he will and will not allow than you do."

"Is that right?" Rachel stepped up and let a fraction of her respect turn to boldness. "You think because Zia screwed up and Turned her boy-toy, Sebastian, and got away with it, that you can do the same?" She grinned and looked at me once. "Besides, she's a female and you know what that means."

Everything about Rachel's last statement worried me a great deal. The cold bitterness in her face was haunting.

Wait a second, I thought—Turn me? I had never thought about that. In fact, that was definitely something I didn't *want* to think about.

Suddenly, Rachel and the few girls with her all turned around as if something had come up behind them. Everyone began staring toward the darkness of the hallway that led toward the kitchen and under the stairs.

To my shock, Rachel jumped backward quickly and clung to the ceiling behind me by her hands and feet. Her eyes went coal black; her teeth grew into fangs, her nails into claws. I gasped, and stood paralyzed.

Then I saw a man's face, though shrouded by darkness I knew it was a man. The outline of his body stood tall and enormous against the wall. His eyes flickered when they grazed the limited light from the den. I shuddered. The hair on my arms rose. I couldn't help but stand from the couch, both from fear and out of respect, which seemed necessary.

Rachel jumped down from the ceiling and left without a word. Many others followed, all of them shuffling through different exits, those at the top of the stairs thinned out to about two. I hadn't noticed, too preoccupied by those who were leaving, but the man in the shadow was also gone when I looked back.

"Who was that?" I whispered to Isaac.

I knew it was Trajan, Isaac's father, but I had to ask anyway for validation.

"My father is the leader," Isaac began, "the Alpha Male. No one here, not even Rachel, is foolish enough to defy him."

Nathan pulled the coffee table forward with one hand and sat on it in front of us. "He'll be going back to Serbia soon," he said, "and most of us won't be going with him. So, there's a lot of uncertainty when it comes to who'll be in charge."

"Nathan is next in line," said Isaac. "He'll be Alpha when our father is gone."

"If I decide not to go with him that is," Nathan said.

Daisy jumped in, "That's where most of the uncertainty lies." She was looking at me.

I was having a hard time trying to absorb all this information. "Serbia?"

"He was born in Serbia, in the Balkan Mountains," said Isaac. "He never liked the States. And his men are in the Balkans."

"So he's just going to leave you?"

"No, if we wanted to go," Isaac said, "we could go, but I've already decided where I'd rather be."

He pecked me softly on the lips. I heard the childish giggling of girls in the background. I had never experienced this before, being someone so important, someone cared for by a person everyone else wanted. I think I understood then why popularity was such an addiction.

"This is a lot for me to take in," I said. Just as I began to ask more about Trajan, Zia walked into the den hand in hand with Sebastian Reeves. I was beginning to see how much of a crash course I was getting in all of this. I hadn't even gotten started in my 'werewolf lessons' for the day when I had to start deciphering news of unexpected couples, and how I was going to break that news to my only non-werewolf friend, Harry.

I shot straight toward Sebastian.

"You!" I said, pointing at him. "What *happened* to you? You disappeared; everybody thinks you're *dead*. How could you *do* something like that?"

Sebastian hugged me, which surprised the hell out of me. He hardly ever spoke to me before.

"Sorry, Adria," he said, "but I had no choice."

Zia stepped up. "It was my fault," she said. "Sebastian and I kind of hit it off when I first moved here—met at The Cove one night. We were…ummm…" She couldn't get the words out. I knew what she was getting at, but I wasn't about to save her from having to say it aloud.

"We were making out one night and things got a little out of hand, if you know what I mean, and I lost control."

I was having a hard time picturing it. My mind couldn't wrap itself around Zia shifting into a werewolf and biting Sebastian. Wondering how that worked exactly was suddenly a curiosity digging harshly into my brain.

I just looked at her, waiting for her to go on.

"I hope you're not mad," she said, tilting her white-blond head repentantly, just enough to make me cave.

"Mad?" I had to think about that for a moment; it wasn't the information I needed or had expected from her. "No, no tell me how it *happened*. I don't understand; is it like in the movies, or what? Do you get really angry or lustful and then shift? Can you not control it? What about the full moon thing? That doesn't seem to apply with you, either." I thought about the barn then. Did I see the moon last night? I thought I saw it, but I couldn't remember. I couldn't remember if it was full.

Zia laughed. "Calm down, girl. No, it's not quite like it is in the movies."

"Nothing ever is," Nathan added.

"And they always butcher the books," said Daisy.

Isaac jumped in, "First of all, the experienced ones, the older ones, can control the Change for the most part."

I needed to sit down for this, so I went back to the couch.

"Anger and lust," Isaac continued, "are the two most dangerous emotions, and can even make an Elder lose it every once in a while. But fledgling werewolves, like Zia and Sebastian, have little control at all."

"So, you turned into a werewolf and bit him?" I said to Zia, still unclear.

"No," she said. "I was in my mediate form. I scratched Sebastian and infected him. If I would've bitten him in full-fledged form, he wouldn't be as pretty as he is now." Zia glanced over at Sebastian flirtatiously. It was weird seeing either of them act that way, especially with each other.

The girl who made the crackers for me stepped forward and pulled up her shirt to reveal her stomach. Or, what was left of it. I tried not to look aghast, but my face betrayed my will. I could see where the teeth went in and dragged across the flesh.

"That's how I was infected," explained the girl. She pulled her shirt back over the scars. "I was lucky; few ever live through a wound like that, especially females."

That was the second time I had heard mention of 'females' and their strange misfortune with werewolf life.

"Zia and Isaac tried to get me to come here after it happened," Sebastian said. "But I thought Zia slipped something into my drink one night. I didn't trust them."

"Yeah," said Zia, "and we couldn't tell him what was happening to him because he *definitely* wouldn't believe *that*."

Sebastian went on: "The Change took days. My temperature rose so high I should've been dead. I was craving raw meat and drank everything I could get my lips on—I couldn't stay hydrated!—but still went through days when I vomited everything I ate or drank. Mom took me to the hospital. They ran tests and did the usual, but couldn't find anything wrong with me. Said I had a few extra white blood cells; that it was normal to fight off infection, or some hospital mumbo-jumbo like that. So, they prescribed antibiotics and sent me on my way. A few nights later, I shifted for the first time, right there in my bedroom. I don't remember anything from that night except waking up in the basement here, chained to the floor."

I imagined it all as he told the story of what happened. Sebastian had gone through his bedroom window, cutting himself on the glass, which left blood.

Alex's face crept up in my thoughts then. I thought back to the night in Georgia when I knew she must've been infected. Then I turned to see Isaac standing beside me. "So Alex was the reason you came to Maine then?"

"Yes," Isaac admitted. "We followed the Vargas family to Georgia from South Carolina and from Georgia to Maine. We follow them everywhere, especially the humans they infect." He paused and then said, "My father and Viktor Vargas are mortal enemies. They've been at war for three hundred years. Over time, that war spread out among their fledglings as Viktor recklessly created hundreds of them to keep my father and his loyals busy."

Nathan said then, "And every time a Vargas fledgling infects a human, we try to…take control of the situation." He was careful to say it, but not careful enough to keep the obvious from me.

"You kill them, don't you?" I asked quietly. "You were going to kill my sister."

Isaac put his hand between my knees. "Not exactly," he said. "We watch them first; see if they show signs of becoming a rogue like the rest of the Vargas bloodline. If they can't be controlled, we have no choice but to kill them."

"No matter the bloodline you're Sired by," Daisy spoke up, "chances are you'll be just like them."

"A fledgling of the Vargas bloodline is dangerous to humans," Zia added. "They're a savage plague."

A horrible thought crossed my mind. I almost couldn't bring myself to ask. "Did one of you kill Julia?" I couldn't bear the answer, but it was imperative that I knew.

"No," Isaac said, shaking his head. "Fortunately we weren't the ones who had to end Julia's life. The Change did it for us."

Zia added, "Yeah, it was probably Alex who infected Julia; not sure, but girls have a hard time living through the Change. The world's werewolf population is about eighty-five percent male."

"We were surprised your sister made it through," admitted Nathan.

I looked around the room then, noticing how many girls were there. There were a lot. There were always a lot.

Isaac was still in-sync with my thoughts. "Most of the girls here," he said, "are not fledglings of ours. Some of them were infected by smaller random bloodlines; a few even kin to the Vargas bloodline."

I felt the color drain from my face.

"You can easily pick them out of a crowd," Nathan said.

I knew that Rachel was one of them. There was no doubt. Now I had more reason than ever to be afraid of her.

I looked toward the exit where Rachel last stood.

"Rachel is a bitch," said Nathan. "She can't help it because it's in her nature to be hateful. But she despises the Vargas brothers, and has never betrayed our trust."

"A woman scorned," said Daisy.

Isaac added, "She has to be put in line every now and then, but she's not a bad person."

"So this place is like a refuge?" I asked, skipping over adding my own opinion about Rachel's character.

Nathan smiled and hit Isaac gently on the shoulder. "Your girl catches on quick, bro."

"Sort of," Isaac said to me. "Most of them follow us wherever we move; a few find us here and there. It seems to grow by five every year."

I had more questions, tons of them, but I was so overwhelmed by everything already.

I looked at Isaac then. "You *really* weren't sick then, were you?" He had already confirmed this before in the barn, but since last night

I still didn't fully understand it. And I was trying to wrap my head around all of these damn lies.

Isaac shook his head.

Zia said, "I really hope you'll forgive me for all the lies and stuff. I'm really, *really* sorry."

"I think your situation sort of lets you off," I replied, numbly. "It's okay, honestly."

"A week before a full moon," Isaac began, "is when all werewolves are the most volatile. Not even an Elder can be one hundred percent sure of himself during that time. We have to make ourselves scarce, just to be safe."

I laughed lightly under my breath. "Sounds like a time-of-the-month thing."

Nathan's mouth fell open. "Sick, but funny. I like her!"

The cracker girl said, "Better than your last girlfriend, Isaac."

I think she soured the mood worse than Rachel had, but I could take it. It wasn't like I expected to be his first ever girlfriend, especially since he was…I had no idea how old Isaac really was.

I *had* to know. And though already the very thought of it was making me nervous, I was fascinated by it just the same.

"Just how old are you anyway?" I asked, arcing my brow at him. "Was that a lie too?"

Isaac shifted, uncomfortably. "You don't really want to know that, do you?" he asked, grimly.

"Of course I do."

"Don't tell her, bro," Nathan said, playfully. "You'll run her off."

"No, really—just tell me."

Isaac breathed in deep. I, on the other hand, wasn't breathing at all.

"I'm…" He hesitated and I was turning blue. "…I'm nineteen."

Silence. I could hear my stomach making funny little noises. "Really, Isaac," I said finally. "The truth."

"I *am* telling you the truth—I'm nineteen years old."

"But…"

Nathan started laughing. Then Daisy and Zia joined him. When I saw Isaac's face finally break into a smile too, I knew I was the butt of some innocent joke. I just sat there, looking at each of them critically, waiting to be let in on it.

"How old did you think I was?" Isaac asked.

"Ummm," I began, gently biting my lip, "well, I don't know. You're sort of immortal, so I assumed—"

"She thought you were really up there, little brother," Nathan said, still laughing. "Better start looking into wrinkle creams and microdermabrasion kits at Lancôme."

Daisy laughed out loud and turned Nathan's own joke around on him. "How do you know about microdermabrasion kits, Nathan?" she mocked, accusingly. "Is there something you're not telling us?"

Zia and Sebastian were eating this up as they stood off to the side; Zia enveloped by Sebastian's arms. I wondered how long that would feel awkward to me.

Nathan's eyes grew perfectly round, but even he couldn't help but laugh.

Isaac kept his full attention solely on me, discounting anymore laughs on my account. "Yes," he began to explain, "I'm only nineteen, but next year on the first full moon after my twentieth birthday, my aging will begin to slow, as it does with all of our kind."

I was instantly fascinated. "How does it…slow exactly?"

"Well, after that," he went on, and by now everyone else had stopped laughing and were listening too, "for every ten human years, we will physically age only one human year."

"Wow. You're like a real life Fountain of Youth."

"I guess you can look at it like that."

"That's amazing," I added, still not fully grasping it. "So then how old are *you*, Nathan."

He stopped smiling then, and I heard Isaac fake a small cough into his hand next to me.

"Nathan is pushing seventy," Daisy happily answered for him.

"Hey!" Nathan said. "You're a brat sometimes; you know that, Daisy?"

Inattentively, I began jotting down formulas in my head, trying to pinpoint this whole human/werewolf aging process and I was coming up short. "But that'd make you…" I thought about it harder just to be sure, "…you'd have to look *seven*-years-old, Nathan, and believe me when I say you definitely don't look seven. More like around twenty-five."

"Technically, I've lived fifty years after Abating," Nathan explained. "But you have to add the twenty years I lived before Abating, too."

"So he's seventy-years into wrinkle cream inevitability," Daisy laughed from behind.

"I think I get it…" I said, and then went back a topic or two. "Wait, what about when you shifted, Zia? I mean, how did Sebastian not know something was…well, not exactly normal?"

"Like I said," Zia began, "I was in my mediate form—easier to disguise, especially if it's dark and other things are going on."

I thought someone might tell me what a 'mediate' form was exactly, but apparently, everyone had forgotten so soon I was only human.

Finally, Isaac spoke up: "It's the form in-between human and full-fledged werewolf," he said. "Like you saw Rachel earlier."

"Oh…"

Isaac and I stayed with everyone in the den for about an hour before we migrated up to Isaac's room. I learned so much in that hour that I should've been mentally exhausted, but I was alert and ready to know more.

Nathan told me some about their father. Trajan Mayfair was actually General Vukašin Prvovenčani, dominant Black Beast of the Prvovenčani bloodline. His was the oldest and most powerful lycanthrope bloodline in existence, and Trajan, the most feared leader in lycanthrope history. He killed his own father to take control of the massive army that his father commanded.

Despite my initial thoughts, Trajan Mayfair was no do-gooder saint. He was a dangerous killer, and only by time and age did he begin to tame his ways.

"My father doesn't mingle with humans," Isaac explained, "unless he has to."

Suddenly, I was no longer afraid of Rachel. I was completely afraid of Isaac's father. This was a very different kind of fear; this fear demanded respect.

"It's another reason he's going back to Serbia. Other than taking control of his army again, there are too many humans and fledglings here. My father has never been tolerable of fledglings, not even his own."

"And humans," I added. "He doesn't trust himself around them, does he?"

Isaac just looked away from my eyes.

"Humans have always been a liability to my father; oblivious to the real dangers of this world and the weakest of all species. Though my father can be counted among the most notorious leaders of our history, it's those like Viktor Vargas, reckless and power hungry, who are the greatest threat to the human race as a whole.

"Unlike my father, Viktor must steal the respect of his loyals. And he does it without regard for the consequences." He glanced at me once. "You see; my father doesn't protect humans because he has a soft spot for them. He protects them only to keep Viktor's bloodline from wiping them out."

I couldn't speak for a moment. I felt insignificant and anxious.

"It's been going on forever," Isaac said, "this war between them. From the time I was born, I can only remember this war. My brothers and sisters and I were..." He stopped and stared at the wall, his jawline more pronounced. "...It shouldn't bother me because I've known nothing else, but spending so much time around humans, and seeing how they live and love, I guess it does make me somewhat envious."

My heart fell heavy for him, and I still had yet to learn exactly why.

"Envious of what?" I urged him softly.

Isaac shook his head. "My father never loved Sibyl. She was chosen because of her strength. At the time, there was no female more powerful than Sibyl."

Isaac looked right at me then. "We were bred merely for war," he revealed. "My training started before I could form a full sentence."

My lips parted gently, stunned. I started to speak, but stopped myself because what I had wanted to say about Isaac's father was nothing kind.

"I love my father," Isaac said, "and I don't condemn him for our ways, but experiencing human ways has made me envious."

"So you *were* born this way. You weren't Turned like Sebastian?"

Isaac shook his head once. "I'm a Pureblood. Like all of my brothers and sisters. I'm proud to be who I am, proud that he is my father; don't get me wrong."

He stood from the bed and went to the window then. I followed and sat on the windowsill. "You don't want to go with him to Serbia?"

He looked down at me, his eyes soft with assurance. "I was going to go, until I met you. Now things are different."

It made me feel guilty. I didn't want to be the reason he separated from his father.

"Adria," he said, detecting that guilt, "I *want* to stay, not only because your life is in danger, but because I *want* to be with you." He moved to stand in front of me and cradled the back of my head in his hand, pressing my face gently against his chest. "I won't lie and say I didn't try to stay away from you at first. I wanted nothing to do with you. I knew that if I followed my heart, I'd just put you in more danger."

I jerked my head away and looked up at him. "I don't care. You can't take it back now anyway."

"I wouldn't do that to you," Isaac said.

"Leave me?"

"No. You're stuck with me." He grinned.

I stood from the windowsill and pressed my lips against his. "I'd have it no other way," I said, and then he kissed me more deeply.

Something had been bothering me since long before I knew the truth about Isaac, and although I didn't want to ruin this moment with him, I had to ask and get it out of the way. As embarrassed as I knew it would make me.

I bit the inside of my mouth gently and crossed my arms, turning away from him.

"What's wrong?" he asked.

I paused for a longer awkward moment than I had meant. "Those girls…" I hesitated once more—just couldn't get the words out in a way that satisfied my need to *not* seem overly jealous, or obsessive. "Well, obviously you're attractive, but…" By now, I had given up trying to word it right.

He smiled knowingly, which made my face burn hotter.

"It's an Alpha thing," Isaac said. "The girls around here naturally and instinctively want a powerful male."

I think even Isaac was blushing a bit now.

"It'll either be me, or Nathan, when my father leaves," he added.

Half of me was relieved by his answer. The other half, undecided. I needed to get used to so many extraordinary things as it was. The possibility of Isaac becoming Alpha wasn't something I could understand yet.

16

ISAAC AND I SPENT EVERY DAY TOGETHER. WHEN I WAS APART from him at school, he was with me in text messages, or watching the school from across the parking lot. To anyone else it might've appeared stalker-like, but Isaac had plenty of reason.

He and many others in the Mayfair house were hell bent on protecting me, including Nathan and Daisy, who had become like my family.

Sebastian finally came back to school, shortly after Julia's funeral, which none of us attended. Her parents decided on a private funeral for family only. They moved away from Hallowell the following day.

Sebastian was welcomed by everyone, even though his excuse for what happened was that he ran away; tore his room up out of rage.

Tori was not so welcoming, however. She hated him for leaving her like that, but hated him more for choosing 'the freak', Zia, over her. So every time she and her new friends passed us, Tori always had something spiteful to mutter. I was proud of Zia for keeping her cool, but only Sebastian and I knew there was more to it than maturity. Zia couldn't lose it, or else Tori and the rest of the school would get one nasty surprise.

"Why do you even go to school?" I asked Zia outside on the football field at lunch.

"Well," Zia said, "I don't really have to. I only enrolled to keep track of you because of your sister. Now, honestly, *you're* my agenda."

I rolled my eyes.

"Here comes Harry," I whispered.

Harry had not hung out with us in days. I tried to talk to him on the phone, but he wouldn't take my calls, and at school, he wandered around alone. This had to stop, and Zia and I had to think of something worthy to tell him. It was no secret that Zia and Sebastian were together. I just couldn't take this anymore, seeing Harry act this way, and knowing it was partly my fault he was so hurt by everything.

I had never stopped thinking about what to tell him since he last spoke to me. But all of that thinking got me nowhere.

Harry approached swiftly, as if he too was tired of the silence. Zia looked at me and I could tell she was as unsure about what to do as I was. With Sebastian in the mix, the situation couldn't be any worse. I winced when he stopped in front of us, his hands buried in the pockets of his jeans.

"I'm sorry, man," he said to Sebastian. "I'm just glad you're not dead, y'know?"

Zia and I locked eyes; we couldn't move the muscles in our faces, but apparently this was going to resolve itself, and I'd be able to breathe again soon.

Sebastian man-hugged Harry, gripping his fist in one hand and patting his back with the other. "Hey, no problem," he said, and then he dropped his voice. "I didn't know about"—he indicated Zia with the movement of his eyes—"I really didn't."

Zia walked around in front of them. "Harry, I'm really sorry. Sebastian and I liked each other before I came to the school."

"I know," Harry said; his posture was awkward, but he was slowly becoming himself again. "It's cool. I just wanted to get this out in the open so we could all get back to normal again. Sucks eating lunch at the loner table."

I couldn't help but smile. This was perfect.

"And Adria," said Harry, "I feel like a real ass for dragging you into this."

"No way," I said. "I should've told you something."

"You were stuck in the middle of it and that's my fault—"

I put up my hand and stopped him.

"But enough of this," he obeyed. "It's done and over with. Have you guys heard what Tori's been saying around the school?"

"Which part?" Zia asked. "That I sleep around? Or that Sebastian hit her when they were going out? Or that she found Sebastian and me together and she busted my lip?"

"Yeah, I guess you *have* heard then," laughed Harry. "That girl is psycho."

"Yeah," Zia grumbled, "there's no way she could bust my lip."

I was glad things were back to normal. The school rival stuff was no big deal. I didn't care that because I was friends with Zia that the rumors about her included me also, or that I had enemies. Nothing anyone at school could do, would ever match what I faced on the outside.

The days were getting colder, and I dreaded the coming winter, especially in Maine. I hoped it would hold off, because I hated snow. I was a southern girl, used to heat and humidity and the occasional tornado.

Friday morning was blustery, and I knew I looked like an Eskimo when Isaac picked me up for school.

"Cold?" he asked, making fun of me.

I pulled the faux fur hood away from my head and scooted over next to him. "I'm not going to make it through the winter."

He wasn't even wearing a jacket; a long-sleeved, tight-fitting thermal black shirt was his idea of warm clothing. Not that I had any arguments—he looked awesome in black.

"It's technically not even winter yet." He laughed, and then said with a grin, "But I'll keep you warm."

He did that already; the hot blush in my face was kind of standard around Isaac Mayfair.

"I had a dream about you last night," he said.

"Oh?" I felt a nervous twinge in my gut. "What about?"

Isaac smiled over at me and shook his head. "Don't worry," he said, detecting the hesitation in my voice. "It wasn't anything like *that*."

We pulled away from my house. I hated how dreary everything was; only adding to the misery of the cold. The sky was gray, blanketed by thick depressing clouds with moving specks of black as crows flew over. The trees had already lost most of their leaves. Just looking at it all made me colder.

"Well, go ahead," I urged him. "You got me all curious now."

Isaac pressed the power button on the radio and shut it off. After a long hesitation, he began: "You were sitting at the edge of a creek and had your shoes off and your feet in the water. You were singing, and I was leaning against a tree, watching you."

I snickered, interrupting him. "Proof there's no truth to dreams—my singing's awful!"

"Well, I didn't say the singing was *good*," he teased with a grin.

My mouth fell open halfway with an unbelieving spat of air.

Isaac laughed and pulled me closer, resting his hand between my thighs. "Anyway, you kept looking all around until finally you saw me. At least, I thought it was me you saw."

"It wasn't you?"

"No," he said. "I got the feeling you were staring right *through* me instead. Then you stood up, slipped your shoes on and walked away."

"That's not what I would've done if that really happened," I said.

No, I would've drawn it out like an overly dramatic run-toward-each other scene; there would have been butterflies and sparkling water; slow-motion; my hair like a feather in the wind. Okay, so maybe it would've been cheesy, but it was better than walking away from him.

"That was it?" I asked.

Isaac turned too early onto Litchfield rather than going toward my school. I was too interested in his dream to ask where we were going yet.

"No, I must've followed you to your house," he went on. "You still knew someone was watching, but you were afraid of me. I think I was a ghost."

My enthusiasm for his dream began to diminish. I wanted to comment about how I didn't like where it was going, but I thought I'd interrupted him enough already.

"You stood near a fireplace then. Gazing out a window with your arms crossed. I reached out to touch your face and…"

I waited, eagerly.

"…And *what*?"

I heard Isaac sigh.

"I woke up."

I felt gypped. It was such a crappy ending. Then I realized most dreams have crappy endings.

"Well, at least I was *in* the dream," I said, laying my head against his shoulder. "That's a good sign."

He didn't say anything.

The car drove far past everything I knew in Hallowell and then past things I'd never seen before.

"Where are we going?"

Isaac slowly pushed on the brakes. His gaze was harsh as he stared out the windshield, one hand gripping the steering wheel.

"Isaac?"

He slowed the car, pulled forward on the road, and made a sharp U-turn.

"I think it's best if you get your Uncle to drive you to school tomorrow," he said, regretfully. "And next week."

Anxiety built up inside me quickly—was he dumping me?

"Isaac, what's wrong?"

"Nothing yet," he said, finally making eye contact. "But that'll change."

I had a feeling then what his strange attitude was all about. "A week before a full moon?" I asked.

"Yes," he answered; a sort of pain lay exposed in his face. "I hate not being in control, Adria."

A truck sped by in the opposite direction, and Isaac wasn't exactly staying on his side of the road. I tried not to pay attention to us narrowly avoiding a head-on collision.

"But you *are* in control. You saved me from Sibyl that night in the barn. You knew what you were doing."

Isaac sighed miserably. "Most of the time I know what I'm doing, but even just a second can be the worst second of my life." He added, "And you see how clouded my mind gets; I could've driven to Portland if you hadn't said something."

Hard lines appeared around Isaac's eyes. He kept his attention on the road, but I began to worry about where his mind was. He seemed deep in thought, frustrated with himself. Both of his hands gripped the steering wheel tight.

I covered his right hand with my left and said softly, "Isaac, pull over up there."

He glanced over at me. I let the softness of my voice show in my face. He needed to understand that I wasn't afraid of him. At least… he needed to believe that I wasn't. The truth was that I couldn't be *more* afraid. I knew it was reckless of me to put so much faith in him when he didn't have much in himself; I knew that he could very possibly kill me, but I wanted to believe in my heart that somehow he could overcome this. And I never wanted him to feel ashamed that I was afraid, or fragile.

Reluctantly, Isaac pulled off the road into a makeshift parking lot. I reached over, turned the car off and pulled the keys from the ignition.

"What was the real reason you told me about that dream?"

His cheeks blew up with air and he let it all out at once. "You don't miss anything, do you?"

I smiled, leaned forward and pecked him on the cheek; his skin was so warm and soft against my lips. "It was kind of obvious," I said. "Now tell me."

Isaac's long face turned into a smirk suddenly. "You're real demanding for, what, one hundred twenty pounds of human girl?"

My mouth fell open. I would've put my hands on my hips, but it was awkward to do sitting down. I settled for crossing my arms. "One-twenty?"

Of course, I loved every minute of this.

"Am I wrong?"

"No, but most guys don't go around guessing a girl's weight. It's dangerous; don't you know?"

"Well, I'm not most guys."

"How'd I know you were going to say that?" I laughed. "Oh well; I guess a werewolf doesn't have anything to be afraid of anyway, let alone someone like me."

The playful tone faded from his face. "That's not true, Adria."

The wind began to pick up; a gust hit the side of the car and shook it just a little. Fallen leaves scattered all around us.

"What are you afraid of then?"

Isaac just sat there, staring intensely out ahead. His hands gripped the steering wheel as if he were still driving. His posture was rigid, his gaze unbreakable. "I'm afraid of losing control. I fear emotion," he admitted. "Most of all, I fear you."

My heart clenched.

Still facing forward, Isaac went on: "Do you remember when Cara brought up my last girlfriend?"

That detail wasn't something a girl forgot easily, but I pretended to have to think about it for a moment. "Oh, yeah," I said. "I remember." Apparently, the girl who made cheese crackers for me, was Cara.

Finally, Isaac rested his back into the seat, letting his fingers fall from the steering wheel, and then he turned to me.

"She was just a girlfriend," he said. "I don't mean to put her down, and I'm not telling you these things because you're here and she's not. She was a decent girl, but I didn't love her."

That should've made me feel better, but the pain in his face was devastating, and I just wanted to make it go away.

I listened.

"She was human too. And she was terrified of me."

"Really? How did she know what you were?"

"Her mother was Turned by an Unknown," he said, before pausing. "None of that's important. What's important is that you know I hurt her. I hurt her bad."

My palms began to sweat, or maybe the moisture had been there all along, and only now did I realize it. A million different kinds of 'hurt' went through my mind, including the worst kind of all: death.

The wind blew against the car again, with more force this time; I could feel a cool draft of air coming in from somewhere near me, nipping at the back of my neck.

"Adria," he said, "you have to know everything about me."

I wondered how I could ever make him believe I didn't fear him, especially now that I know I looked every bit afraid. I could sense his sadness, his regret, the hatred he felt for the part of him that could not be tamed. Sometimes the look of fear and anguish are not so different.

"I know you didn't mean to," I said softly.

Once I said it, Isaac's posture hardened.

He went back to the subject of the dream quickly.

"Dreams are just subconscious metaphors," Isaac began. "They're life's way of warning us of future events, explaining the past and deciphering the present."

"You think your dream was warning you?"

He nodded slowly.

"Wait a second," I said, "but you said you were a ghost in that dream." I couldn't believe I was even entertaining Isaac's dream theory—I refused to accept him being dead; that part had to be the metaphor.

"Yes. And I think it represents my need to protect you without being in your life."

All of my organs stopped working in that moment. So, maybe this *was* about him breaking up with me, after all.

Like his death, I refused to accept that, too.

"Look at me, Adria."

I couldn't. I didn't want him to see me cry, and I was going to if this was heading in the direction I feared it was.

"But in one way like my father," he went on, "I'll ignore that need and I'll ignore the warning. As much as I know I'm a danger to you,

I'm also selfish. My heart will go against everything my mind tells me." He sighed, and said, "And later on, I'll regret it."

I started to cry anyway.

Wiping away the tears, I turned to him. The topic of his last girlfriend, I wasn't going to let him avoid. I needed to know the truth. "How did you hurt her, Isaac?"

Isaac looked down at his lap. It felt like a long time before he answered. "I gave her what she wanted—I Turned her."

I started to speak, until I realized I wasn't sure what to say. Being a werewolf myself was something I never thought about much. Truthfully, I avoided those thoughts as much as possible. The things I had seen, the terrifying transformations, the pain; everything about it made me want to run the other way. Everything but Isaac.

"I'm sorry."

What more could I say to something like that? I wanted to; I felt like I should, but anything I could think of sounded stupid.

"She was relentless," Isaac continued. "Threatened to have her mother do it if I didn't. My family didn't trust, nor like her. They warned me she was unstable."

"Why didn't you just let her mother do it?" I asked. "If you didn't want to be the one."

"Because her mother was a rogue werewolf. We, my brothers and I, were hunting her mother. There was no hope for her."

"Well then you saved her," I said, with confidence. "Don't you see? If you hadn't, she'd be dead no matter what."

"She *did* die," Isaac said, draining that confidence right out of me. "I killed her, Adria. I could've refused to Turn her, to let someone else do it and my conscience would be clear, but I didn't."

"The transformation killed her?"

"Yes," he admitted. "And I knew that it was a risk, but I did it anyway."

"Isaac," I said, with intent and calm, "I know you hate what you did, and I know this probably won't make you feel any better, but I just want you to know…" Our eyes locked; I could've stared forever into his eyes. "…I will never ask you to do that for me. I don't need to be what you are to be with you. All I care about is that we're together."

I meant every word. Isaac Mayfair was my world now. Asking for anything else would be asking too much. The thought of being a werewolf was frightening, yes, but the process killing me was much worse.

His lips were soft and tasted like fading mint. Every time he kissed me, it felt like an assurance that my life was complete, even a little magical. And I knew it was too soon, that we'd practically just met yesterday, but already I could feel our bond was strong. It grew stronger every day. And I knew that love would follow, sooner rather than later—I could feel it.

He pulled away slightly; I could still feel his cool breath on my lips. "It does make me feel better," he said.

We sat quietly for a moment.

"I was wondering," I said, finally breaking the silence, "why is it only girls that can die during the transformation? Kind of sexist, I think."

Isaac chuckled and fell back against the seat again. "Honestly," he began, still sort of laughing, "no one knows how or why it turned out that way. Just like how some human diseases affect different sexes and races more than another, I guess."

"Well, it makes girls look weak."

He held up his index finger. "Not true," he said. "Girls that do survive the transformation are usually stronger than men. Zia can take down Damien and Dwarf easily."

"Wow, really?" I pictured Zia taking her brothers on at the same time, and winning. It was a comical mental image, which I'd mess with Damien about later.

"I guess Zia could beat you then too, huh?"

"In her dreams," he said with a big grin. "She's too new."

He added then, "I should get you to school."

The abrupt change of subject caught me off guard. If all this talk was Isaac's attempt to cover up his mention of someone else taking me to school, it wasn't going to work with me.

"Not unless you promise to take me the rest of the week," I said.

"I can't do that."

"Yes, you can."

"Adria—"

"No, you take me to school, or I stay home."

He looked uncomfortable, and although I got the sense I was slowly winning this game, I knew he didn't like it. It wasn't a joke to him like it was to me.

"I know you can control it," I said, putting the joke aside. "Maybe you should learn to trust yourself more."

"Maybe you should learn to trust me less."

I sighed.

Then I smiled wickedly, thrust open the car door and ran out into the cold. "No promise, no deal!" I said, as I ran away from the car, climbing over a small stone wall and down a path. I dashed straight into the woods, looking back only once to see how far behind he was. Who was I kidding? Isaac was a werewolf and could catch up to me easily. But he was playing fair, still barely past the trees, and obviously running like any human would. I ran hard; trees and bushes whipped by. I jumped across a small flowing stream and then over a fallen tree, surprised I could leap that far. I could hear Isaac behind me, the sound of leaves crunching and sticks snapping underneath his fast and heavy feet.

It was so cold. I swore the temperature dropped ten degrees since he picked me up. The only thing that kept blood flowing through me was how hard I ran. It pumped fast and intensely through my veins. I was beyond the point of being out of breath.

"Is it a promise?" I kept running.

"No!" he shouted.

When I thought the woods would never end, I finally made it to the outskirts and ran out into an endless field. I stopped, trying to catch my breath and admire the sight before me at the same time. Isaac stood behind me then, not the slightest bit winded.

"It's beautiful," I said, with unsteady words.

It was just a field. I had seen hundreds of them in my life. Somehow, even those underneath a bright blue sky and blanketed by springtime flowers were nothing compared to this one. It appeared endless, stretched across the horizon by a blanket of frost-covered, dead grass. The sky suspended over it with thick, draping gray clouds that hung so low they seemed to touch the grass in the far distance. The air smelled so clean, as if never touched by human pollution. Only the swish of windblown trees and the low whicker of grazing horses could be heard. There were three out ahead, standing closely together, completely oblivious to the cruel world around them.

"Must be someone's farm," said Isaac.

"Let's get closer," I urged, taking him by the hand and pulling him along.

"That's not a good idea."

"Oh, come on," I said. "No one will see us. I just want to look at them."

I ignored his warnings, even the hard reluctance in his body as we walked along the border of the trees. I hoped we weren't trespassing, but usually signs were posted on the trees and there were none that I could see.

"Adria," he said, tightening his hand to stop me, "I mean it; we should just leave."

We were already close enough to the horses that I could count the black splotches on one of them.

I let go of his hand.

"Why?"

Isaac backed up a few steps into the cover of the trees, but he didn't answer.

In the corner of my eye, I saw the salt and pepper speckled horse rear up on its hind legs. The other two followed, neighing frantically. At first, I thought they were going to run right toward us. I pulled back and stood next to Isaac, holding onto his waist. The frightened horses ran a full circle before dashing through the field and away from us, the sound of hooves hitting the ground left in their wake.

Isaac watched out ahead where the horses had been standing. A look of guilt lay in his face. The cold air was finally beginning to affect him too; his cheeks and around his eyelids were slightly red.

"We should go," he said simply.

"No," I said with concern. "What's wrong with you?"

He looked at me. "I'm a predator, Adria. They can sense it."

I lowered my gaze, shamefully.

"Don't do that," he said. "I just didn't want to scare them off since you wanted to see them so badly."

Part of what he said was true, I believed. The rest of him was bothered by it, that such peaceful creatures were afraid of him. That was how I would've felt if it were me. But Isaac hid that small truth from me, and I let him believe that he did it successfully.

The cool kiss of tiny raindrops touched my face. The trees shielded us mostly from the rain, but in the field, it came down like a delicate veil of mist.

"It's going to snow soon," Isaac said, interlacing our fingers.

Surprisingly, I wasn't as disappointed to hear that as I thought I'd be. I guess Isaac just made everything better.

"You run fast for a human," he said.

I shook my head. "No, no, no," I scolded him, "you're not getting out of this one. Are you going to drive me to school every day, or not?"

My body shivered. Isaac reached behind me and pulled the hood of my coat over my head, adjusting it to fit snugly.

"Adria, listen to me," he began. This time I did, but that sense of victory I had before was gone. "I don't want to hurt you." He placed both hands on my freezing cheeks, warming them instantly. "I hate to bring it up, but you saw me that day when Rachel was in my room."

"But you were out of it," I argued. "I can take care of you when you're like that. What's wrong with that?"

I knew he was right, and I had known it all along, but I had been relentlessly trying to trick my human mind into believing that he could never hurt me.

Isaac let out an uncomfortable breath, and drew me into the tight fold of his warm arms. "If I begin to Turn and you're there…"

"I *know* you can control it, Isaac." It didn't seem to matter how many times I said it.

He pulled away from me, his hands gripping my arms; the desperate look in his eyes paralyzed me.

"No, you *don't* know that," he growled. "Would you ever put a child in a cage with a bear? *Would* you?" He shook me. "Learn a lesson from the horses—they know what I am and what I'm capable of, and I'm still in human form."

I didn't want him to be right, so I pulled away and started walking back through the woods. I crossed my arms tight at my chest; my fingers were finally starting to feel the sting of the cold.

I heard Isaac's footfalls behind me every step of the way.

I didn't want him to be right!

But I knew that he was…

"Adria, please stop."

Hesitantly, I stopped.

"Look at me."

Reluctantly, I turned, and I looked at him.

His face and his eyes softened, but there was a lot of pain and regret in them, too. "I…I know we haven't known each other long, but…but you're very important to me. From the moment I saw you, I…felt something I've never felt before."

I did too, Isaac…I could hardly breathe.

"I want to know you," he went on. "I want to know everything about you, past and present, inside and out—please, let me protect you the only way I know how. I…I wouldn't be able to live with myself if anything ever happened to you because of me."

A tear tracked down my cheek; I reached up, wiping it away. Then I went back into his arms where he held me tighter than ever before.

17

IT FINALLY DID START TO SNOW. I EXPECTED SCHOOL TO LET out early and the roads to be deserted when the first flake fell, but life in Maine was much different than in Georgia. In the South when it snows just a little—because it doesn't snow often—life comes to a halt. Bread flies off the shelves in the grocery stores, wreckers gear up rather than salt trucks. School is closed. An inch of snow is the major newsmaker. In the north, well, it seems the only thing that changes are the coffee and hot cocoa sales at Finch's Grocery.

Saturday morning I agreed to help Beverlee with the register again.

Beverlee moved the mop around near my register, cleaning up after a customer had dropped a glass bottle of soy sauce. "Looks like Nathan won't be working tonight," she said. She dipped the mop in an industrial-sized yellow bucket, squeezing back the handle to wring the blackened water from it. "He's called in more than any employee I've ever had."

"I'm sure he has a good reason," I said, knowing that was entirely true. "Want me to help you with that?"

She gave the floor one more swish of the mop before lifting it back into the bucket. "No thanks, I've got it." She looked winded, but then again that mop was huge and had to be heavy. After wiping her hands on her apron, Beverlee placed them on her hips and stood there looking at me.

"Do you have plans tonight?"

Oh no, I thought. That uneasy look on her face gave her away. I knew I couldn't tell her no. Besides, I didn't have any plans anyway, and Isaac was 'incapacitated' for the next few days.

"No, I don't. You need some extra help?"

"Would you mind?" she said, unease turning into relief. "With Nathan gone, I have no one to stock that new shipment, and it's double the size it was the last time. But you don't have to lift anything heavy."

"No, it's cool," I said. "I'll lift what I can."

"Maybe Harry can help you out," she offered.

That was a great idea, actually—suddenly, I wasn't dreading the work as much.

"Yeah, that'll be perfect," I said aloud. "I'll call him in a few."

Beverlee gave the mop handle a push and the yellow bucket's wheels began to squeak across the floor. The bell above the door chimed as a customer entered, bringing a gust of cold air in with him.

"Good morning, Mr. Deter." Beverlee waved from the bread aisle.

The elderly man held up two fingers and waved them as he slipped down an aisle.

"Watch him," Beverlee whispered behind me, "he's a shoplifter. Stole a lighter last week and a pack of cheese the week before. We can ban him from the store, but he always comes back."

I stuck my head out to see around the aisle where the man stood reading the label of a soup can.

"Cheese?" I whispered back. "Who steals cheese?"

Beverlee laughed lightly. "People who can't help but steal, I guess. Just keep an eye on him."

The bell chimed again.

"Good morning, Mrs. Perry," I greeted, remembering her from my first day at the grocery store. She was one of Finch's most loyal customers. "Come for some coffee?"

I thought I was getting the hang of this customer service thing.

"Well, hello," she said, hugging her big purse against her stomach. Her head looked like a wrinkly cabbage buried under a giant hat. "Good to see you again. No coffee today. Just peanut butter and hot cocoa."

I smiled. "Well, I guess I don't have to tell you where to find it."

"No, no," she said, "but thanks anyway, sweetheart."

She slipped down an aisle too, her thick-soled granny shoes made a squishy sound as she walked.

The snow was picking up, and since the night before, Hallowell already had six inches on the ground. Being Saturday, the streets were filled with kids. A few flying snowballs had smashed into the window of the store, and I hoped the glass was thick. Those snowballs could easily pass as baseballs.

I felt awkward standing there doing nothing, so I went to the front door to sweep the dead leaves from the giant rubber mat. It was a less conspicuous way to watch Mr. Deter, too. He was still reading the soup cans. I got bored with him fast.

I got bored with everything fast.

It wasn't Beverlee's fault, or even that I was stuck working. When you want to be with someone else so badly, nothing else you do can take your mind off it much.

Honestly, this sucked.

All I wanted to do was see Isaac. How could he expect me to stay away from him an entire week before every full moon? Nathan never had to stay away from the world for that long, so why did Isaac? Nathan's older, I thought. He probably had more control than Isaac did.

I swept the floor absently, not even realizing my aim was doing no good.

My cell phone rang in the leg pocket of my cargo pants.

"Harry," I said, "I was going to call you later. What's up?" I placed the broom against the wall.

"Mind if I come over later?"

"I'm working at the store tonight," I said. "I was going to ask if you wanted to help out. Nathan called in."

"Yeah, I can do that. For how long?"

"The store closes at seven. We'll probably stay after to stock for a couple of hours."

Harry agreed.

"I have to go," I said, seeing Mr. Deter come up the aisle to check out. "Got a customer to ring up. See you around seven?"

"I'll be there."

I walked around the counter and keyed-in the amount of his items on the register. It was an old-fashioned store, without the advantage of bar code scanners. Beverlee said Mrs. Finch refused to 'upgrade to the Devil's technology'.

"Find everything all right?"

Mr. Deter nodded; he wasn't much the speaking type.

"Good then. That'll be $14.84."

For a second, Mr. Deter looked confused as he began counting out his money. He handed me a twenty and I gave him his change.

"Have a great day, Mr. Deter," I said. "And stay warm."

The bell chimed over the door as he left, waving with two fingers above his head. More leaves blew inside that had been pressed against the building and untouched by the snow.

Beverlee came up beside me.

"I think you overcharged him," she said.

"Nope." I pointed to my shirt. "I saw him slip a package of triple A batteries down his shirt pocket when I was on the phone with Harry."

Beverlee smiled hugely. "So you charged him for them. Nice move."

Mrs. Perry approached, the squishing of her shoes on aisle two getting louder.

"Harry said he'd be here later."

"Oh good." Beverlee was delighted. "I was going to change my mind about you working if he couldn't help you."

I rang up Mrs. Perry's peanut butter and hot cocoa. She and Beverlee talked for the longest time—more town gossip stuff, which I shamefully could admit, I was starting to pay more attention to lately. I pretended not to be interested when Mrs. Perry said something about Lester Mann's dogs found dead in the woods, ripped to pieces. They talked a lot about 'that poor dead girl, Julia Morrow', but Beverlee did her best to change the topic quickly with me standing nearby. By six o'clock, I had heard enough gossip to start my own scandalous town newspaper. But I never expected to learn so much, either.

After Mrs. Perry left, Joan Something-Or-Another, came in. She expressed concern for her neighbor's son, David Shanks, who had been so sick with 'pneumonia' they had to hospitalize him.

"He was hanging out with that new crowd," Joan said to Beverlee, "up past The Cove."

Beverlee knew as well as I did that Joan was referring to the Vargas family, but she pretended not to.

"Jonathan Forrester," Joan went on, "he lives over on Academy; I heard he was coming down ill, too. It might be something health officials need to worry about."

This was getting bad.

Shortly before seven, I called Isaac. He needed to know what was going on, but there was no answer, and I had to explain everything in a voice message.

I was worried about everyday life and people around me now. I felt vulnerable without Isaac or even Zia to protect me. How could they leave me alone for days like this, to fend for myself?

Maybe it really was more dangerous to be around them when they were like this, I thought. If Isaac had to leave me alone, unprotected, especially when Alex and the Vargas family wanted me dead, then Isaac was right. His uncontrollable nature was more of a threat to me than the Vargas brothers were. This revelation not only struck me numb, but it changed everything.

If Isaac and I were going to be together—and I would have it no other way—something needed to happen. Something needed to change. I just knew in my heart that me being human was going to put a serious divide between us. It was starting to already.

I couldn't let that happen.

"Here are the keys to the store," Beverlee said, standing at the front doors. "Keep these doors locked at all times, except to let Harry in."

"There he is now." I pointed to the parking lot as headlights moved in, illuminating the snowfall.

"Carl will stop by in about an hour," Beverlee continued, "just to check on things. He keeps my emergency key to the store, so he'll be able to get in if you're in the back and can't hear him." She seemed nervous about leaving me in the store without her.

"I'll be okay, Aunt Bev. Go home and get some rest." Beverlee always worked long hours on the weekend; up before the sun even.

She stopped babbling and smiled with confidence. "All right, I'll be back at nine-thirty to pick you up."

Beverlee pulled open the glass door to let Harry inside. Snow fell off his shoulders and the back of his coat as he stomped his shoes clean onto the mat.

"Thanks for the job," he said.

"You're more than welcome, Harry," Beverlee said, putting money into his hand. "Glad you're with Adria, too."

Harry looked surprised. "Didn't expect to get paid before I worked, but I'm not complaining. Thanks!"

Beverlee slipped her hood over her head and went to leave. "Lock the doors," she demanded one last time.

Harry and I went to the stockroom near the bay door. Boxes piled high against every wall. Old shopping carts with three legs had been stored near the giant cardboard recycling crate. Every kind of junk food and cola imaginable was stored back there, along with a lifetime supply of toilet paper and headache-inducing laundry detergent. I rummaged an unopened box of aspirin and took a few just to be on the safe-side. Strong-smelling anything always gave me headaches.

"What do we start with first?" Harry asked, looking a little overwhelmed.

"None of that stuff," I said, pointing. "Just these boxes in front of the bay door." I whipped out my box cutter and sliced open the tape on one box to look inside.

"Y'know, you could just read the *side* of the box to see what's in it."

"Oh shut up!" I laughed. I tried to hide the embarrassment on my face, but I couldn't.

"It'll be easier to take boxes to the aisles if they're not opened," he said, all brainy-like.

Harry lifted two boxes into his arms and started to carry them out.

I stopped him, smirking—it was my turn. "Harry," I said, standing there with my hand on a dolly, "it'd be a lot easier to use the dolly."

His face turned bright red.

In an hour and a half, we stocked everything from canned goods and deodorant to paper plates and garbage bags. I was exhausted and my back hurt.

"I could never do this for a living," I whined, sitting on the floor of the cereal aisle with my back against the generic brands of pancake mix.

Harry was still placing boxes of cereal neatly on the top shelf in front of me.

"Shouldn't have tried to carry the cans like that."

Groaning, I reached behind to massage my back with my fingertips. "I know, but you don't know it's a bad idea until long after you've done it."

"Well, you just do the light stuff then," Harry said with his back to me. "I think I saw a box of mini marshmallows over there." He failed to suppress the laugh entirely. It came out like he was snorting.

I swung out my foot and nudged his shoe. "You're so cruel."

He agreed, still laughing.

"So, how are you and Isaac doing?" he asked, carefully, putting another box into place. "I notice you haven't been texting tonight."

It never occurred to me how obvious some of my new habits were to others.

"We're doing great."

"Just great?" He turned to bend over and take out three more boxes of cereal.

"Well, yeah," I said. "Great is pretty good, I thought." That sounded backwards to me, but I went with it.

"How great?" Harry finished shelving the cereal and started breaking down the box it all came in. He tossed it on top of the pile we had made over time.

"If you're implying something is *not*-so-great between us, then you're wrong."

"I never said that."

"It sounded like it."

"Why are you getting defensive?"

I supposed he was right: I *was* getting defensive. I had to be careful. Harry would want to know why, and I would have no idea what to tell him. But it was too late to pretend that nothing was wrong. I pushed myself up from the floor and cut open a case of instant oatmeal boxes.

"You don't have to tell me," Harry began, "but if something happened and you need to get it out…"

"I know, Harry. Thanks," I replied. "Nothing happened. We're still together, just trying to work out one minor issue, but it's no big deal. Nothing major." That was probably the biggest lie I'd ever told.

He knew I was lying, too; that look on his face made it obvious.

"Hey, isn't your uncle supposed to be here?"

I glanced at the clock on the wall above the customer service booth.

"Probably just the roads."

The snowfall had reduced to light flurries within the past hour, but outside, everything was covered by it. Only one snowplow had driven past the store since before Beverlee left. I took that as a sign the weather wasn't going to get any worse. Traffic, although light, was moving along at a normal rate.

I started to go back to the oatmeal boxes when I noticed a dark figure standing in Finch's otherwise empty parking lot. Moving out of the pool of light shining above from the fluorescent, I stood closer to the end of the shelf to get a better look.

"Thirty more minutes and he won't need to come anyway," Harry said from behind.

I walked closer and edged my way toward the window. The figure stood just out of the glow from the street light. He, if it was a man, wore dark clothes from head to toe. The way he stood there, still as a statue and staring toward the store, made my nerves short out like electrical wires.

"Me and Sebastian don't hang out much anymore," Harry went on, still shelving merchandise. "I mean, I get it—girlfriend and all—but it still sucks. Y'know?"

"Harry," I whispered, as if the man could actually hear me from that far away, "come here."

I felt Harry standing behind me then.

"Do you see that guy?" I asked, taking my eyes off the parking lot for just a second.

"No," Harry answered. "I don't see anybody."

I did a double-take. The man was gone.

"No," I said, moving quickly to the store window, almost pressing my face against it. "He was standing right there. He was staring at me."

I turned around to face Harry.

"I can't believe this," I said.

"Don't get so worked up, Adria." Harry started to walk back to the aisle. "Could've been anyone. You're really jumpy tonight."

I turned around again; the man, with a grinning, maniacal face dripping with blood, stood an inch from the glass.

I shrieked and stumbled backward, my foot catching under a metal newspaper rack. I fell hard on my side and newspapers came tumbling down.

Harry came running over.

"Holy shit!" he said.

Harry grabbed me and pulled me to my feet. The man's eyes swirled black; his knifelike teeth glistening with blood.

Suddenly, Harry fell over the same newspaper stand that I did. He almost took me down with him, but let go of my arm just as he hit the floor.

"What the hell!" he shouted.

The man came closer to the window; his wicked, smiling face put the fear in my heart. His hands were behind his back; he pulled his right arm out slowly and pointed his index finger upward; the nail two inches and razor-sharp, black like his eyes; his hand was covered in blood. Blood stained the snow beneath him.

"I imagine uncles taste better than German Shepherds," the man said, so cold and menacingly through the glass.

I gasped. Harry had gotten to his feet and was trying to pull me backwards with him, but I pushed him away from me. I threw myself against the window, my face and the werewolf's face separated by nothing more than a false sense of security. I banged my palms once against it, feeling the entire window shake and shudder.

"What did you do to him?" I screamed. "What did you do to my uncle?" I banged the glass once more; the palms of my hands stung.

The man grinned, revealing his deadly teeth.

Harry grabbed me and pried me violently away from the window. I was mad with rage, trying to fight my way free, but Harry was too strong; I felt my shoes scraping across the floor as he pulled me into the nearest aisle.

The werewolf let out a menacing growl from outside, jerking back his head. The last I saw of him was how his hot breath had melted the cold from the glass.

"We have to leave!" I said. "*Now*! Can you drive me to my house?" I ran into the back of the store and grabbed my coat and canvas backpack from a file cabinet.

"Adria, what the hell was that?" he shouted, following behind me. "I'm not going out there. I-I'm not going *anywhere*."

I forced my coat on angrily because it wasn't cooperating. "Harry, *listen* to me." I stopped directly in front of him; he couldn't hide the fear in his face. "That was a werewolf. I know it sounds stupid and you probably won't believe me, but I'm telling you the truth. Now, we have to find my uncle, all right?"

Harry's head drew back in disbelief. "A *what?*"

"I don't have time for this," I said, pushing my way past him. "If you won't take me, then I'll walk."

I pulled the store keys from my pocket and unlocked the front door before tossing them at him. "Lock up if you decide to leave. In fact, lock up after *I* leave."

I went out into the cold night, leaving Harry standing there in shock, completely disoriented.

I ran down the snow-covered sidewalk and past the streetlights, far away from Finch's Grocery. I ran until I was out of breath and my throat burned from the cold. My shoes were wet with snow, all the way through to my socks. The streetlights became fewer, and darkness began to surround me. A couple of houses were on each side of the street, but nestled many feet away and encroached by trees.

I unlocked my cell phone and called Beverlee. There was no answer and I broke down and started to cry.

The phone rang, and BEVERLEE lit up on the screen then.

"Aunt Bev," I answered frantically. I fumbled the phone to my ear and dropped it in the snow. "Where's Uncle Carl?" I said, after finally getting the phone back into my hand.

"Adria, calm down, okay? I need you to calm down."

Her voice shuddered quietly, as if she had been crying, too.

"I can't calm down. Please, just tell me what happened."

I heard Beverlee take a deep breath.

A car drove past me; the sound of snow crunching under its wheels.

"Where are you?" she asked suddenly. "Did you leave the store? Are you outside?"

"*Beverlee!*" I couldn't help but yell at her. I needed to know the truth, and she was angering me by holding it from me for so long.

"Carl is in stable condition," she said finally, the tears choking her voice, "but he's not been conscious at all since they brought him in."

"Oh no, what happened? Beverlee, what happened to him?"

Headlights bore down on me from behind. I pulled the phone away from my ear and turned swiftly, on my guard. It was Harry. Thank God, it was Harry.

"Harry's here," I said into the phone. "I'm coming to the hospital."

Harry hung his head out the car window and motioned for me to get in. I ran around the car and slung open the door, jumping inside with the phone still pressed to the side of my face.

"He was in an accident," said Beverlee. "No one knows for sure, but by the looks of the car it might've been a deer, possibly a moose, that ran out and hit him."

Oh-my-God, oh-my-God, I kept saying over and over in my head.

"Please tell Harry to be careful," she urged.

"I will."

I hung up and just sat there, gripping the phone.

"First, your Uncle," Harry demanded. "And then you have some explaining to do."

All I could do was nod, agreeing. I had to catch my breath. I had to calm myself down and think clearly.

"We need to go to the hospital," I said. "Uncle Carl was in an accident."

"Okay, we're going now."

I got quiet again. I kept picturing the so-called accident in my mind. I saw the werewolf bash into the side of my uncle's car, tossing him from it. I saw the car become crushed and mangled beyond identification, because that was exactly what would happen. Werewolves were enormous, formidable beasts. A car impacted by one would be like hitting another, better-built car head-on.

But the blood. The werewolf at the store was covered in blood. His teeth, his hands, all dripping with blood. He did this. He mentioned my uncle. But what exactly did he do?

"Oh no…"

I was never going to be able to think straight.

"Adria," said Harry, "you have to tell me what that was. I'll believe whatever you say, if you just start explaining."

Harry needed answers as desperately as I did.

"I told you—it was a werewolf."

"I know, but I thought you were screwing with me."

I swung around to look at him. "Why would I joke about something like that?" I was shouting, but trying not to. "You saw what I saw. You know it wasn't normal."

"Yeah," he admitted, "but the dude could've been wearing contacts, or something. Anyone can look like that."

I stared at him in that are-you-for-real sort of way. Nothing in any local costume shop could duplicate that nightmare. Harry knew it, too.

"Okay, so it was real," he conceded. "But that didn't look like any friggin' werewolf I've ever seen."

"And how many werewolves have you seen exactly?" I asked, hotly.

The car slid a bit when he turned left at the end of the street.

"Well, none…in person," he said. "But like on the—damn, Adria, you know what I mean!" He slapped the steering wheel. "How do you know so much anyway?"

"Because I've seen them Turn. Because I've been chased and attacked by them," I snapped, "and because my sister is *one* of them!"

Harry shut up in an instant.

It was like telling him I just robbed a bank and shot someone, that look on his face.

"Yes, you heard me right," I said. "Alex is a werewolf. That man you saw back there was a werewolf. There's quite a few in this town, actually."

I was steering too close to revealing the Mayfair's secret. Sebastian's secret. Zia's secret.

"I can't believe this," he said, and then shook himself from the stun. "But why did he look like that? I thought werewolves were supposed to look like, well, like werewolves."

"He was in-between his human and werewolf form," I told him.

Blue, red and yellow lights flashed on the road up ahead. As we got closer, I recognized the totaled car immediately.

"*Jesus*," Harry mumbled.

We crept along past the accident scene slowly. The yellow lights were coming from a wrecker, which already had the car halfway lifted onto it. It was nothing but a twisted heap of warped metal.

How Uncle Carl survived that crash was beyond me. I couldn't get the reality of it out of my mind, how he might have survived. I felt guilty for thinking it, but I knew that Uncle Carl would be better off dead than one of them.

All the way to the hospital, I tried to prepare myself for the unthinkable, about losing my uncle the same way I lost my sister. Who would be next? Harry? Aunt Bev? Me?

The nurse at the desk directed me to the waiting room where Beverlee joined us. She hugged me so tightly I thought she'd never let go. Her face was stained with tears where they had run down her cheeks and through her makeup. Her hair was wild, and the butterfly barrette she always wore hung hopelessly on one side of her head. I reached up to fix it for her. She hardly noticed.

"I can't lose him, Adria," she croaked. "I just can't."

I hugged her close to me. "You said he's stable, and that's a great sign. Just try to be positive."

Harry stood nervously off to the side, giving us our space.

"I-I don't know what happened to the dog," Beverlee said, her voice trembling. "He's probably out there in the cold."

I pulled away from her.

"What dog?" I asked, confused.

"Carl adopted a German Shepherd from the animal shelter," she said. "It was supposed to be a gift to you. He had just come back from Augusta. I was on the phone with him. The car. I heard him yell and the dog whimper. Oh God, I thought it happened because he was talking on the phone while driving." She buried her face in her hands. "That still could've been why. Adria, oh God, it's probably my fault!"

I held her close again, rubbing her back with my hands. "No, Aunt Bev, it wasn't your fault." I felt so awful for shouting at her earlier on the phone. Now I was the one trying to calm *her* down. "You said they think it was maybe a deer, remember? Why do they think that? Did they say why?"

Beverlee dried her eyes the best she could, and began pacing; a tissue crushed in her fist.

"There was no other vehicle," she began. "No second set of tire marks; and his car was found on the side of the road, not against a tree, so he didn't lose control or drive into anything. That's all I know." She wiped her nose with the tissue.

I couldn't bring myself to say anything aloud about there not being a dead deer in the road. Beverlee would have gone back to the cell phone theory, blaming herself.

But Beverlee gave me hope that I didn't have before. Maybe the blood was from the dog. It had to be. The werewolf's only words indicated that it was a dog he attacked, not my uncle. Yes, that gave me hope, though very little.

A nurse opened the waiting room door.

"Mrs. Dawson, you can go back now," she said, gesturing her to follow.

I took hold of Beverlee's arm. "Can I go?"

Beverlee looked across at the nurse who nodded her approval.

I went over to Harry. "Wait for me, okay?"

"Don't worry about me. I'm not leaving anywhere without you."

18

WE FOLLOWED THE NURSE DOWN THE STERILE-WHITE HALLway. I never liked hospitals, the smell of them, the bright lights, the cruel atmosphere, the death. The last time I was actually in one, my great-grandma was recovering from heart surgery. She died two days later.

I held Beverlee's hand the whole way.

The nurse stopped us at the door to Uncle Carl's room before opening it. She held a lime green clipboard pressed against her breasts.

"Dr. Derringer will be here to talk to you soon," she said. "Your husband is awake, but the pain medication will keep him from making much sense for a while."

Beverlee listened carefully, tears glistening on her cheeks, but then her face lit up. "He's conscious?"

The nurse smiled and pushed open the door slowly. I felt like I was taking a deep breath before jumping off a cliff into water. I expected to see flesh ripped from my uncle's bones, maybe even an arm or leg missing. I wanted to shut my eyes and not look at all, but some invisible force locked them wide open.

Machines were hooked to him on both sides: an IV taped to the top of his right hand, a blood pressure cuff resting around his bicep.

An annoying little machine with flashy colors and lighted numbers displayed his heartrate and blood oxygen. One leg and one arm were in casts; bandages were wrapped around the upper part of his head with thick gauze taped over his left temple. Blood was there, soaked up in the dressing. A long, clear tube hung from the left side of his chest as bloody fluids pumped through it into an ominous contraption that sat on the floor. It made such an eerie sucking noise that I wanted to plug my ears.

Uncle Carl's head fell sideways on the pillow so that he was facing us. A tiny clear tube rested in his nostrils, feeding him oxygen.

The nurse set the clipboard on a table and began adjusting this and that, poking and prodding his tubes and needles.

Beverlee took the chair close to the bedside.

I didn't feel comfortable sitting down. I didn't feel comfortable being in the room at all. My uncle looked horrible, and technically, it was because of me. I choked back the tears and they made it only as far as the edges of my eyelids.

"I'll be back in about half an hour," the nurse announced, just before leaving.

I walked closer to the bed, every step more hesitant than the last. Uncle Carl's eyes were partially closed; they were bruised and swollen.

"What is that?" I whispered to Beverlee about the machine on the floor.

"His left lung collapsed," she said. "They had to insert a tube into his chest to help it inflate."

A shiver went up the back of my neck. I didn't even notice when my hand went over my mouth, or how long it had been there.

Beverlee leaned in close to Uncle Carl's face. She kissed his bruised cheek. "Carl?" she said, in a low voice. "Honey, can you hear me?"

His eyes opened a crack, and he mumbled something neither of us understood.

"What was that, honey?" She was trying really hard not to cry anymore. It was a struggle for her.

"It...*hit* me," he said. Still, his voice was so low I could barely make out the simplest of words.

Finally, I pulled a chair next to Beverlee's. Leaning forward, I said to Uncle Carl, "What hit you?"

"An...animal," he said weakly. "I-I don't know...huge."

The more he struggled to speak, the worse he was in pain. His face tightened in agony. The heart rate numbers went up on the machine beside him.

"Shhh," Beverlee said, brushing his eyebrow with her fingertip. "Just try to sleep."

He took Beverlee's advice; shutting his eyes and allowing his face to rest on the pillow.

"I just can't believe this is happening," Beverlee whispered aloud to herself.

Secretly, I began inspecting Uncle Carl's visible wounds, though most were bandaged or covered by the hospital gown. I didn't know what I was looking for anyway. A scratch? A deep cut? Bite marks? Any wound would look like any other wound to me, unless it was blatantly obvious. But I needed to know.

I thought of Isaac suddenly and then my heart sank. If Uncle Carl was infected, Isaac and his family would want to kill him. I panicked inside.

My cell phone rang in my pocket and startled me. Beverlee looked up, motioning with her eyes to hurry and answer it. Uncle Carl barely stirred. I pressed the phone to my ear and stepped into the restroom to talk.

"I *was* at the store," I said to Isaac, "but I, well, I had to leave in a hurry."

"Nathan said he found the store keys in the parking lot," Isaac said on the other end.

Harry must've dropped them, frantically trying to get into his car to come after me.

"Adria," Isaac warned, "I know something's wrong. What happened?"

I hesitated, peeking my head around the door to see Uncle Carl lying on the bed.

"My uncle was in a car accident," I whispered.

"Is he all right? Are you at the hospital?"

"Yes and yes."

Silence.

"Adria, please don't keep things from me."

"I have to go."

I hung up on him. Just like that, I shut the phone off and dropped it in my pocket. I couldn't believe what I'd done, what Isaac must be thinking. It tore me up inside.

But I couldn't let them kill my uncle.

I wasn't going to let them kill my sister, either.

I wanted to crawl inside a hole and die. How cruel life was to make a person choose between the people she loved most. I cursed the Powers That Be, God, or whoever was listening at that moment—I didn't care. I pressed my back against the wall and slid down onto the floor. The restroom was pitch dark, only a tiny slither of light beamed in through the cracked door. I buried my face in my hands and cried. I cried and cried until my throat felt closed up and I couldn't breathe. I tried to keep Beverlee from hearing me; she didn't need to console me, of all people. It was difficult to cry softly when your body wanted to do exactly the opposite. But I managed to get through privately.

The whole world spun around in my mind. I saw the face of my mother, screaming with rage at Jeff. I saw my dad walk away and never even say goodbye. I saw my great-grandma lying in the hospital bed as her heart rate machine flat-lined. I saw Alex, her face ravenous and evil. And I saw the face of Uncle Carl.

"Oh my God!" Beverlee screamed from the room. "Oh my God, someone help him!"

I exploded out of the restroom. Nurses came running inside, crowding around Uncle Carl's bed.

Everything moved in slow motion.

I ran toward Beverlee, grabbing her by the waist, trying to pull her away so the nurses could resuscitate him. But it felt like I was under water, struggling to move, stuck in time. I heard Beverlee screaming, her body thrashing and frantic, yet I heard nothing at all. Surreal. Time was cruel like life; it slowed down so that you could truly experience the worst moments of it; only if you made it through them did you get to say, 'It all happened so fast.'

The next thing I knew, Beverlee and I were standing outside the room. The door to Uncle Carl's room burst open and he was rolled down the hallway in his bed.

We were forced to sit in the waiting area again. Beverlee was inconsolable. She stood next to a giant window overlooking the snow-covered streets. I left her alone. It was where she wanted to be. Alone.

Harry and I sat next to each other, my head resting on his shoulder. We stayed like that for an eternity. The clock high on the wall ticked and ticked. I heard water dripping from a faucet near the visitor coffee pot. The sizzle of coffee hitting the hot plate when a woman filled her cup. Intercoms with voices reverberating through the halls. Hospital gibberish. Secret codes for sickness and death.

Finally, a doctor came in.

"Mrs. Dawson," he said, "I'm Dr. Derringer."

He was smiling. In a time like this, a smile was the most important facial expression a family waiting could hope to see. Anything else, even the tiniest downturn of the mouth, always meant bad news.

The doctor shook Beverlee's hand. "Mr. Dawson is going to be fine," he said, reassuringly.

That was really all I heard. It was all I needed to hear. Relief and happiness took over my ability to pay attention. The doctor went into detail with Beverlee about what happened: pneumothorax, bleeding in the chest; I was too happy to try putting the grim pieces together.

Harry looked up at the double-doors. Isaac, Nathan, Zia, Sebastian, and Daisy entered the waiting room.

Panic mode set in. That elated feeling I had, fled at the sight of them. I paused, thinking, and then ran over to Isaac and pulled him off to the side.

I shoved against his shoulders and whispered hatefully, "I won't let you kill my uncle." Tears streamed down my face again. I wanted to be held by Isaac at the same time. All these mixed emotions were tearing my atoms in half.

Isaac grabbed me and pulled me against his chest, his arms wrapping protectively around me. "We're not going to hurt your uncle."

"But he was attacked," I said. "I know he was attacked and by what."

He whispered into my ear, "Your uncle wasn't infected, Adria."

I looked up at him. "How do you know that?"

"We can smell them: the blood, the infection; the only ones in this hospital are us." He hesitated a moment. "And one other on the first floor."

"Who?" I demanded desperately. "Who else is here? Is it the one from the store?" My whole body tensed up.

"Shhh," Isaac said, holding the back of my head. "No, it's a new one. Probably the guy you told me about in your voice message, David Shanks."

I heard Harry's voice behind me, talking to Sebastian and the others about what happened. My ears perked up. I hoped he wouldn't mention any of the 'forbidden information'. Harry was smart. I thought surely he wouldn't.

"Isaac," I moaned, "I have to tell you something."

"Adria," Beverlee called from across the room, "I'm going in to see Carl."

I left Isaac and walked over to her. The doctor had already left, and a nurse was waiting to take Beverlee back.

"They said only I could go back to see him right now." She hugged me tight. "I want you to go home, or leave with your friends and stay with them, but I don't want you hanging around here, okay?"

"But—"

"It's fine," she urged me. "They're not going to let you go back for a long time anyway. Go get some sleep and I'll pick you up tomorrow and you can visit him."

She turned to Harry then, who had walked up after me. "Do you mind taking Adria home?"

"Not at all."

Beverlee hugged Harry too, and then Nathan—Nathan coughed once, still pretending to be sick—just before she slipped out the door with the nurse. I watched her go, feeling I should be with her. Isaac came up behind me and I felt his arms slip around my waist. Instantly, they comforted me. I shut my eyes and inhaled the air. Then I felt his lips press into the back of my hair.

"What did you need to tell me?" he asked.

I glanced over at Harry, hoping he didn't hear Isaac's question. Harry was too into listening to Daisy talk in her English accent about how much she hated hospitals.

"Dreadful tombs," she said. "That's what they are."

"I'll tell you later," I told Isaac. "Can we just go?"

Zia stepped up with Sebastian at her side. She looked to see if Harry was listening, and then leaned into me. "Girl," she said, "you know you can't come with us; not right now—we shouldn't even be *here*, but Isaac insisted."

"So, I'm just supposed to go home?" I argued. I dropped my voice a little and added, "Zia, one of them came to *Finch's*. He threatened me. Look what he did to my *uncle*." What I really wanted to do was scream at the top of my lungs.

I saw Harry look over, but I noticed that Daisy's conversation with him was also her way of keeping him occupied.

"She can't go home," Isaac spoke up. "Not now. It's worse than I thought."

"He's right," Nathan graciously jumped in. "At least *we* aren't out to get her."

Isaac let go of my waist and took my hand. "We'll have to take our chances. I think I'll be fine for another night or two, but after that…"

Nathan nodded.

"But *I'm* not fine," Zia snapped, her voice still a whisper. "And neither is Sebastian—you *know* this!"

I wasn't used to seeing Zia so incensed, so on edge. If I hadn't known better, I would've thought she hated me, but she was only worried about what she and Sebastian might do to me.

"What about Harry?" I asked of Isaac.

"Absolutely not," Zia demanded.

"Look, he knows," I blurted. "He was with me when the one came to the store tonight. He saw everything and I told him what he was."

I thought Zia's eyes were going to pop out of her head. Sebastian and Nathan even stiffened.

"I *had* to." I let go of Isaac's hand and stepped in front of him. "But I didn't tell him about any of you. I haven't told him much of anything really…only about Alex."

"Don't blame Adria," Isaac said. "It's probably better if Harry be a little more on his guard around here anyway." He looked straight at Nathan as if trying to justify his words. "Viktor isn't going to stop this. It'll only get worse."

Something secretive passed between Isaac and Nathan. I saw it. Isaac knew as much.

Harry walked over and joined us then, though the conversation ended immediately.

"Ready for me to take you home?" he asked.

"Thanks, Harry," Isaac replied, "but she's going to go to our house tonight."

"That's cool," Harry said, slipping his hands inside his jean pockets. He stood in that awkward, uneasy way he always did when he felt out of place.

"Harry can come along," Daisy said, smiling hugely from beside him. "If you want to, of course."

Not even Zia could say what she was thinking. No one wanted to hurt Harry's feelings, least of all her and Sebastian. But by the looks on their faces, it was a certainty that Daisy would never hear the end of later.

"Sure, that'd be awesome," Harry replied.

"Good, it's settled then," Daisy said.

Uncle Carl crept up in my thoughts again, not that he ever left; the pain and guilt of what happened to him haunted me, and likely would forever.

Isaac took my hand and led me out of the hospital. All night I gripped my phone, worried I might put it down somewhere and miss Beverlee's call. Finally, after a couple of hours, I tucked it safely away inside the pocket of my cargo pants.

"No call from her is probably a good thing," reassured Isaac, sitting with his back against the headboard of his bed.

I sat next to him, curled up in the bend of his arm; his chin rested upon my head. "Not true," I said. "She didn't technically even call me when he was *in* the accident. I called her first."

"I'm sure she would have when she had the opportunity."

That was probably true, but I couldn't convince myself of it.

The Mayfair house was quiet for such a feral and populated haven. A few footfalls shuffled past Isaac's room; voices faint as they faded down the hallway. Zia and Sebastian were in the basement; she stayed with him when Nathan had to chain him to the floor. I would never go down there. The very thought of that place frightened me.

I moved from Isaac's bed and went to look out at the snow. The wind blew lightly against the side of the house. It hadn't snowed in hours, but what had already fallen would probably be there for days. It was quite beautiful, actually. Not some evil nuisance come to halt my life as I always thought of it before. The white glistened in the darkness, such a heavy blanket of glitter that was frail and soft. There was something mysterious and magical about snow.

Two shadows moved into the light from the porch below. They grew larger as they moved outward into the yard. Daisy and Harry, bundled in thick coats, walked side by side; tracks in the snow were left behind them, disturbing the smoothness of it. I watched until they were no longer in sight.

"Isaac?" I called, with my back to him. "Will they hunt Harry, too? Since he knows?"

"I don't know," he said, softly. "They want you because of Alex. I think Harry'll be safe as long as he doesn't let anyone know what he knows."

I stared at the footprints left in the snow. "He doesn't even know Daisy is one. How is she so casual about it?" I turned around at the waist, my arms crossed. "What if she loses control and hurts him?"

Isaac shook his head. "Daisy has complete control of her transformations. All of my sisters do, except Camilla. She's the youngest."

"Is that part of being a powerful female?"

Isaac nodded slowly in response.

"Daisy will keep Harry safe."

I turned away from him again. "Why didn't that werewolf just kill me? If they wanted me dead, or even Turned, that one could've easily done it."

The bed moved as Isaac stood up from it.

"Nathan and I have been wondering about that."

I wanted there to be more to his answer, a theory at least. Something. Their concern about it was surely what I saw pass between them earlier at the hospital.

Earlier at Finch's Grocery, everything swarmed me at once, the realities of me being what I was and Isaac being what he was. Finally, I turned around and looked Isaac hopelessly in the eyes. "No matter what," I began, "you'll outlive me, Isaac. Either I'll grow old and die, or something will end my life too short. My heart might give out and surgery will fail to repair it. Or, worst of all, I'll be Turned by someone other than you, and either die in the process, or become one of *them*." I felt the nerves in my lips jerking, my eyes watering.

Isaac, for a moment, couldn't look at me.

"I promised I'd never ask it of you," I said. "I meant that. I could never put you in that position—I wouldn't let you."

I walked away from the window and away from Isaac. Something inside me knew that what I was about to propose would require I not be near him.

"What if I get Nathan to do it?"

Isaac's eyes turned black in half a second. He rushed at me so fast I never saw him move; my back suddenly pressed against the bedroom door; my throat wedged behind his powerful hand, and though he wasn't hurting me, the breath left my lungs. With his razor-sharp teeth an inch from my face, a growl rattled Isaac's body. I froze. I couldn't move if I wanted to; my body and mind disconnected completely from one another. Isaac moved his head around in a circular motion, cracking his neck' veins bulged, pulsating, but I had to trust that he wasn't going to hurt me, that this display wasn't an act of violence, but instead, one controlling a violent trigger.

He shook it off. I felt his hand on my throat ease until finally he let go. The lids fell over his eyes, and when they opened again, the blackness was gone.

"I-I'm sorry," he said, pushing away from me. He backed farther away, punishing himself, his head lowered in shame and regret, it seemed. He went to his knees in the center of the floor.

I knelt in front of him and placed my hand on the side of his face. "You didn't hurt me, Isaac. You see?"

The pain in his face was unmistakable. He was breathing so hard. Nothing I could say was ever going to make this better.

"Please tell me," he said, "that you don't really want that."

"I don't," I admitted. "Isaac, I just don't know what to do. How am I supposed to go on like this, knowing what you are? That any future we have together is limited by my humanity?" That word, humanity, felt acidic on my tongue. I felt betrayed by destiny that I should be so different from the one I knew I would love.

I thought Isaac would cry. Everything about his face suggested it: the hardness of his eyes, and the tightness of his mouth.

The door to his bedroom opened, and Rachel stood there, smirking across at me. Isaac's head jerked up quickly, angrily, suspiciously. "Rachel," he growled, "this is a bad time."

"It's always a bad time with you." She grinned. "Isn't it?"

The girlfriend in me wanted to stand up to her, punch her in the face. The human in me kept me quiet and still.

"We overheard you talking," Rachel added. Two girls—werewolves surely—stood behind her in the hallway, their smiles just as slippery. "I thought by now you'd propose the Blood Bond to your precious human."

Isaac was on his feet so fast I hardly noticed. Rachel was sent flying backwards, slamming hard enough against the wall to crack the drywall. But she was back on her feet instantly; her defiance frightening. I didn't have to see Isaac's eyes to know they had changed colors again.

The two girls backed away, the smiles dissolving from their faces at once.

"What is she talking about?" I asked, but he didn't answer.

Without moving her head, Rachel averted her attention to me. "They say that if one survives the transformation, the other often can too. Don't know why you won't just Turn her, Isaac."

"One what?" I asked, baffled. I felt the frustration boiling inside of me.

"If you don't leave now," Isaac threatened, "my brother's approval will no longer protect you."

Rachel's eyes slowly moved back to face Isaac. Staring each other down, I got the worst feeling from the silence. I stood up carefully, but I couldn't take it anymore; I wanted answers.

"Blood Bond?" I asked, walking up to them. "Isaac, please tell me what she's talking about."

Still, he ignored me.

Rachel broke her stance first, leaving Isaac there, stiff and ready to kill her. She reached out and touched my cheek. I remained as I was, refusing to let her intimidate me anymore.

"You *are* pretty," she began, "I'll give you that much, but that's *all* you have."

My hand to Isaac's chest stopped him, but I knew he wouldn't honor my request for much longer. It was only because of me that he hadn't already killed her, that he hadn't turned into the violent, brutal creature that he was by nature.

"Rachel," I said, "what are you saying?" I really just wanted her to be honest with me, to stop playing her hateful, puzzling games for once. I hoped the sincerity was visible in my face, and I hoped she would respect it.

Her hand fell away; it had felt soft against my skin.

Nathan stood in the doorway then, and Rachel's posture changed. Still defiant as ever to Isaac, but now with less mockery. She held her chin high. The girls who had been with her had already disappeared.

"Any more of this, Rachel," Nathan warned, "and you're on your own with my brother. Do you understand?"

She didn't answer him, just gave me one last look before slithering out of the room. Nathan passed Isaac an apologetic nod before following her, shutting the door behind him.

"She's more trouble than she's worth," Isaac growled, still staring fiercely at the door.

"Isaac," I said softly, pleadingly, "what is a Blood Bond?"

Something about him seemed different suddenly. Behind the pain-stricken exterior, I saw in him, a sliver of a thought. It was faint, but just enough that it was there. His gaze met mine and it held there, suspended in time.

Then it all fell apart.

"No…" he said aloud, to himself it seemed.

He began to pace, uncertainty and fury in every step.

"Tell me, Isaac. *Please*." I approached him. "Don't do this to me. What's wrong?"

"No, I can't," he said. "I won't do it." It seemed he was arguing with himself.

"You won't do *what*?" I tried to take his hands, but he carefully pushed me away from him.

Much like he had done to me, I grabbed Isaac and pushed *him* into the wall. It barely stunned him, but he let me have my way by not rejecting it.

"You won't do *what*, Isaac?" I had had enough of these broken sentences, these secretive little topics that somehow were different, yet connected to one another.

He shut his eyes in surrender. I heard Sebastian howl from deep inside the basement again, but nothing could break this moment. Nothing.

And then Isaac said, "I think it's time you meet my father."

19

Absently, I stepped away from him, and my hands fell to my sides. He grabbed my coat from the foot of his bed and urged me to put it on.

"But—"

"No, Adria," he said, placing his hands on my cheeks, "it's the only way you'll understand any of it."

What had I done? Did I push Isaac too far with my unwavering persistence? To most girls, meeting your boyfriend's parents was a simple, possibly unnerving event. For me, it was something very different.

Isaac kissed me fully on the lips. "I need to do this," he said, and I could taste the sweetness of his breath. "You'll be safe with me. Just trust me."

"…but, why do I need my coat?" Between confusion and fear, there was no hope for me. I could hardly form a sentence anymore. All I wanted to do was stand my ground and refuse.

"He isn't here," Isaac revealed, zipping my coat up. "He's in the mountains, far away from here."

I just stood there, more baffled by the second. Isaac grabbed his car keys and then my hand. We were out the door and in his car in seconds.

"What about my uncle?" I reminded him. "I can't just leave."

"We'll be back by morning. You have your cell on you, right?"

"Yes," I replied, patting my leg pocket just to be sure.

The question was merely his way of assuring me that it was okay to leave, that the phone was my link to Beverlee.

The car trudged through the thick, undisturbed snow down the long driveway. It got easier to pass once we made it onto the main road. Only silence filled the air around us, and the sound of the heat blowing gently from the vents. Isaac watched straight ahead, focused, distressed. I could only imagine what he was thinking. No, honestly I couldn't even do that. To pretend I had any clue as to the importance of what was going on, was absurd.

I sat with my head against the car window. The world flew by outside. A blanket of glittering white surrounded by night. Houses dotted the side of the highway. An old factory rose high on the horizon, one-dimensional, like a silhouette against the night sky. Lights from 24-hour gas stations and the occasional oncoming car were the only source of light for miles. Mostly there was nothing but trees and asphalt, winding black roads with yellow lines moving eerily in my vision. I watched the stars a lot; hard not to when they were the only things that seemed attentive to me. Isaac was lost somewhere in his thoughts, so deeply I was afraid to disturb him.

At least an hour into the drive and the stars and the moon were the only light source left. Street and headlights were non-existent, like houses or anything else that signaled signs of modern life.

Finally, I fell asleep.

And I dreamt.

I was sitting at the edge of a creek with my shoes off and my feet in the water. Such a peaceful place, surrounded by spring. The smell of honeysuckle lingered in the air. I could sit here forever. Water trickled gracefully over smooth rocks in the creek's bed. I reached out and let it run through my fingers. The wind blew through my hair, ruffling the bushes nearby. The sky was never bluer; thick, cottony clouds drifted gradually in spots.

"Who are you waiting for?" asked my mother, Rhonda. She stood at the bank, her shoulder propped against a skinny tree.

I looked up. "No one."

She walked toward me, but I continued to watch my own reflection in the water. A hand touched my hair. "It's not safe for you out here, Dria."

"It's perfectly safe," I responded. "And I'm not waiting for anyone."

"What are you waiting for then?"

"I…" I paused. I was about to say that I wasn't waiting for anything, but then I thought that maybe I was, after all. "I don't know," I said, unsure. "Do you?"

I glimpsed my mother's reflection in the water too, smiling softly as she combed her fingers through my hair.

"Death," she answered.

I stood and turned to face her, but my mother was gone.

Suddenly, the cool wind turned warm on my shoulders. I looked to my left into the trees. Something was there. It felt like someone was watching me. My skin crawled all over.

"Adria." I heard Isaac's voice, and I woke up. "Come on."

Lifting my head, I peered out the window, expecting to see something other than darkness and trees. Still, nothing but darkness and trees and devouring white snow everywhere.

"Are we there?"

"Not quite," he said. "Put your coat back on. You're going to need it."

I let the disturbing dream fade from my mind. Maybe some other time I would tell Isaac about it. Or…maybe not.

"Where are we?" I wondered aloud, standing outside the car somewhere deep in the wilderness. I felt the cruel sting of cold air through my pants; my breath exhaled in puffs of smoke. Wherever we were, it was much colder here than in Hallowell. Even the snow was deeper; my boots were covered by it.

Isaac reached into the backseat, and then walked over with my canvas backpack in his hand. He positioned it over my shoulders.

"Sugarloaf," he answered. "Werewolves tend to stay deep in the mountains away from the cities. My father has an underground sanctuary about an hour from here. Can't get to it by any road."

"An *hour*?" I gazed harshly out at nothing but forest and snow and darkness. "We're going to walk an hour in *this*?" I was ready to take that stand now and refuse.

"Not exactly," he said, pulling me along.

We left the car parked on the side of the road and entered the forest.

"Isaac?" I moaned, uncertainty lacing my voice.

"We have to get away from the road," he said. "Just in case."

"In case of what?" It was difficult to walk through the thick snow, much less keep up with his much faster pace.

He stopped next to a tree stump.

"Don't be afraid," he said; he held both of my hands in his. "You trust me not to hurt you, so I'm going to trust myself because of that."

I nodded nervously, and then he began to undress. He didn't have to explain further—I knew exactly what he was about to do. My heart sped up; my legs began to shake; my stomach swam.

Isaac handed me his clothes and shoes, and then stepped backward and away from me. "Just don't move, speak, or walk towards me. Do you understand?"

I felt my head nod in quick, nervous, jerking motions as I shoved the clothes into the backpack.

Isaac gave me one last loving gaze, finally stopping his backward trek many feet away from where I stood.

His whole body jerked forward, plunging him onto the frigid, white ground. He was on his hands and knees, his head rolled up and backward, the whites of his eyes churning black. The first growl ripped through the air, echoing off every looming tree. A burning scream forced from his lungs and his body began to thrash, throwing him onto his back where he writhed in agony.

Everything told me to back away farther, every sense and emotion. But I had to be still. No movement. No words.

He leapt up then, his legs growing along with his massive body. His face contorted; I heard bones snapping, his flesh ripping. Birds sleeping in the trees above went wild and flapped their wings in a fleeing rage.

Isaac howled, standing feet taller in a dominating stance. His enormous, razor-sharp hands pulled backward. His snout heaved with hot, visible breath. He howled again and then dropped his massive head and looked right at me. I felt the perilous graze of his eyes scan over me.

No movement. No words.

Towering on two feet, Isaac approached me, his much heavier footsteps crunching the snow loudly in his wake. I trust you, I thought. I trust you…

I was terrified.

I shut my eyes tight as he got closer, his form so enormous that I felt engulfed by its shadow. I shook all over, uncontrollably, feeling his hot breath moisten the skin on my face. He was right there, an inch from me. I could hear the saliva sloshing around in his mouth, the heavy breath from his nostrils. Only when I heard a low guttural growl from deep in his chest did I slowly open my eyes. In a split second, Isaac hoisted me up and pressed me between his colossal chest and the fold of his arm.

I never saw it coming.

The whip of tree limbs thrashed against Isaac as he ran; his body protected mine. Branches and even rocks crushed hopelessly under his giant, beastly feet; rock reduced to dust. He moved so fast, covering a distance I could never possibly imagine. I had to shut my stinging eyes. The battering wind was too cold; snow from the trees pierced my face like tiny shards of glass. If it weren't for the warmth his body gave off, I would have frozen to death.

I clenched desperately to his fur, but the hold he had on me was all that I needed. His chest was rock hard; his arm I knew had a grip stronger than a boa constrictor. One slip-up and Isaac could so easily crush me like brittle bone.

We moved so fast through the mountain that I was lucky to make out anything as we raced past. The sound of water thrashing against rocks was all that I heard distinctly. I opened my eyes a crack, just in time to see the ravine out ahead. The trees ended and my heart fell into the pit of my stomach. Isaac leapt over the deep chasm and skimmed the waterfall. Only seconds felt like an eternity suspended in mid-air as I held my breath. But he covered the ravine flawlessly, landing hard on the other side. The whipping trees were back as we pressed on. One caught me, cutting a tiny slit along my cheekbone.

Finally, we stopped.

My eyes crept open as Isaac laid me on the cold ground. My hands and legs had fallen asleep. Tender ribs caught me off guard. He had held me tighter than I realized.

Isaac went to his knees and raised his head; pain reverberated in his screams. I covered my head in the snow with my arms, my breath hot in their confines. I couldn't take it anymore, seeing him in such agony. I wondered why when I saw Alex Turn she didn't show to be in as much pain as Isaac. She didn't writhe on the floor of our den. Her body didn't thrash about.

Isaac lay naked on his side, the snow around him melting from the excessive heat of his human body. I could even see the ground, wet and dark as though only touched by rain.

I ran over to him.

He reached for me, his finger running gently across the cut on my face.

"It's nothing." I pulled the backpack around and set it on the ground, rummaging through it for his clothes. "Isaac?" I said, handing him the long-sleeved shirt. "Why does it hurt you so much to Turn?"

"Because my concentration is filtered elsewhere."

He lifted and sat in an upright position, one leg bent upward to shield his nakedness. "Usually the concentration is to keep the pain to a minimum," he said, slipping on the shirt, "but making sure I don't hurt you is more important."

Next, he put on the pants, and lastly his shoes.

"The entrance is there," he said, indicating it with the tilt of his head.

I stood and turned, but saw nothing but the usual: darkness and trees.

"Right there between the rocks," he said, pointing. "Stay close."

Not until we came right upon the mouth of the entrance did I see it. And not that I had technically forgotten why he brought me here, but suddenly it plagued my mind again.

We passed the threshold and stood between the towering boulders.

"Remember," he said, taking my shoulders, "stay close to me. My father doesn't know we're here, and really, I'm not supposed to be here."

"What?" Worry twisted every muscle in my body. "But I thought—"

Isaac quickly placed his hand over my mouth. My voice had echoed down the dark passage. Wincing, I realized, and he slowly moved his hand away. "I thought you were bringing me here to meet him?" I scolded in a whisper.

He whispered back, "I did…"

Isaac paused, looking at me with warm eyes.

"Adria," he said, "do you remember what I said to you about how in one way I would be like my father?"

I thought back to that day in Vaughn Woods, remembering everything he said to me almost word for word.

"Yes…you said you would ignore the need and the warning."

He looked down and away from me. I couldn't read his emotions at all.

"I *will* ignore the need to protect you without being in your life," he began, "but in another way I will *not* be like my father. I won't…"

It seemed like a warning and a promise.

Isaac held my hand through the cold, dark tunnel underground. Wind whistled through cracks in the ceiling until we were too far away from the entrance to hear it. The passage snaked left and right, and then minutes later I felt like I was walking down a steep hill. I could see nothing, hardly even the white of my hands. But Isaac could see perfectly in the darkness; without his guide, I would've tripped many times over rocks and uneven flooring. I briefly wished I had a flashlight; a primitive fiery torch would've even been welcome.

I was beginning to feel a gnawing pain through my wet socks. My feet were thawing. I noticed that the air was getting warmer, the rosy tip of my nose no longer chilled to the touch. I could inhale with my lips parted and not feel the sting of frigid air drying and scraping my throat anymore.

We were close.

We came to the end of the tunnel. Warm firelight glowed against the cave walls in the short distance. Shadows moved along them.

There were voices.

Isaac stopped about twenty feet away. He turned to me; his hair looked darker in this light, his eyes, more fierce. "Don't speak to anyone if we're seen," he whispered. "Let me do the talking." He leaned in even closer, his expression fixed. "Those here are not like me or Nathan. They're soldiers, loyal to my father, but more beast than man."

The mere fact that Isaac seemed worried at all put me completely on edge.

He led me around the first corner where the stone and dirt hallway turned into a V. The firelight source, I was surprised to see, was my wishful primitive torches mounted along the rock walls. I peered down the left tunnel as we passed quietly; guards were posted far off in the distance. I was glad Isaac took me in the other direction. Soon we came to a section of the hallway where the rock separated. Ducking halfway, we squeezed into a hidden niche. It was a good thing I wasn't claustrophobic.

More voices reverberated through the space. Generous firelight brightened the blackness of the cave from a room just beyond. We crouched low behind a rock wall; a jagged oval-shaped opening allowed us to peer inside the room unseen. My fingers pressed against the moistness of my palms, sweating like mad from both the heat and my rattled nerves.

The room was vast, towered by rock and earth that had been carved perfectly over time. The ceiling shaped like a dome, which seemed to cradle the room beneath it. Three more entrances were visible, one just behind the long black table where a man sat at the head, a delicate woman on his lap. Guards, werewolves that wore the skin of men, stood at each entrance with swords sheathed to their backs. They were ridiculously tall even in their human form.

I was trembling. Isaac put his arm around my waist, pulling me toward him.

Six chairs were on each side of the table. Random food, and what looked like old maps and yellowish-brown paper lay strewn across the tabletop. Thick, dusty books were stacked next to candelabras—I truly felt as though I was in the wrong time.

"Milord," said a man, standing near the entrance at the other end of the table, "he is here."

The man at the head looked up from the woman. I knew the man was Trajan, Isaac's father; there was no mistaking it. He was the power in the room; when he simply moved his eyes, all attention shifted to him; he was the one I saw in the painting above the fireplace in the Mayfair house. Unapproachable and imperial. He appeared in his middle forties, rugged and unshaven, scarred and beastly, yet handsome beyond words.

Trajan didn't answer the man. And then I noticed something, something disturbing. I felt my cheeks flush under my already warmed skin. A tiny gasp of disbelief escaped my lips.

The woman sat facing Trajan, straddling his lap on the chair. The long, thin white dress she wore covered what was happening underneath it. I didn't want to look, but the shock of it forced me to. "Oh my God," I whispered, "…is she?"

Isaac nodded, but there was sadness in his face.

He began to explain, until four more men entered the room, the two in the center obviously led by the guards beside them. A dark piece of cloth lay against the front of their shirts. I recognized it as what had probably been placed over their eyes by the guards, before coming here.

One of the visitors gawked, realizing instantly what I had realized about the woman. It sickened me, to see this man so excited by a seemingly sad sex act. I don't know why it was sad, but it loomed in my heart. Maybe Isaac's expression rubbed off on me, or maybe it was the woman. Something about her, even though I could barely see the side of her face, was tragic. There was no emotion in her except for sorrow and emptiness.

I had to shake it off.

Trajan carefully took the back of the woman's head carefully into his giant hand. Pressing his lips against her forehead, he whispered something to her.

I was completely confused.

Trajan, this man of total domination and power, a werewolf known to be cruel and deadly, *respected* the woman. No—he *loved* her...

Another woman stepped out of the shadow near the exit behind Trajan's chair. She took the woman's hand and led her out, leaving Trajan free to the visitors.

"Nothing says power," the gawking visitor began, "like having whores at one's disposal."

No time at all for me to quietly display my disgust, Trajan was out of the high-back chair, pressing the man against the stone wall. Every guard in the room stiffened, one hand raised to the handle of their swords. The quiet visitor withdrew, feeling for the exit behind him, only to be grabbed by one of the guards who brought him here.

Trajan held violently to the man's throat. Rage had become him. The muscles in his neck thickened and pulsated, the glint of his eyes were golden in the light of the fire. Gold on black and fury.

Isaac held me tighter. I was shaking all over.

Without a word, Trajan crushed the man's neck in his hand. I felt my heart stop, literally, for two seconds. Vomit churned in my stomach as the man's neck fell over to one side, dangling grotesquely. The tongue lolled out of the corpse's mouth so unnaturally, so horrific. Tears burned the edges of my eyes.

"I s-swear to you—" the other visitor had started to say.

Trajan stepped into the man's space, his hands balled into fists at his sides. Tilting his head to one side, he said calm and dangerously,

"Innocent and precious is the beloved that your friend so foolishly insults." He tilted his head to the other side. "Do you share his views?"

The man shook his head rapidly. "N-No…" The guard holding him jerked his body forward, forcing him into a deep, painful bow. The man screamed out and grimaced under the pressure. "I m-mean…n-no, Milord," he corrected himself.

Trajan walked gradually back to his chair. He looked across at the man, brought one hand out from behind his back and gestured. "Sit," he said, just before sitting himself.

The man took the chair, his body shaking worse than mine was. A lone candle sitting in a silver tray fell over onto its side as his fumbling hands grazed it. Apologizing profusely, the man picked the candle up before it caught a stack of papers afire.

"What information," Trajan started, "do you have for me?" He never looked at the man; it seemed the man was not worthy of such a gesture. Instead, Trajan began scanning a nearby text.

"Viktor," the man began, "he has—"

Trajan put up his hand, and the man stopped cold; worry plagued his expression; his eyes grew wide with dread; his face stricken pale and nauseous.

Then Trajan looked in *our* direction, and I gasped.

He *knew*.

I slid down, sitting fully on the dirt floor, praying silently. "Isaac," Trajan said, his deep voice echoing, "go to my chamber and take the Dawson sister with you."

Isaac stood carefully from our not-so-secret spot behind the rock wall. He held his hand out to me, but it took a moment for me to gather the courage to accept it.

"Adria," he said to Trajan. "That is her name, Father."

Was he *insane*? I froze, all except for my hand, which tightened around his in alarm. Isaac's comment wasn't a correction—I think even he knew that would be unwise—it was merely an introduction, a dangerous introduction that could so easily go the wrong way if one syllable was out of place. Being the son definitely had its advantages.

Trajan nodded so lightly that it was almost as if he never moved his head. He sat with his elbows resting on the table, his fingers touching in a steeple.

The frightened man gawked at me from across the cave room. It felt intrusive. "Forgive me," he said to Trajan, "but is that the sister? The one who—" The man swallowed the rest of his words and slunk back into the chair—the simple threatening turn of Trajan's head was enough to steal his voice from him.

"Leave now," Trajan demanded Isaac.

"Yes, Father."

Isaac bowed halfway and pulled me through the room toward the exit behind Trajan's chair. I didn't want to go that way; for a second I felt my feet become heavier. But Isaac kept me closest to the cave wall, away from the man's reach…away from his father's reach.

Every ravenous eye in that room was on me, except for Trajan's. I could feel them all, like tiny spotlights alerting hunters of my whereabouts. And though Trajan was not looking, he was the one I feared the most.

We slipped into the tunnel and made our way through the torch lit hall.

"Is he going to kill me?"

"No," said Isaac, as we turned a corner.

"What was that man talking about?" I asked in a hurry. "The sister who *what*?" The hallway snaked around another corner, and then we descended a set of makeshift stone stairs. "Isaac? I've got a bad feeling about it."

"So do I," he said, pulling me along.

We came to another room where four guards, three on each side, were posted at the entrance. Like the ones in the room we just left, they were giants; I felt like an insect standing before them.

"Isaac, you shit," said the one closest to the tall wooden door. "What are you doing here?" He glanced over at me, inspecting me. He raised his head and sniffed the air—they seemed to do that a lot, I noticed. "Human. Ah, I see," he said, with a disturbing grin. "Come to show her what it's like, have you?"

Isaac was not amused.

"You know it's forbidden to speak of her, Raul."

The werewolf smiled a big, toothy smile. It was an odd way to apologize.

Raul stepped aside to let us pass.

Isaac closed the door softly behind us. The room smelled of flowers and scented oils. There were so many candles placed throughout that the room was bright with intimate light. The space was enormous. A giant bed sat centered against the stone wall; the most delicate fabric dressed it lavishly. Great pillows, large enough to sleep on themselves, laid out across the floor. A desk and a sofa sat against one wall, a claw foot bathtub against another, where three women sat on short wooden stools in front of it. Two more women stood to the left of me, one holding a white robe. All of them were dressed the same: black gowns, their heads covered by thin black veils. They were servants.

20

I HEARD THE SOUND OF TRICKLING WATER. ANOTHER SERVANT knelt near the bathtub; steam rose up out of the water, swirling around to veil her face briefly. The woman who had been in Trajan's lap sat blankly inside the tub, her dainty white arms resting along the sides. Briefly, I wondered where they drew the water from to fill the bath.

A servant bowed deeply in front of Isaac.

"Shall we leave you to her, Milord?"

All of the proper addressing of titles and such was foreign to me.

"No," said Isaac. "I won't be here long."

She bowed once more and then went back to stand where she was before.

The woman rose from the bathtub; water ran smoothly down her pale, lithe form; her semi-dry hair flowed to the center of her back. She was human—I was sure of it. But she was…different; frail and innocent beyond my comprehension. In my heart, I knew that no part of her was capable of savagery.

A servant dressed the woman, slipping another white gown over her body. It seemed the woman did little on her own: another servant had to lift her arms for her, while a third brushed out her hair from behind.

Then the strange woman looked across at me; it felt as though she was staring right through me. I felt like I was in Isaac's dream again, but I was the one watching through the trees. I was the ghost, and she wasn't aware I was there.

"Who is she?" I whispered to Isaac. I never took my eyes off the woman. She was beautiful and soft, pure beyond words. Pure. Yes, that was the perfect words to describe her.

Isaac's breath tickled my earlobe. "She is Aramei, my father's wife. She is his soul."

Softly stunned, I could only stare at her for several long minutes. Aramei wasn't a child, after all.

Two servants led Aramei to the bed where she sat on her own. Still, the act of sitting seemed only achieved due to repetition. Nothing in her face suggested she even knew where she was.

I felt sorry for her.

Lacing my arm around Isaac's, I asked, "What's wrong with her? Is she sick?"

"No," he answered, absently. "It's the price she and my father pay for her immortality."

I stopped blinking. "Immortal? How?"

"The Blood Bond." Isaac walked with me toward Aramei. Reluctance weighed my feet down again, but this time for a different reason: I worried Aramei might be scared of *me*.

She didn't stir.

I realized, as I got closer, that Aramei was the woman in the painting with Trajan.

"It's a sad story," Isaac said.

He sat down on the end of the bed. I sat next to him though I felt I was being disrespectful.

I watched the servants tend to Aramei while he told me the story.

"There was a war between my father's clan and Viktor Vargas', many years ago in the Carpathians. My father was wounded on the battlefield and he woke up in a barn in one of the nearby villages. Wounded so badly, he wasn't strong enough to shift back into his human form."

A servant lit two more candles on the bedside, while another rubbed Aramei's skin with scented oil.

"Aramei, the poor daughter of a fisherman, found him in the barn."

"While he was in his werewolf form?" I couldn't imagine being her and seeing something like that.

"Yes," Isaac said. "And she wasn't afraid of him; not like a human should be anyway. She pulled the swords from his chest and back. She even sewed the gash on his throat. My father could have killed her. In fact, when we're wounded severely enough that death is a possibility, blood is the one thing that can sustain and heal us. But my father was powerful even then and could control his rages, and the pain."

Aramei lay against the pillows on her side. A servant covered her middle body with a silk sheet. Her feet were so delicate, so small.

"If she were anyone else," Isaac continued, "my father would have killed her without a thought. He almost died himself because he couldn't do it."

"He fell in love with her."

"Yes. He did."

The servant stroked Aramei's hair and face softly as a mother would do to her child.

"When he was healed enough to shift," Isaac went on, "he wouldn't shift because he didn't want to scare her—I know that sounds dumb, but—"

"I know why," I interrupted. "Trajan was afraid if she saw him shift into a man, it would be too overwhelming."

Isaac nodded slowly. "A beast is one thing, but a beast that is also a man is many things. He left one day and couldn't ever go back. He knew that just being near her would sooner than later only get her killed."

Isaac looked into my eyes. I knew what he was thinking. He was thinking about me being human, about the danger he posed. And I found it disturbingly beautiful how similar mine and Aramei's stories were, that I would meet the real Isaac wounded in a barn, too.

He turned away.

"A few years later," he continued, "Viktor's men were ravaging villages and Turning the men. He wanted an army that could defeat my father's. Aramei's village was one of them. By the time my father made it there, her family had been killed or Turned. He found Aramei lying in the woods, bloody and dying, but she hadn't been infected."

Isaac took a deep breath, watching Aramei.

She shut her eyes.

"My father fed her his blood, bonding her to him," he revealed.

The dancing candles cast shadows upon the walls. The light dimmed slightly as a servant gently blew the candles out near the bathtub.

Isaac turned back to me with severity in his face. "Our blood, male werewolf blood, will protect a human from age and disease. It can heal grave wounds and ward off sickness. It'll make them immortal. Though just like us, a human can still be killed."

It was the answer to everything, this Blood Bond. My mind was running a million miles a second.

"Milord," said a servant, "will you be sleeping with Milady this evening?"

A weird lump caught just below my throat suddenly. I stopped blinking again.

"No," Isaac told the servant. "Adria and I will be leaving soon. You can lay with her until my father comes."

Isaac placed his hand on my leg and turned back to me.

"The price," he continued, "of her immortality, is her mind. Aramei hasn't been herself for at least two hundred years. She knows only my father, and few people can be left with her." He glanced at Aramei and then back at me. "She can never be left alone. Tonight you've seen her calm, emotionless. But sometimes she goes into uncontrollable episodes. Sometimes she cries and hurts herself. Other times she's violent toward others. You never know what it's going to be."

"That's awful…"

As Aramei lay there sleeping, I saw nothing but peace in her. I couldn't imagine her any other way.

"But why was she…on Trajan's lap like that?" I had to ask. It was obvious Aramei was no 'whore' like that stupid man had said; but I couldn't understand the relationship between her detached personality, and what I saw at the table.

Isaac's gaze strayed toward the floor, his posture suggesting pity and regret.

"She's barren," he said, lamentably. "The blood made her barren. She had been trying to give my father a child since before the blood started taking its toll on her mind. Her thoughts, they sort of…stuck that way. My father will never tell her she can't have children. Her mind is too fragile. He'll do anything for her; let her have her way with him whenever and wherever she feels the need."

After a moment he added, "My father is her life, as she is his. If one of them died, the other would follow."

It was the most heartbreaking thing I'd ever heard.

It was also a devastating end to my so-called answer to everything. I stood carefully from the bed and watched Aramei from afar; my hand cupped my mouth and nose.

A servant curled up next to her, stroking her hair; Aramei was like an angel laying there.

Isaac moved in front of me, taking my hands away from my face. "Now do you see why I can't do it?" The way he said it, with such devotion, crippled me. I put my hands to my eyes, trying hopelessly to wipe away the steady stream of tears. "Adria, you *have* to be the way you are. I'll never risk killing you with the Change. And like my father, I'll keep you in my life, but *unlike* him, I'll never leave you to *her* fate."

My tears won. They kept coming. Isaac crushed me devotedly against him. I could hear his heart beating so fast. I knew I was going to have to accept the way things were, that Isaac and I would not be forever.

The giant wooden door came open softly; Trajan stood in the doorway. He wore a dusty old black leather trench coat with no shirt underneath. I tried not to look, but couldn't help but notice how muscular his chest was, though not as scarred as I would have imagined.

"Adria Dawson," Trajan said in a calm, low voice, which still managed to frighten me. "The one to win my son's heart." He let the door close as he walked into the room. I saw his gaze fall on Aramei as she slept. I could tell that even after a few hundred years, his love for her had not withered an ounce.

"Father, I had to bring her here."

Isaac never let go of me.

"Your reasoning," said Trajan, "is what disturbs me the most."

Isaac glanced over at Aramei. "It was important that she know."

All of the servants scurried out of the room, leaving Aramei alone in the bed. She stirred just slightly, but that seemingly normal movement caught Trajan's vigilance.

"Yes," Trajan admitted. "It is important that she know because you feel that she must be given a choice." A hidden pain lay quiet in his face.

I spoke up. "She...Aramei, I mean, didn't have a choice, did she?"

Trajan looked at me; another seemingly normal movement, but it meant so much more coming from him: Either I had offended him by speaking of Aramei, or I was worthy of the gesture.

"No, Adria," he said, still composed. "I was selfish. I took everything from her. Death would have been kinder."

"That's not true," I said, pulling out of Isaac's embrace. "She would've wanted you to do it, because she loved you that much."

Trajan and Isaac locked eyes.

"And how would you know that?" Trajan asked of me.

Isaac moved to stand behind me, resting his hands around my arms. "Because I'm falling in love Isaac, and because I don't want to be without him, or him without me, *ever*."

Silent words passed between them.

Trajan turned away. I could feel Isaac's hands get warmer against my skin. He kissed my hair.

"As long as I am the Alpha," said Trajan, now approaching Aramei on the bed, "there will be no Blood Bonds. If my son goes against me, you will both regret it."

I said nothing in response, and Isaac knew better.

Aramei's eyes opened carefully and she gazed up at Trajan. She reached out a delicate hand to him. Trajan leaned over, placing his arms underneath her small body and lifting her into them. He held her like a child. She draped her arms around his neck and rested her head against his naked chest.

Like in the previous room, Trajan whispered something to her, which I could not hear. I knew they had to be words of love and affection.

He sat on the bed with her in his arms.

"Onto other matters," Trajan announced. "Seems our skittish little visitor out there told me something quite interesting." He turned to see Isaac, and then me. "Something you both should know."

"What is it, Father?"

Aramei lifted slightly and turned to sit upright facing Trajan. She wrapped her bare legs around his waist and laid her head back down against his chest.

I was just glad that was *all* she wanted to do.

Trajan's giant arms enveloped her tiny frame.

"Viktor Vargas has found a potentially strong female in which to make his mate," said Trajan.

"I feel sorry for her," said Isaac, "whoever she is. Why does that matter, anyway?"

"Because your girl there," Trajan said, nodding once toward me, "is the one he wants."

Isaac's body jerked around; eyes already churning black like oil; it felt like the oxygen had been sucked right out of the room. "*What?*" His voice growled and echoed.

"Calm," demanded Trajan—I thought he would come off the bed with churning black eyes, too. "Never here, Isaac. *Never* in front of her." He held Aramei closer.

Isaac calmed, as much as he could. I, however, was as far away from calm as I could be.

"Why would he choose me?" I asked.

"Because your sister survived," Trajan revealed. "And because siblings are almost always alike in that way."

"That's why they haven't harmed you," Isaac growled, pacing. "It's why Viktor called Sibyl off the night in the barn, too. Why didn't I *see* this?" He balled his fists.

I was in shock; I couldn't say anything.

"But Viktor could've done it already," Isaac said to his father. "He's had opportunities: the barn; even one night at The Cove, Viktor was there, feet from her."

Isaac was enraged; I stayed far away from him, letting him pace furiously back and forth.

"He wants her to be willing," said Trajan. "Her sister was supposed to bring her first, and when that didn't work, he sent others to scare her."

"*Oh no*…The bastard used my *uncle* to threaten me." The realization hit me hard. I was even more the reason Uncle Carl was in the hospital than I knew.

Remembering I had my phone on me, I reached inside my pocket and yanked it out, desperate to check on my uncle. No signal. That was no surprise, considering.

Trajan looked at me. "Adria," he said, "your family is safer without you there."

"But Father," said Isaac, "what am I supposed to do? I will kill every last one of them."

"And I don't doubt that you're capable," Trajan replied. "But Viktor is the one who wants her, and he is also the one you cannot defeat."

Isaac raised his fist and sent it crashing down on the desk against the wall, breaking it in half; splintered wood, papers, and other items flew up and around him before scattering about the floor. My breath caught and I froze, only my eyes moving to see if Trajan was going to get up from the bed with reprimand. But he remained calm, holding Aramei as if she was all that mattered.

"Viktor Vargas will soon be dealt with," he said.

Isaac turned swiftly. "I'm sure you said that to your men three hundred years ago."

I never even saw Trajan place Aramei onto the bed; he was kneeling over Isaac, gripping Isaac's throat, crushing him against the rock floor. A picture of the man I watched die earlier in an eerily similar predicament flashed through my head.

I screamed. "Please! Please don't..." I rushed over and knelt, my knees touching Isaac's head. I didn't care if it would be the last thing I did. One hand held Isaac around the chin, the other I put up in front of Trajan pleadingly. "*Please...*" More tears streamed down my face.

Slowly, Trajan's haunting figure rose and stood tall over us. With his back to us now, Trajan said to Isaac, "One day you yourself will know the perils of being an Alpha."

Isaac got up from the floor; if he was in any pain, he wasn't showing it.

"Forgive me, Father," he said. "I'm—"

"You are your father's son," Trajan said, proudly. He inspected Aramei once more, and then turned around to face Isaac again. "Adria is strong," he said. "I can smell it on her: the control, the impending power." His voice got lower. It was as if he didn't want me to hear, yet it wasn't entirely a whisper.

"You might have to do it yourself, before Viktor does."

Isaac shook his head and stepped back, letting his father's hand fall away from his shoulder.

Aramei lifted from the bed, the silk sheet barely covering her. "Vukašin," she called out, using his real name, but the rest I couldn't make out. She was speaking in a different language. Trajan went over to her, cradling her head in his giant hands, and kissing her eyelids.

"Until I go back to Serbia," Trajan said, as Isaac led me toward the door, "I will be staying here with Aramei. I won't risk her with Viktor and his vendetta."

"And what about Adria?" Isaac asked, stopping at the exit.

"My men and I will do with Viktor what is decided when that time comes," he began. "But as Aramei is to me, Adria must be to you. An Alpha protects his own. It is the way it has always been."

As promised, Isaac had me back in Hallowell by morning. I had fallen asleep during the long drive. All that had happened, emotionally and physically exhausted me.

I saw someone die. I couldn't decide if my lack of caring was affecting me the wrong way. It worried me.

When we arrived back at the Mayfair house the shrouded sun was just barely rising over the vast blanket of white. Cold and gray would be this day too, even with sunlight; I knew because I could feel it, like when you know it was about to rain.

Isaac guided me up to his room. He straightened and fluffed his bedding for me so I could go back to sleep. I felt him cover me gently, just to my waist.

He went to leave; his footsteps quiet across the floor.

"Isaac," I said, holding out my hand, "stay with me."

He paused, but only long enough to know that I meant it. I wasn't ready for anything more, but having him next to me already felt natural. I needed him. We needed each other.

I fell fast asleep curled up in his arms, and I never slept as soundly as I had that day. I was in more danger than most humans could possibly imagine, yet in Isaac's arms, I felt completely at peace.

21

The cell phone vibrating against my leg woke me. I crept awake, a little disoriented. 1:42 p.m. showed next to Beverlee's name. I answered quickly.

"Carl is doing better," she said. "You can visit him this evening. Are you with Harry?"

"That's so great," I said, with relief. "I was so worried. No, ummm…" I glanced down at Isaac lying next to me. "No, I stayed at Zia's place."

"That's okay," she said. "In Zia's room, right?" she added skeptically.

"Definitely."

"All right, hon, if you need me to come pick you up to bring you to the hospital, just call me."

"I will. I love you, Aunt Bev."

I knew she was smiling on the other end. "I love you too."

Isaac opened his eyes as I reached over and laid my phone on the nightstand. I had the feeling maybe he wasn't sleeping after all.

"Uncle Carl is going to be fine."

He smiled softly at me and then brought me back into the fold of his arms.

"That's awesome." Then he sighed heavily and pulled me closer. I buried my head under his chin. "Now we just have to figure out how to keep you away from them without making it seem like you're abandoning them."

There was a tiny knock at the door.

"Yeah?" Isaac said.

Zia peeked her white-blond head around the corner.

"Safe to come in?"

"It is," Isaac answered.

She practically tiptoed inside as if still unsure whether she was intruding upon something.

I smiled across at her. "It's all right," I said. "Don't get any ideas."

Zia snickered and plopped down on the end of the bed.

"You two have been asleep all day. What'd you do last night?"

Isaac sat up straight. I stayed curled up next to him. "I took Adria to see my father."

"Oh." Zia's smile was replaced by a more serious expression. "You mean Aramei?"

I felt Isaac nod next to me.

Zia looked sadly at me then. "Tragic, isn't it?"

I didn't want to answer, but my face did it for me.

"Well"—Zia slapped her palms against her jeans—"that's none of my business. I guess you're both too tired then to go skiing with us, huh?"

I rose finally. "I'd love to, but I need to go see my uncle later."

"I'll be taking her to the hospital," Isaac answered. "She'll be forced to endure me looming over her pretty much everywhere from now on."

Forced? Hardly.

"I'll need to talk to Nathan, Seth and Xavier, too," he added. "Father told me that Viktor wants Adria as his mate."

Zia's body went rigid, pushing her instantly to her feet; her mouth formed the letter O.

"It's true," Isaac said. "But I won't go into it right now. Not again." He combed his fingers through my hair. "Just tell my brothers if you see them before I do, that the circumstances have changed."

"Okay, I will," Zia agreed.

She lightened up then, though her bright smile seemed forced. I sort of felt like a little girl shielded from all the bad words and bad people. But that was okay. For now.

"I probably should tell you," Zia said to me, "Daisy and Harry really hit it off. He's still here; passed out on the sofa in the den."

"Wow, seriously?"

"Yep," Zia said. "I'm almost jealous!"

I laughed. Isaac eased his way out of our girly conversation and went to change his shirt. I couldn't help but watch. He was perfect, even though his sculpted chest was scarred; I even noticed a large birthmark along his ribs. He had 'flaws' and that was why he was so perfect to me.

"Girl, you're not even listening to me!" Her mouth and eyes were wide with over-exaggerated shock.

Isaac secretly smiled across at me. He knew I had been watching him instead of listening to Zia.

Blushing, I turned back to her. "Sorry, I was just—"

"Distracted?" She grinned. "I'm glad your uncle is doing better," she said, changing the subject from whatever she had been going on about before.

"Thanks," I said, as she hugged me.

"Who all is going skiing?" Isaac asked.

"Sebastian, my brothers, Harry and Daisy," she said. "That's all I know so far. Y'know, I've never been skiing before. I kind of like Maine; except for the trouble that came shortly before us."

"Don't get too comfortable here," Isaac said. He slipped on a pair of socks and slid his feet down into a pair of black Doc Martens. "Depending on how this all turns out, we may be moving again."

Zia's face fell, but when she placed her hand on the door and looked back at me one last time, she was smiling again. "See yah later, Dria," she said, before slipping out of the room. She called me Dria, like my sister used to. It kind of made me feel good.

"What was that supposed to mean, about moving?" I was still on the center of the bed, sitting with my knees drawn up to my chest.

Isaac leaned over me, easily lifting me into his arms, my legs wrapped around his waist. I draped my hands on his shoulders; he kissed one arm, and then the other.

"I don't know how any of this is going to turn out," he said. "I have no idea what we're going to do about Viktor, and that worries me. It's why a meeting with my brothers is imperative."

"But if you move?"

"If *I* move?" he challenged. "If *we* move, Adria. I would never leave you here, or anywhere. It's too dangerous."

I started to speak, but he hushed me with a peck on the jaw line. "I know you don't want to leave your family; and I would never ask you to do that, not even for me, but it may be the only thing that saves them."

My head fell in despondency.

"I know," he whispered, trying to console me. "We'll figure it out."

"I know we will," I said, raising my chin.

We rode around for a while to waste time before visiting hours at the hospital. Spent an hour at Harvey's Coffee Shop, and then drove into Augusta. I wanted to get something nice for Uncle Carl, and flowers just seemed weird. We ended up at a bookstore where I bought *On the Shoulders of Giants: The Great Works of Physics and*

Astronomy by Stephen Hawking. Uncle Carl loved science; I just knew that it would be the best gift ever.

When I saw him lying in the bed, I tried not to think of how he looked last night. It was hard not to; all the same machines were still hooked up to him, even an extra one that I refused to ask Aunt Bev about. I didn't come here for that. I came to see my uncle getting better, and to make him smile seeing my awesome gift-picking abilities.

He couldn't smile when he saw it. He couldn't even hold it and flip through the pages. I guess I hadn't thought about any of that. I imagined him ripping open the bag, lifting it out and turning it this and that way. I imagined the biggest grin across his face as he read the book details.

None of that happened.

His car had been totaled. He almost died when at first he seemed to be stable. And I would never forget that it was all because of me. Even being in his car at that very moment was because of me. If only he hadn't gone to Augusta to adopt a dog *for me*, he wouldn't have been on that road. And even if the dog was out of the picture, Uncle Carl was still in his car to check on *me* at Finch's.

Me, me, me.

Beverlee came over and stood beside me.

"I know he loves the book, Adria," she said. "The doctor said Carl's going to be here for a while. I'll be home as much as I can; I've even talked to my sister about coming to stay with us so you won't be by yourself so much."

I just let her talk. I didn't have it in me to say much about anything in return. Nothing mattered really, anyway.

She knelt in front of me, placing her hand on top of mine. "He's going to be okay."

I smiled weakly, giving her the okay to stop worrying about me and my feelings. The smile was totally fake, of course, but as long as she didn't know that.

Isaac had been waiting for me out in the waiting room.

"Let's go to your house and get some of your things," he said.

The sun had set while I was with Beverlee. I recalled it getting darker outside from the hospital room window. It was also snowing again, but only light flurries. The ride to my house was quiet. All I could think about were things that required every bit of my attention, things that sucked any happiness from me that might've been there. Isaac left me alone; I guess he felt I needed the time to think, to grieve.

Pulling up into my driveway, I saw that the porch light wasn't on. I never noticed before how eerie that old house was in the dark, even though I'd seen it a hundred times just like that.

Isaac put the car in park.

"Are you okay, Adria?" He turned sideways, one arm resting on the steering wheel.

"Yeah, I'll be fine."

"You will be, or you are?"

Leaning across the seat, I pressed my lips gently to his cheek, just under his eye. "I am," I said. "I wouldn't be if you weren't here, though. Thank you."

A smile softened his face.

I placed my hand on the door handle of the car, and abruptly Isaac grabbed me.

"Stop," he demanded, smelling deeply of the air; his eyes darted around apprehensively.

Suddenly, Isaac threw the car back in drive and slammed on the gas. My body lurched forward and then backward, thrusting me harshly against the seat. I fumbled for the seatbelt, but couldn't get it on. The car swerved through the snow, mud, and slush, tossing me sideways.

"Isaac!"

"Hold on!" he shouted.

I braced myself against the dashboard, one foot pressing on the door. *Slam! Clunk!* The hood of the car caved in. Steam and anti-freeze whistled and spewed from the wreckage. The car was dead. Black eyes and dripping teeth bore down on us through the windshield. I screamed. My body pressed so hard against the seat I felt it jump the track forcibly and fall backward.

The windshield crumbled into a thousand nugget-like pieces of glass. The beast's head entered the opening and roared, blood and thick saliva dripped from its blade-like teeth. I managed to get into the back seat, cowering low halfway into the floorboard.

I heard a *pop!* and then a long, grating sound as Isaac's seat pushed backward and snapped completely off its tracks. I moved over just in time before it crushed me. Isaac's door flew off, landing feet away in the snow. Another deafening roar ripped through the car, and Isaac, massive and beastly, burst through what was left of it. The wreckage tossed with me in it; I held onto the back of the front seat; trees and white ground flip-flopped in my vision many times before the car landed upside-down. Snow cushioned one side of my face, the roof of the car pressed against the other; the taste of blood filled my mouth, and I could feel something hard and cold penetrate my side. At first, no pain followed, but then a burst of pain surged through my body like an electric shock.

I tried to call out for Isaac, but it seemed my voice was gone. A giant mass of gangly black fur and gnashing teeth skidded across the ground in my limited line of sight. I tried desperately to pull myself out of the car, dragging my body forward with…I didn't know with what—maybe I wasn't moving at all. Maybe I wasn't really there. Something wasn't right.

I could see the deadly fight, the torn flesh; I could see the dark red stain on the bright white snow. My vision went in and out. More than two werewolves? I wasn't sure. I heard voices in my head, not my ears, but my head. I couldn't make out what they were saying, but I knew they were talking to me. The voices were familiar, but intuition told me they were not real. I saw my mother's face. She was so beautiful, like she used to be before she met Jeff and let herself go. She held out her hand to me, and in it, the tiny ceramic cat she gave me when I was six.

It fell from my fingers and shattered on the sidewalk.

I saw her lips move to tell me not to cry, that she would glue it back together; but I only heard her voice in my head.

The car jerked violently, and my eyes sprang open, though they might not have ever been shut. The sound of metal ripping apart should've been much louder, but something muffled everything around me. I felt my cheek lift away from the coldness of the snow. I could've sworn in a glance that I saw a naked woman lying dead; hair as black as paint contrasted heavily against the snow around her.

The voices were back. Alex was there with me. No, not really there. At first, I thought she was. I thought she came to help me, but she stood in the field outside our house in Georgia. The grass came up to her ankles. I took her hand and she helped me up. The sun was bright over the Georgia sky, but the wind was mild and it wasn't so hot. I saw the house had been painted. No longer did I live in a dirty speck in a green, treeless pasture.

"Drink it," Alex urged, holding out a cup of water. Words actually came from her lips. "I drew it from the creek for you. It'll be hot soon."

The creek? There was no creek by our house. But I reached out my hands and took the cup from her anyway. And I drank.

Was I dreaming? I *had* to be. Where was Isaac?

Suddenly, I was running fast and hard through the field with Alex close behind. We were laughing hysterically. I never felt so happy, so free. And when I saw the horses out ahead I ran straight for them. At a safe distance, I stopped, out of breath; my hands propped upon my knees to keep my balance. Alex ran up from behind.

"You think they'll…let us ride them?" She was also out of breath.

Time moved forward, jumping ahead in strange jerking intervals. Alex went toward the horses. Closer. Closer. I noticed that as she got closer, I stood farther away by hundreds of feet. Alex waved at me from afar, smiling so hugely. I waved back with the same smile, but my heart doubted her.

"Adria," said another familiar voice. "He's coming…he's coming, Adria."

This voice was echoing from somewhere else, from where I was truly supposed to be.

This field wasn't real…

The horses reared up. Alex was no longer my human sister. She took one horse down and devoured it. I cried out in horror and felt my feet run toward her of their own accord. "No!" I shouted; rage filled every part of me.

By the time I made it there, Alex was gone.

The field was covered in snow, the sky gray and frigid, dominated by thick winter clouds. The horse lay dead in a pool of blood. I fell to the ground beside it; blood and snow soaked up in my hair. And I just lay there, staring out at the endless nothing until the dream became nothing and everything went black.

22

The heat of a fire warmed my skin. It crackled softly somewhere nearby. So weak, at first I couldn't even open my eyes; my body drained of energy, and sore beyond tolerance. I could still smell the offensive stench of blood. But it wasn't my own. My blood could never smell like that. My blood was human. Some kind of cloth lay beneath me. My feet were bare and I could tell I wore clothes that were not mine, either. Thin. A nightgown maybe.

I opened my eyes a slither. Viktor Vargas sat at a table in the room, watching me.

Had my nightmare gotten worse? No, this was real. I would have preferred to lie in that bloody field and die with the horse, than to be here.

My first instinct was to try to run, but I was too weak. I shut my eyes and hoped that it would all be over soon, that he would infect me with his...disease, and the transformation would kill me quickly.

Isaac, I thought.

I was strong enough to lift my shoulders suddenly.

"Where is he?" I demanded, weakly. "Where's Isaac?"

Viktor strolled over and sat beside me. I shrank back against the wall. "Get away from me," I lashed out. "You sick bastard!"

He was unfazed.

A woman walked in. Familiar. I hated the cunning of her walk, and the way she looked at me; a venomous smile tugged the corners of her lips.

"Isaac," she said. "He almost had me—such a strong boy. That part he got from me, of course."

"Sibyl," I spat.

She looked mildly surprised, until I realized it was sarcasm. "Oh," she said, "he told you about me, did he?"

The dead, naked woman—a flash of memory raced through my mind: she was the one I saw lying in the snow…

Sibyl walked toward the fireplace, a skin-tight dress hugged her voluptuous curves and dragged the floor behind her. How could someone so hateful, so vile, be so stunning? Just like the monster that sat near me. He was calm and mysterious. I hated them both.

"My son," Sibyl said, prodding the fire with a poker, "will make quite the Alpha one day—"

"So then he's alive?"

Sibyl rose up, grinning over at me. "He'll make quite the Alpha one day…*if he lives*."

What was that supposed to mean? Was it a threat, or was it a prediction based on something that had already happened? I felt the tears rushing up from behind my eyes. I looked at Viktor who confused me more and more as he just sat there, listening to us.

Finally, Viktor spoke: "Sibyl," he said, his voice deep and abrasive, "bring food and drink for our guest."

I would've thought someone just asked her to wash their feet; her thin hands dropped to her sides and her face went cold and mystified.

"Why would you treat this one as so?" she asked, as she stepped closer. "Give her to the sister and be done with it. It is Alexandra's duty to kill her. Those were the requirements of her initiation, her so-called *unwavering* loyalty."

I felt my body jerk forward, but I couldn't go anywhere. I couldn't move; every bone suddenly attacked by pain. I lay back completely against the pillow.

Viktor pressed his hand to my chest. "No one will harm you." He turned back to Sibyl. "She was not brought here for that reason." He stood and approached her, authority in every step. He grazed the side of her face with his fingertips.

Sibyl shut her eyes softly and breathed in deep, taking in his sadistic scent. "Then why is she here?"

Viktor didn't answer. His silence did that for him.

"You *wouldn't*," she ripped out the words, and took two steps away from him, her face overcast with revulsion. "You mean to *receive* her?"

Still, Viktor did not speak. Sibyl looked at him one last time, and then left angrily.

"I know what you want," I said, and he turned around. "You're crazy if you think I'll let you. Now tell me what happened to Isaac!"

The sound of his boots went across the wooden floor slowly.

Where was I? There was no window in the room. I needed an idea so that I could figure out how to get away.

"I left him where I found him," Viktor answered.

"Please just tell me; is he alive?" My heart was breaking; I wanted to cry and throw up at the same time, but I could do neither.

No answer.

"Was that you who attacked us in the car?"

Viktor laughed lightly. "You offend me," he said, with a twinge of humor. "I am an Alpha Elder, over four hundred years old. Sibyl's size could never compare to mine."

It didn't surprise me that it was Isaac's mother who attacked us, who nearly killed both of us yet again.

"You were severely wounded in that car," he said. "Lucky to be alive, I must say."

Keeping my attention on Viktor's every move, I also tried to examine myself. My arms and legs were blue and purple. A finger-length gash on my shin had been cleaned and stitched up. My back was sore, and something protruded through the thin nightgown below my ribcage. I touched it. More stitches. A burning pain shot through me.

"And it was because of Isaac that you were almost killed in that car," he said.

I felt the side of the bed move as he sat down again. I didn't want to look at him, but I did anyway.

"No, it was because of *you*."

Viktor smiled. "Isaac shifted inside the car with you in it, Adria. Neither I, nor Sibyl did anything to harm you. Isaac is young. He'll not be able to control the Change all the time." He moved a strand of hair from my face, and added, "And you see how well he can protect you."

Disgusted, I jerked my head sideways even though I knew it would hurt. "Trajan will deal with you," I snapped. "Isaac can take care of everyone else in your…dysfunctional family: your sons, even my traitor sister—*all* of them." It hurt me to say that about Alex. It would always hurt, no matter what.

"Trajan," Viktor said, "will not kill me, Adria Dawson. I admit—because I am not so awful that I have too much pride—that Trajan is more than capable of destroying me. He is the most powerful and feared Black Beast since his father before him. If he wanted me dead, I would have been dead centuries ago."

"That's a lie."

Viktor's dark brow rose just slightly. That confident, knowing expression never left his face. It haunted me.

"Believe what you want," he said, "but don't let your human weaknesses get in the way of your good sense."

Thankfully, he left the bed and began casually pacing the room.

"If you had the opportunity," he went on, "to be with the Mayfairs long enough, you would have started to see the truth."

"What *is* the truth then?"

He stopped. His back was to me, but I got the sense he suddenly felt more confident than before.

"I'll tell you anything you want to know," he said. "All you have to do is be willing." He faced me, his expression more sincere. "I am not the atrocious villain you think I am."

"Believe me, you are," I answered. "You're the one who forced me here, who sent people to attack me. Because of your 'family,' people in this town are dying. You're the reason my uncle is in the hospital! Your son is why my sister is one of you!" I was shaking, uncontrollably; I felt my blood pressure rise, my stomach swirling.

"Calm down," he said, softly. "You are in no condition—"

"To *what*?" I shouted. "No condition to tell you what you don't want to hear? No condition to tell you I'll *never* be willing, and that you'll have to kill me?"

"Oh, I won't kill you." The sincerity in his face faded, replaced by something more displeased, arrogant. "I'll still infect you, whether you're willing, or not."

"Then what does it matter?" I lashed out. "Why don't you just get it over with then?"

"Because a willing mate creates a stronger bond."

My face scrunched up. "Do you know how *disgusting* that sounds?"

No reply.

"I'll never submit to you in any way," I threatened. "*Never!*"

"I'll give you some time to think about it," he said, placing his hand on the doorknob. "You have until morning. Feel free to..."—he gestured with his hand—"...look around the place, if you wish." Something about the way he said it seemed to have hidden meaning.

I was appalled; shocked that he actually thought I would change my mind. Viktor Vargas was not only a power-hungry abomination—he was completely mental.

There was a clicking sound as the door locked from the outside. I was alone in the room.

It was strange, but I already felt stronger than moments ago. I hadn't noticed I was sitting straight up in the bed; must've managed it while shouting at Viktor. Amazing what anger can do to a person. Getting ahead of myself with a false sense of independence, I tried standing, but my legs buckled and I tumbled onto the floor, dragging the blanket off the bed with me. The wound under my ribcage shot me with excruciating pain; my hands went up instinctively to put pressure on the area, but that proved to be a mistake. Pressure made it worse. Blood soaked through my gown. Carefully, I lifted the gown above my waist. The gash was deep. I counted twelve stitches, two of which had split when I fell.

With difficulty, I turned my body, put my back against the bed and just sat there on the floor.

I must have cried for an hour, in the same spot with my knees pressed to my chest; I didn't care that it hurt. I thought about Isaac the most, feeling this dread in my heart. If only I could see him, just to know that he was okay. Eventually, anger took over. I wiped my face harshly with my hands, mad that I let Viktor cause me to cry at all.

I looked up and all around this room. Nothing of interest. Nothing out of the ordinary except the rotting wooden chest set against a corner. I glanced at the door, checking to make sure no one was coming. No shadows moved across the floor through the crack underneath; I heard no voices, no movement. Then I grabbed the bed firmly, expecting to fall this time so I'd be ready for it. Pulling myself up, I bit through the pain and walked over to the chest. Winded, I sat down on the floor next to it. I hoped to find something inside I could use as a weapon. Anything to give me any chance at all.

The hinges creaked as I lifted the heavy wooden lid; I was surprised I could lift it. The wood smelled old, like dust and water damage. It also smelled strongly of salt, just as the ocean did when I saw it for the first time.

Old weathered books were inside. Parchment. Maps. I was no expert, but I knew this stuff had to be antique. A broken compass and a spyglass telescope lay in the bottom next to a case that held tiny glass vials plugged with corks. There was liquid inside the vials, but I wasn't about to find out what kind.

I leaned farther over the chest, reaching as far into the bottom as I could. There was nothing that would help me to escape, or fend off a werewolf. I never expected there to be, really, but when all you have is hope, you tend to do what you can with it. I settled with what looked like a journal: a thick, leather bound book with coarse vellum pages; twine tied the spine together, though it had snapped in sections and the pages were loose. A tiny spider crawled out of the water-damaged pages and scurried up the side of my hand. Gently, I blew it away. I never liked to kill them.

The journal opened with a slight crunching sound. The pages were so worn and thick they stuck together in spots and curled unevenly in others. I was almost afraid to touch them they were so fragile.

I held history in my hands, an unmistakable feeling that awed me. But I couldn't read the text; a deep ink flourish in an unknown language.

Disappointment swept over me.

There were medieval-like drawings with names underneath:

Veliki Vojvoda Vukašin Prvovenčani
Vojvoda Viktor Vargasavič
c. 1514
Entry M. Duvellain – Praverian Third Order

The first sketch depicted two men with dark hair, beards and mustaches. They stood side by side in a portrait pose; strange armor dressed them. Trajan and Viktor. A drawing on the next page showed them in a field of soldiers, a battle, where men with black eyes and long claws lay dead all around them. In every drawing, the one thing that remained the same was Trajan and Viktor standing together. I flipped several pages, skipping many in between, and stopped at another sketch that was different. With Trajan and Viktor, there was also a woman, a soldier like them. Next to their names another name read:

Vojvoda Natasa Vargasavič
c. 1519
Entry M. Duvellain – Praverian Third Order

If only I could read the language!

I slammed the journal shut and tossed it back into the chest. "That's what he wants," I said. "That's what he meant by telling me to look around. Why else would a random, out-of-place chest be sitting in the room with me?"

I didn't care. So *what* if those pictures of him and Isaac's father seemed friendly. They were obviously not on the same side now. The past was the past.

At least, that was what I kept trying to tell myself.

Viktor succeeded only in making me curious, raising my worry somewhat, I could admit, but that was all. Nothing he could do or say would turn me against Trajan, and certainly not Isaac. It insulted me he thought I was so easy to manipulate.

The isolation of the room was my only comfort. Hours went by; the sound of bodies moving quietly past the door, voices that seemed to whisper, until eventually I heard nothing at all. I could feel that it was the dead of night. It seemed I was the only one awake, accompanied by the constant smell of mildew and salt; the unsteady exhale of my breath. I lay in the bed staring into the fading flame of the fireplace. It danced sideways as if constantly licked by a draft in the wall. A draft, I thought, and raised my head from the pillow suddenly. I went to investigate. The giant wooden shelf to the left of the fireplace covered something. I tried to move it, but it was too heavy for me even if I had been in tip-top condition. The draft came from behind it, where I noticed there was once a window now barricaded by boards. Frustrated, I moved over and stood in front of the fire; smoke rose from the wood in a steady coil. My mind in overdrive, trying to find a way out of this place, I began to wonder where the smoke was going. Two ceramic pots sat on the floor holding frail, dead flowers. I pulled the dried stems from the pots and lay them on the floor beside me. Pouring the water over the flame, I snuffed it out. I got down on my knees and leaned over the sizzling smoke, twisting my body at an angle so I could see upward inside the chimney. Nothing but blackness. I peered further, hoping I was just missing something, that maybe it was so dark outside that I couldn't see the opening, but I knew in my heart that there wasn't one. At least, not the kind of opening that I could crawl my way out of.

"He wouldn't put you somewhere," said a familiar, frightening voice, "where you could find a way out."

Startled, I hit my head on the fireplace; soot and dirt fell off the stone and dusted me. My hands were black from holding onto the inside wall.

Sibyl closed the bedroom door behind her and stood in front of it.

"What do you want?" I snapped. I wasn't afraid of her—at least, not as much as I should've been; I got the feeling no one knew she was in the room with me. I pretended to be more interested in wiping the soot from my hands onto my gown, but really, I wanted to scream for help. I felt Sibyl was more of a danger to me than Viktor was.

Sibyl slithered across the room. Immediately, I glanced at the door. It was unlocked. I could try to run for it.

"I came to talk, that's all," she said.

"Yeah, I kind of doubt that," I said, with a snarl. "And what if I don't want to talk?"

"Oh, I think you will."

My legs hurt, but I remained standing. I needed to be strong, to show her I wasn't as weak as I really was.

She grinned faintly, and then walked toward the chest, grazing her fingertips across the lid. "Viktor didn't tell you why Trajan won't kill him, I presume."

She had my attention suddenly.

"No, he didn't, but I don't care."

"Of course you care—what if *I* told you the reason?" she said. "Would you do something for me in return?"

The atmosphere shifted. She wasn't here to hurt me, but I got the distinct feeling if I didn't give her what she wanted, she'd have no second thoughts about it. Dilemma. Sibyl's offer or Viktor's?

"What do you want?"

Sibyl opened the chest and pulled the journal out, smoothing its cover under her hand. She pressed her lips to it softly and then set it back inside, leaving the lid open.

She turned to face me.

"I simply want you to tell my son what I'm about to tell you."

Relay a message? It couldn't be as simple as that. Everything about this felt wrong, dangerous.

I went toward her a few steps. "That's it?" I said, leery. "Tell Isaac? Why?"

"That doesn't matter." She smirked. "What matters is that he knows. You wouldn't want to keep things from him, would you? You would tell Isaac because he has a right to know. Because you care for him."

Hesitation froze me. There was some kind of catch. There had to be. "Exactly how am I supposed to tell him anything in here? And when Viktor is done with me, things will be different. *I'll* be different…" I swallowed hard; I didn't want to think about that.

"I'll get you out of here."

No, this was too good to be true. I stepped away from her again. I waited for the catch, the fine print, but so far there wasn't any.

"A Blood Bond," Sibyl began, "is a tricky thing." She laughed suddenly, whirling her index finger above her. "Tricky is an inadequate word, really. It's more a complex, deal-with-the-Devil sort of thing."

She sat on the side of the bed, crossing her legs and pressing her palms against the mattress.

I didn't budge.

"Young werewolves," she went on, "think they know about the Blood Bond, how it really works. Only the Elder's know because it's the Law. A Blood Bond is forbidden by anyone who is not an Elder, and anyone who breaks that law must be killed by the Alpha of his pack." She sighed. "When a Blood Bond is made, the human is tied to that first drop of blood for eternity, or death, whichever comes first, and death usually does."

"I thought it made humans immortal."

Sibyl's grin spread wider. "It does. But if the blood that made that bond ever dies, so then does the body it bonded to."

I tried to put it together in my mind, what she was getting at, but I couldn't.

"Aramei is very precious to Trajan," she said, cryptically. "And Trajan protects Viktor. It should be obvious why."

"*Protects* him?" I couldn't grasp this at all. I refused to believe something so wicked. Trajan wouldn't protect Viktor, not now, I thought. But if Trajan was so powerful, then why would Viktor still be alive after all this time? Maybe the things Viktor had tried to tell me were true.

Then something clicked in my subconscious.

My hand went up to my chest, and I shook my head, trying to find any reason to substitute the revelation infecting my thoughts.

Sibyl smiled; I wasn't looking at her, but I could feel that wicked smile move over me.

"You figured it out," she said. "Yes, it was Viktor's blood that Aramei drank first—not Trajan's. When Viktor dies, so does Aramei."

I stood there in mute. Sibyl moved from the bed and approached me. I felt the stiff heat from her body so close to mine.

"Trajan's blood does keep Aramei alive," she whispered, walking around me in a circle, "but Viktor's blood is what *gave* her life."

Shock beset me.

"Such a sad, pathetic little situation really," she added, her words laced with sarcasm and amusement.

"You want me to tell Isaac," I said, "because it will pit Isaac against his father."

Sibyl nodded.

"My sons should know the truth about the parent they choose to give their loyalty to, the one they choose to admire."

I swung my head to the side so I could face her. "Then why didn't you just tell Isaac this yourself?"

"I told you why."

"Because it's the Law?"

"Part of the reason," she said, "yes."

"But you're telling *me*. You're breaking the Law now."

"I don't care about that anymore," she said. "The other reason I don't do it myself is because Isaac despises me. Can't blame him, I admit."

"You're right about that."

A smirk barely broke in her face.

"You're jealous," I said, "aren't you?" I wasn't actually trying to mock her, but it seemed to come out that way.

Sibyl snarled, grinding her teeth behind her closed lips.

"Viktor is a fool," she barked. "He's only ever wanted what Trajan had: the respect of his men; the fear the very mention of Trajan's name inflicts upon others; the love of women." Sibyl smiled then, as if reminiscing. "It's even how I came to be here, trapped in Viktor's snare."

"Seems to me you *like* being in his snare."

"I do," she admitted, proudly. "And that's why I have to get rid of you."

"That's what I thought—jealousy. Well, trust me, I don't want to be here and I'll never be willing."

Sibyl smiled a soft, dangerous smile.

A loud *crash!* caught us both off-guard. I turned around swiftly, facing the door. The door swung open, and Viktor came rushing inside, pushing Sibyl violently into the massive wooden shelf. I thought at first he was there to keep her away from me, but the shouting in the hall told me right away that something else was going on.

Viktor grabbed me by the arm.

He made it as far as the exit when I saw something move fast behind me. I dropped quickly to my knees, missing the swipe of Sibyl's deadly fingernails coming right for me—she hit Viktor instead. I gasped sharply; the look on his face; I thought demons were about to burst out of his eyes at any moment.

"She'll *never* replace me!" Her eyes were the abysmal black I had seen so many times before.

I crawled on my hands and knees out of the way, hoping by some miracle that they'd would be distracted enough by each other that I could take advantage of the open door.

Sibyl's body went flying across the room; Viktor's hair didn't even stir.

"Tell him! Tell Isaac!" Sibyl screamed at me through fanged teeth, but before she could another word out, Viktor had me in his arms carrying me out the door.

"Father," Ashe said, running up, "he got in! He killed William! William's dead!"

I knew then that I must've been in the Vargas house. Werewolves in their mediate form ran through the hallways, most in the same direction. Viktor gripped me so tightly he was hurting me. I tried to fight him, but it was a wasted effort.

I began to lose hope, until I heard Isaac's voice; I couldn't make out what he was saying, but I knew it was him. Relief and worry washed over me at the same time—he was here for me, but I knew he couldn't defeat Viktor.

I didn't know what had happened, but suddenly I was lying face-first on the stairs, my wrist twisted beneath me from the fall. I caught my breath and my balance before looking up to see Isaac at the bottom of the stairs. Blood covered his face and hands. I thought I would roll right down the stairs when Viktor moved past me, knocking me into the stair railing, but I held on tight and only skidded one step, wincing from the strain of my injuries.

When Isaac and Viktor clashed, it shook the house like thunder. Fully transformed within seconds, I watched in horror. I pulled myself up, holding onto the rail, and then shakily flew down the steps on my unsteady legs. I had to help Isaac; it was crazy and stupid, I knew, but I had to do something.

I could only tell them apart by their size difference. Isaac was like a pup next to Viktor Vargas. I thought I would faint as Viktor struck Isaac so hard I heard a frightening *crack*; I grabbed my ears and cried out.

When three other werewolves rushed from different rooms and leapt into the fight, Viktor tossed them all like ragdolls out of the way. One soared above me, crashing into the stair railing; splintered wood shot in every direction; instinctively I covered my head and face with my hands. The other werewolves recoiled instantly, obeying Viktor's unspoken demand to stay out of it—he wanted Isaac for himself.

I ran for the nearest weapon: a small, but heavy, lion statue on a nearby shelf; but just as I went to smash it across Viktor's back, Alex grabbed me from behind.

"Not a good idea, little sister." The rancid smell of her breath choked me. "That'll only piss him off."

"You're *not* my sister," I screamed. I spun around, and my hands came up fast, pushing her away hard enough that she let go of me, but she had me in her grasp again in no time.

She held me there, forcing me to watch as I struggled against her. She knew Viktor would rip Isaac apart, and Alex wanted me to see it happen. I thrashed around in her grasp, but she was so strong.

Isaac lunged at Viktor and buried his teeth into Viktor's collarbone; an excruciating howl ripped through the air. Isaac was *beating* him. I even felt Alex's hands loosen from around my arms out of disbelief.

Isaac had Viktor on the ceiling, pressing his head against a massive wooden beam. Isaac's brute head reared back, mouth wide open, and came back down on the other side of Viktor's neck. Viktor fell to the floor like a slab of meat; in seconds he was in human form again. He lay there naked, slumped against a coffee table.

Then Ashe, and one other, stepped forward to help, but Viktor, grasping his bleeding throat, ordered them away.

"I *want* him to kill me," Viktor growled.

But Isaac refused to give in. He was going to kill him. And in turn, he was going to sentence himself to death by killing Aramei.

I jerked my way free from Alex again and stumbled forward, catching my fall by holding onto someone's shoulder. I didn't care that it was Ashe. He didn't seem to care either.

"Stop!" My hands were out in front of me.

The room became quieter.

"Isaac, don't kill him!"

Isaac's head, teeth dripping with saliva and blood, turned to see me. His eyes drifted to and from me and his prey.

My voice dropped, and I pleaded, "*Don't…*"

It was in that very moment that I decided not to tell Isaac about Aramei. In that crucial moment in time when everything I knew became clear: Isaac could not know the truth, because sometimes the truth does more harm than good. If Isaac knew his own father chose to risk the lives of his sons to save Aramei, Isaac would've been abandoned twice—first by his own mother, and worst of all, by the father that he revered.

Isaac let go of Viktor, but stood over him in warning as I approached. I moved against Isaac's beastly chest and looked down upon Viktor.

"Humans are so soft," Viktor said. "You would want me to live after what I've done to you? *Stupid* little girl."

He didn't know. Viktor had no idea why I stopped Isaac. I wanted to keep it that way. From the corner of my eye, I saw Sibyl watching me from the second floor.

"I guess being human has its disadvantages," I deceivingly agreed.

Zia and the rest of Isaac's family entered the house in their mediate form.

"No!" Viktor roared at his fledglings, keeping them at bay. "Let them leave, all of them." He looked at Isaac then. "One as powerful as his father," he said. "Of your brothers, I always knew it would be you." Viktor's eyes met mine then, and I felt a remarkable sentiment in his gaze. "In more ways than one, I see," he added.

The comment was directed at me, but what did it mean? The possibilities weighed heavily in my heart.

Isaac's massive body hardened. I stopped him. "Let's go," I said softly, hoping he would continue to listen to me. Already, I felt I had asked too much of him.

"We'll stay to make sure no one follows," said Nathan.

Zia took me by the arm.

But Isaac wasn't following…

I tore away from Zia.

"What are you doing?" I shouted at Isaac. I wished he could speak in werewolf form. He wouldn't even look at me.

But Isaac knew something that I didn't—Viktor was not ready to give up.

It wasn't over.

In a flash, Viktor sprung up and bounded toward Isaac in mid-air. Claws and teeth at the ready before his feet fully lifted from the floor. My body flew backward, crashing into Ashe who tossed me aside as if I were weightless. I skidded into the kitchen, landing pressed against the legs of dining chairs. It felt like my brain bounced around inside my skull as I hit the metal bar holding the massive tabletop to its base.

I couldn't move; beasts were all around me. I couldn't tell who was who, except for Isaac and Viktor, who had fully shifted again by now. Viktor was a titan among the others. And Isaac, I knew him now enough to distinguish him over anyone and in any form.

The house began to come down all around me, the table barely shielding me from broken glass and projectile debris. A giant chandelier hit the table hard, shattering in all directions, reflecting light like glitter as it rained down onto the floor. I wondered how the table was still standing when everything else was destroyed. I hoped it would hold. I hoped it wouldn't crush me.

Stunned, I slowly pressed my hands over my ears. The roaring, the gnashing of teeth; I couldn't take it anymore.

Savage fighting everywhere. Blood everywhere.

But Isaac was still beating Viktor.

I couldn't breathe' I watched in horror and fascination.

Isaac's beastly claws came down on Viktor and sliced his neck once. Once more and I knew Viktor would be dead.

Everything moved so slowly. In the back of my mind, somewhere beneath the pandemonium, I wondered if I would be able to say how fast it all happened.

And then the unthinkable happened.

A beast more colossal in size than Viktor, held Isaac's arm just before that fatal blow.

Isaac was thrown right through the wall of the house.

I gasped and felt my insides dissolve into mush.

"Nooo!" My scream was the only noise.

I painfully rolled out from underneath the table, watching everything and everyone around me and I crawled forward. Many others bolted with Trajan's presence, scattering in all directions. Viktor stood wounded, blood soaking his fur.

I looked directly at Trajan, so tall against me, so enormous, so absolutely frightening, but somehow I managed to get to my feet. "An Alpha protects his own…" I said loud enough for him to hear me, my words poisoned with resentment.

I wasn't afraid of him; for the life of me I didn't know why, but to run felt wrong.

Trajan let me be. I couldn't believe it, but I didn't have time to care. I ran through the new opening in the side of the house and found Isaac in human form, lying naked in the snow. Blood covered him; his hair thickly wet with it. I fell to my knees next to his body.

"Isaac!" I touched his face and head all over; blood quickly stained my hands and clothes.

He wasn't responsive, but his body shivered in the cold. His skin wasn't hot like it normally was after he shifted form; the snow around his body didn't melt away. I stumbled to a nearby parked car and opened the back door, searching everywhere for something to cover Isaac with. I pushed the button in the front to pop the trunk where I spotted a duffle bag stuffed full of laundry. I tossed everything until I found a large bath towel.

I covered Isaac with the towel as best I could. He had started to gain consciousness while I rummaged through the car, but he was weak.

"My father…" he said. "Was that…my father?"

I looked toward the house. Indecision crippled me.

And I couldn't lie to him.

"Yes," I said, and I leaned down and kissed his forehead softly.

Isaac lifted with difficulty; I couldn't believe all the blood, that he was still alive.

"My father has always been greedy," he said, holding onto my shoulder for balance.

"Greedy?"

"He won't let anyone else kill beasts of rank," he said. "Not while he's Alpha. It can threaten his position."

The secret was still safe, but it was painful for me. Isaac didn't know that rank had nothing to do with what Trajan did, that Trajan was saving Viktor's life. But I knew. I knew and I hated myself for it.

Isaac climbed to his feet, gently lifting me with him.

"My father will kill him," he said, staring toward the house. I could sense a big part of him was angry—*he* wanted to be the one to do the honors.

I couldn't say it, that I knew otherwise. Trajan would not kill Viktor Vargas.

"I need to get you out of here," he said.

He kept looking back as we walked toward the main road where his car had been parked. I thought at any moment he would barrel back into the chaos and finish what he started, but we sped away from the Vargas house, and I hoped I would never see it again.

23

On the way to Isaac's house, over the winding black roads and snow-covered land, I kept looking back, afraid that we would be ambushed again.

"They won't come," he said, as he pulled me nearer.

I could hardly keep my eyes open, but in a short time we were pulling into the driveway, and Isaac killed the engine. He carried me into the house, and though I was more worried about his injuries than mine, I couldn't bring myself to object.

The house was rich with warmth and firelight; the fireplace blazing behind the hearth, licking the cool air coming from the chimney above. Briefly, I glimpsed the painting of Trajan and Aramei, and I softly shut my eyes.

My bare feet began to thaw as Isaac walked with me up the staircase. I could feel my toes coming to life with pain. My back and ribs began to throb even more, but I hid my discomfort from him well. Carrying me into a spacious bathroom, Isaac carefully sat down on the side of a deep tub with me enveloped in his lap. He reached out and turned the squeaking faucets, letting the tub begin to fill up with water. Steam rose from the top of the water, fogging the nearby window, which had already been covered by frost and snow. Only one light burned low over the pedestal sink.

"Isaac," I mumbled tiredly, noticing how weak my voice had become. "I'm fine."

Of course, he didn't believe me. I was a bloody mess; the gown Viktor dressed me in drenched with Isaac's blood. Glancing down, I noticed that both of my legs were covered in bruises and cuts, but I ignored that too. Isaac was more important.

"Look what he did to you," I said, my voice trembling with tears. I traced a long, bleeding gash down the length of his neck with the tip of my finger.

"Adria," he murmured, staring deeply into my eyes. "This is why it has to be you," he whispered softly, devotedly. "Why I already know that you're the one. Because you curb my envy for human life, by allowing me to experience human love."

Tears began to stream softly down my face.

He pulled me closer, letting my head fall against his chest, and he held me there, his strong hand cradling the back of my head.

"I've never known anyone like you," he went on. "So much love for your mother who you stayed with to protect. That you would risk your life for your uncle. And your sister—even after everything she's done to you, I know you still want her in your life." He held me tighter, and over my quiet tears I still managed to hear the beating of his heart. "And for me…" he said, even more softly than before, "…you know what an abomination I am, how dangerous I am, yet you risked your life for me, too—"

He stopped abruptly as though his mind had been snapped into another place; his deep gaze immersed in some powerful thought or memory. I started to speak, to stir the peculiar silence, but he came back out of it so quickly.

"And I love you, Adria Dawson, with that same undying passion."

I began to feel…strange. My legs felt heavy, my arms weaker every time I moved them even just slightly. A steady stream of tears poured from the corners of my eyes and I looked up at him, vaguely realizing how heavy even my head had become. "If that's true," I said, though I didn't doubt it for a second, "then do one thing for me."

"Anything," he promised.

I pecked him lightly on his soft, warm lips.

"Promise never to call yourself an abomination."

There was a faint, yet unmistakable smile in his eyes.

Suddenly, I felt his lips on mine again, but I couldn't recall the few seconds before, when he leaned in to kiss me. I could taste his sweet mouth; his perfect, deep kiss as he held my face in his hands. I could tell, even with my eyes shut, that the room was getting darker, the air colder. I shivered. My bones were frozen and strange, as if I were still lying out in the frigid snow with Isaac, surrounded by darkness and winter and blood.

I heard voices. Just like the night when Sibyl attacked us in the car, there were voices in my head; odd, indistinct whispers.

I couldn't open my eyes.

My body felt light like air; my chest devoid of breath. When I tried to lift my hands, it felt as though a cumbersome veil of magic lay over them, preventing any movement. I tried to speak, but my lips were as heavy as stone.

In a flash of a second, I gained control of my mind and felt my lids open just a slit. I was incredibly dizzy; Isaac's face spiraling around in my gaze.

"Isaac?" I said, but I realized the words never actually left my lips.

My lids slammed shut over my eyes again and I felt my body lift viciously into the air; nothing but blackness and cold all around me as if I were being hurled through time and space. I screamed out Isaac's name once more.

The voices were getting nearer; I could hear the hot breath of whispers upon my ears, feel fingers grasping around my elbows. "Get her back into the water," I heard one voice say, but it had sounded muted, as if she were speaking through a thick wall.

"Get her back into the water!" a different voice said so plainly that it jolted me alert.

I looked up and I was knelt by the creek again.

"Adria," Alex said, standing over me, "we need to get you cleaned up."

Confused, I looked all around me toward the water and then back at Alex. Her dark hair rested softly over her shoulders. Her eyes were beautiful and serene like they had always been before she was infected by evil. She smiled down at me.

I looked at myself; still wearing the bloodstained gown, still covered in bruises and cuts and soot from the fireplace in my prison.

"Where's Isaac?" I asked; my words still detached from my tangled mind. "How are you here?"

I felt trapped in some vivid dream, though everything was too real, too convincing to be a dream.

Water flowed gently over the rocks, and the wind brushed lightly through the trees. Flowers were in full bloom, lined perfectly along the creek's bank; vines crawled over the forest bed and wrapped themselves around every tree, every branch in an intricate display of green.

Alex was suddenly kneeling in the water with me and I was naked. I didn't know how she got there so fast. I didn't know how I got there at all. The water was warm, almost hot. Instantly it soothed me. I felt my eyes close once more as Alex guided my body backward and I lay within the creek, propped against her lap. Tenderly, she washed my hair, combing her delicate fingers through every strand. I glimpsed the blood staining the water around me as it washed away.

"She's waiting to speak to you," Alex said, and I looked up to see her face. "She's watching you; can't you see her?" And then Alex pointed through the trees and I lifted from her lap, wearing a new gown; thin and clean and white. My hair was completely dry; my body left no evidence of taint.

I looked raptly through the trees, but saw no one. I could feel a presence, one so compelling, yet so absolutely cryptic. And when I turned around again, Alex was gone.

I heard the ground crack lightly like a branch burning in a fireplace, and then I looked down. The creek bed had dried up; nothing left but dust-covered rocks and tiny pebbles and parched earth. The flowers on the bank behind me were gone; the crawling vines withered and brittle. The sky was eerily gray, yet I saw not a single cloud moving across it.

But in front of me, everything was still beautiful. Everything was in full bloom—it was a wonderland.

I took a step forward and the vines under my feet turned to dust and blew away. Another step and the flowers on the bank withered and died in an instant. I stopped then, afraid to kill any more beauty with my presence.

Aramei walked toward me through the bright and colorful forest and reached out her frail hand.

"You must drink it," she said, but her lips never moved.

I went a few steps toward her, but she never appeared any closer. I tried again, but the distance between us refused to change.

"Drink what?" I asked, but my lips never moved either.

"The water from the creek," she replied.

I glanced down at the dried-up creek bed and then back at Aramei.

"But it's gone."

She reached out her hand once more, and although she appeared to be many feet away, I looked right down into the palm of her hand as if she were standing directly in front of me. A single droplet of water rested there. I could see my reflection within it.

I looked up at her, unsure, confused by her words.

But I could never distrust an angel, and Aramei was the closest thing to an angel that I would ever know.

I took her hand into both of mine and I leaned over, placing my lips over the droplet of water. And I drank. My eyes shut softly, and I drank more and more and more until my body was hurled through the blackness of time and space again.

And I woke up.

I lay in Isaac's bed, surrounded by crisp, white sheets and fluffy pillows. I was curled up inside a thick, warm comforter. It was early morning; the day had barely gone through an hour of dim sunlight, still subdued by thick, dreary winter clouds. A muted ray of light pushed through the frost-covered window and pooled on a spot on the floor. The room had been cleaned, everything positioned neatly into its own place. I could faintly smell lemon furniture polish underneath a stronger layer of fragrant candles. One burned on the nightstand beside me; the tiny flame steady and calm.

Someone had dressed me. I wore the same clean, white gown I had worn in my dream. My hair was clean; brushed so thoroughly that it felt like silk. My cuts had been tended; the bruises on my legs had already started to fade. Brushing my hand over the wound under my ribs, I noticed that the stitches were gone. Gently I touched it through the thinness of my gown, feeling a small mass where a scar was already beginning to form.

"Are you feeling better?"

I saw Isaac then, sitting in the far corner of the room, enveloped by the shadow. I heard the chair move as he stood from it and walked toward me into the subdued light; the sound of his boots gently moving across the floor.

He sat down beside me on the bed and reached out, brushing the back of his fingers along my cheekbone.

My eyes closed of their own accord, and I breathed in his scent; it was more prominent than ever before, more intoxicating.

"What happened?" I asked, slowly opening my eyes. "I don't remember…"

Isaac leaned in and kissed me tenderly.

"You passed out," he said, pulling away. "Everything must have overwhelmed you all at once after I got you here. We were in the bathroom, and I was going to clean you up; we were talking and… well, you passed out." It seemed like he had wanted to say something else, too, but changed his mind at the last second.

He brushed his fingers through my hair and he smiled.

"Zia and Daisy helped me," he said, "with the bath and getting you dressed. Oh, and cleaning the place up."

The thought of him seeing me naked in such a state, had never even crossed my mind. It wouldn't have bothered me. I knew in my heart that Isaac would never do anything to violate me.

I thought of the dream then, worried that my intimate time in the bathroom with him before, may not have been real, either. I looked up into his eyes and paused for a moment, taking in every second of the way he looked so devotedly back at me.

"You promised me," I said. "That you would never call yourself an abomination. Do you remember?"

"Yes," he said, smiling. "But you fainted so conveniently before I could request *my* terms." His smile became more of a grin then.

"Oh?" I said, a little surprised.

"Uh huh." He nodded. "You have to promise me that a week before every full moon—"

I put up my hand, stopping him. "No," I demanded, "you can't ask me to do that. Isaac, I *want* to be here; I—"

He placed his fingers on my lips to hush me. His face was unreadable, but still, he was smiling, his dark eyes soft with adoration.

"You have to promise that you'll be at my side," he said, and my heart quickened. "Because I know that without you here, I'll become something far more dangerous."

I almost cried, but instead I choked it back and smiled, nodding slowly. "I promise."

After a thoughtful hesitation, I added, "But why the change of heart? I thought you were afraid."

For a moment, Isaac's gaze strayed from mine. Patiently, I waited for his answer, but at the same time, I was desperate for it.

"I feel like I can trust myself around you now," he said, still not looking at me. "I could never hurt you."

Isaac stood and went over to the window, pulling the curtain open the rest of the way. More soft, gray sunlight flooded the room. I could see the tops of the trees outside covered in glistening white, but nothing fell from the sky.

"Isaac," I said, as he turned around to face me. "For now—and I'm not sure how long now will last—I can live with the way things are, but..." I stopped and inhaled a deep breath, looking down at the sheets. It wasn't all that I had wanted to say—I needed time alone, away from everyone and everything. I needed to think.

"I need to go home for a day or two," I spoke up. "Just to be able to clear my head. And I need to be with my aunt."

Immediately, I could see the obvious protest in his face; the last thing he wanted to do was leave me alone after what happened. But if

I knew Isaac as much as I thought I already did, I wouldn't technically be alone; he'd watch me like he watched me at school.

"I'll be all right," I assured him.

He had made it back to the bed by now, and sat beside me. "Okay," he said, nodding with reluctance. "If that's what you need…"

"It is."

24

Isaac borrowed Nathan's Jeep and took me to see Uncle Carl in the hospital later that day. Beverlee asked why I looked so 'worn'. Good thing she couldn't see any of the wounds underneath my clothes. There was no way I'd find a worthy excuse for any of that.

Uncle Carl was doing good, considering.

"The book is great," Uncle Carl said, weakly. "Beverlee read some of it to me earlier. Awesome stuff."

The smile on my face was genuine, despite all the worries beneath it. It was the best thing ever to see my uncle able to talk again. I stayed with him until visiting hours were over, and I picked up where Beverlee left off on page fifty-six.

I went back to my own house that night. I wasn't afraid to be there anymore; I was hardly afraid of anything. I had a lot of thinking to do, many dark secrets to tuck away properly inside my head; choices to make and the equally devastating consequences that all of them came with, to consider.

"I really don't like this," Isaac said, as we stood together on the front porch, the house keys dangling in my hand.

"Think about it, Isaac," I said. "After last night, this is probably the last place they'd expect me to be."

I glanced over and saw Sebastian, Dwarf and Damien watching us from the barn entrance. Just as I expected—babysitters. As much as I didn't like it, I also didn't have the heart to say so. Besides, I knew it was for the better, anyway.

Isaac kissed me deeply, and then reluctantly walked down the porch steps, looking back twice before he made it to the car. He stopped with the door open, maybe in case there was the possibility I might change my mind; and I admit I almost did. I didn't want to spend even an hour away from him, but this time to myself was important.

The house was cold and empty. As I walked through the kitchen, and then the rest of the house, I made it a point to look at absolutely everything, trying to find something that didn't feel changed. Uncle Carl's favorite chair was empty; the navy and red zigzag afghan that usually hung over the back of it lay sloppily in the floor. Dust had begun to settle on everything. Aunt Beverlee had always kept the house dusted; once every other day at least. The fireplace had been abandoned; no lingering warmth or the smell of recently burned wood came from it. I went upstairs to find Uncle Carl and Beverlee's room a chaotic mess: clothes were strewn across the bed; the chest of drawers half open.

The door to Alex's room was always shut. I stood in front of it for the longest time before deciding to go inside. It had been cleaned. Everything had a neat little place on the shelf, or dresser, or desk. All of Alex's clothes had been tucked neatly in the drawers and hung away inside the closet. Beverlee had hoped that Alex would come back, despite her being banned from the house, and so she did whatever she could to make Alex feel at home. Just in case.

From across the room, I noticed a photo of Alex and me together that had been taped to the dresser mirror. I walked over and took it into my hand, staring down at the memory. Alex's loving, smiling face looked back at me. Quietly I laughed, recalling that moment. We were sitting together on the beach in Savannah; her arm around my shoulder. Minutes before the photo was taken, Alex had dumped a bucket of sand crabs on me as I lay on the beach.

I put the photo away inside a drawer. I couldn't look at it anymore.

I slept alone in my room, but I knew that Isaac was nearby, watching over me. I slept without dreams. I slept without a memory of them if there were any, and that was a good thing.

I stayed home from school the next two days. It was like Georgia all over again, skipping school to mentally recover after what I'd been through. No one came to my house, not even those who had tried to kill me before. No one. But I saw Isaac's car from the window in Uncle Carl's office upstairs. Sometimes I saw Damien's. Beverlee finally came home only once to get some clothes to take with her back to the hospital.

"They're going to start Carl's physical therapy," she said, so happily. "As soon as next week."

I rushed to hug her. "That's great, Aunt Bev!"

"Yes, it's wonderful," she said. "I'll have to hire someone to build a wheelchair ramp out front for when he gets to come home."

"Did they say if they expect him to walk again?"

Beverlee had mentioned at the hospital that Uncle Carl was paralyzed from the waist down.

She buried her hand in the bottom of her purse and fished out her keys. "He's already moved his legs a little."

Beverlee hugged me one more time before she hurried out the door.

I spent the rest of the day inside, having no real recollection of anything other than my current thoughts. How does a person overcome things so tragic and unbelievable? I thought about the world around me, the oblivious world filled with billions of oblivious minds;

and I contemplated everything: my solitary life, the differences between it and every other life; and I thought that maybe I wasn't so different, after all. Everyone had their own troubles, their own battles to fight. Everyone eventually faced darkness and hardship. Mine was just a little out of the ordinary—and I could live with that.

But I never came to a decision, and so my time alone to think had been not wasted, but spent making me more torn between lives than before. I knew that I didn't want to live as a werewolf—that was one thing for certain. I could never imagine going through such horrific pain. And Aramei, the Blood Bond, I didn't want that either, though I admitted it was more acceptable than the latter.

Remaining human, continuing on with my mortal life, trapped inside the body of an inevitable death, was also something I didn't want.

But those were my choices.

For now, I decided that choosing none of them would be the best choice. Day by day, to live and enjoy what life I had at that moment, was ultimately the only decision I *could* make.

Isaac was waiting outside in the driveway when I went to leave for school the next day.

"Need a ride?" he asked, smiling, though we had discussed it late the night before over the phone.

The sun was out. It wasn't helping to melt the snow much, but it was nice to see it; the gray gloom of clouds and weather was beginning to get to me.

I smiled back, tossed my canvas backpack into the front seat, and jumped inside his new Jeep; newer and shinier than Damien's.

"Where'd you get *this* Jeep?" I asked, testing out the feel of the leather seats. "Better yet, where'd the other car go?"

Briefly, I thought about that car, but all I could remember was flipping around inside of it.

"Nathan and Xavier ditched it behind our house," he said.

"What are they"—I chuckled—"the clean-up crew?"

Isaac laughed, too, and pulled me next to him. "Sometimes."

Almost to my school there was a long silence between us. We pulled into the parking lot. He put the Jeep in park, turned the key, and gazed out the windshield. His thumbs tapped undecidedly on the steering wheel.

"Nothing happened, Isaac," I said. "Alex didn't come back for me."

"I know."

"Then what's the matter?"

His thumbs stopped tapping, and then he looked at me. "I thought about leaving with my father to go back to Serbia…"

My heart sank like a stone. The bright morning was turning gray again.

"…but it only crossed my mind," he went on. "Just my conscience hard at work. But don't worry—I'm still selfish."

"If you left me, it would hurt worse than anything."

"It would me too. I could never leave you, and I won't."

He lightened up then, pulling away from the wheel and slipping his arm around me. "Good news is Viktor is dead and his family is leaving."

"Really?" I questioned. I was careful, still.

"Yeah, Nathan found out from Rachel; Ashe is Alpha now, and they're heading north."

It was all a lie, one that I knew, and Isaac did not.

"Are you going to follow them?"

"Xavier and Seth might," he said, "but right now it's too early to know anything."

Isaac touched my earlobe with his fingertip; a shiver went up the back up my neck. "Adria? Why didn't you want me to kill Viktor?"

I knew this was coming. I knew it the moment I saw the look in his deadly black eyes as he stood over Viktor that night.

I thought about the answer carefully. I had been thinking about it since. Finally, I answered, "I guess I just don't want to get used to seeing people die."

He regarded me quietly, and then a smile crept up on his gorgeous face. He kissed my lips, and then my forehead.

"How is that wound?" he asked, placing his hand softly against my stomach.

"It hasn't hurt for a while," I remarked. "Kind of weird. It looked really bad before."

He patted the area lightly before pulling his hand away; he then reached over into the back seat and grabbed a black shoulder bag.

"What's that for?"

He grinned. "I need something to carry my stuff around in at school, don't I?"

I blinked. "Huh?"

"I'm enrolling. Kinda had to be a senior, so we won't have any classes together. Thought that if I'm going to live in Hallowell, might as well become part of everybody else in this town."

"Are you…I mean, really? Seriously, you're going to go to *school* with me?" I never expected this. I mean I completely expected to have to werewolf-proof my aunt and uncle's house, but I never imagined Isaac would attend school.

I threw my arms around him and planted kisses all over his face. "This is perfect!"

Isaac laughed. "I take it you have no objections then," he said. "I worried you might not like the idea much."

"Are you kidding? No way."

I walked with Isaac Mayfair, my werewolf boyfriend, and by the looks of it, the hottest guy in school, to the office. Everyone watched: the guys with envy and discomfort; the girls with their hormones in overdrive; even Tori, which I quietly thought was hilarious. I couldn't force the smile off my face. I was never the type who liked public attention, but this was just fine by me. Didn't hurt to let it happen every once in a while, I supposed.

Still living up to his best friend title, Harry was still Harry towards me despite being totally in love with Daisy Mayfair. It made me happy to see him and Daisy together, to see him in such high spirits. And of all the surprises lately, Daisy surprised me the most: she could skateboard with the best of them. Who would've thought?

My life in Hallowell was finally beginning to feel normal. I was in love with a werewolf, and some of my best friends were werewolves, but somehow the not-so-normal managed to fall into place, too. Even with the hole my sister left in my heart, I was able to go on without her. And I knew secrets, terrible secrets I had to learn to live with, but I intended to do just that. For Isaac's sake. For as long as I could.

But there was just one thing I still couldn't quite shake—the wound underneath my ribs. It was already completely healed, and I didn't have to be a doctor to know that, judging by the severity of it, it was not normal.

And I was afraid to know the real reason why.

KINDRED

The Darkwoods Trilogy #2

Available now!

OTHER BOOKS BY J.A. REDMERSKI

Speculative Fiction/Contemporary Fantasy
DIRTY EDEN

Crime & Suspense
KILLING SARAI *(#1 – In the Company of Killers)*
REVIVING IZABEL *(#2 – In the Company of Killers)*
THE SWAN & THE JACKAL *(#3 – In the Company of Killers)*
SEEDS OF INIQUITY *(#4 – In the Company of Killers)*
THE BLACK WOLF *(#5 – In the Company of Killers)*
BEHIND THE HANDS THAT KILL *(#6 – In the Company of Killers)*
More to come…

New Adult Contemporary Romance
THE EDGE OF NEVER *(#1 – The Edge Series)*
THE EDGE OF ALWAYS *(#2 – The Edge Series)*
SONG OF THE FIREFLIES
THE MOMENT OF LETTING GO

Young Adult Paranormal Romance
THE MAYFAIR MOON *(#1 – The Darkwoods Trilogy)*
KINDRED *(#2 – The Darkwoods Trilogy)*
THE BALLAD OF ARAMEI *(#3 – The Darkwoods Trilogy)*

About the Author

J.A. (Jessica Ann) Redmerski is a *New York Times, USA Today* and *Wall Street Journal* bestselling author and award winner. She is a lover of film, television, and books that push boundaries, and is a sucker for long, sweeping, epic love stories. Things on Jessica's wish-list are to conquer her long list of ridiculous fears, find a shirt that she actually likes, and travel the world with a backpack and a partner-in-crime.

To learn more about Jessica, visit her here:
www.jessicaredmerski.com
www.inthecompanyofkillers.com
www.facebook.com/J.A.Redmerski
www.pinterest.com/jredmerski
Twitter - @JRedmerski

Printed in Great Britain
by Amazon